See you on th

Kerry Whelan

Copyright © 2020 Kerry Whelan

ISBN: 9798683718275

All rights reserved, including the right to reproduce this book, or portions thereof in any form. No part of this text may be reproduced, transmitted, downloaded, decompiled, reverse engineered, or stored, in any form or introduced into any information storage and retrieval system, in any form or by any means, whether electronic or mechanical without the express written permission of the author.

Rpb0121

Prologue

In Ireland of 1916 all the emotions of loyalty, love, bravado, ambition, and power came together as the nightmare of all nightmares. To the close community of Shaw's Bridge, South of Belfast, every sense was laid bare. War in Europe had no winners, only survivors if they were fortunate.

A hundred years later history, as always, has been rewritten. Twisted and abused to suit the power brokers of the day. The real lives of those who lived those dark days disappeared like the morning mist over the River Lagan. Only ghosts return to tell the tale of their fate and destiny in the most unexpected ways.

Contents

Part One	"Lagan"
Chapter 1	Monday morning news
Chapter 2	The Dutch Blue Guard
Chapter 3	Lagan Days
Chapter 4	The Match
Chapter 5	Home to Roost
Chapter 6	The Grand Entrance
Chapter 7	Late back my dear
Chapter 8	Young Citizens Volunteers
Chapter 9	Morning Service

Chapter 10   Departure

Chapter 11   The Last Farewell

Chapter 12   Come back, son

Part Two   "The Somme"

Chapter 13   Poacher raids

Chapter 14   Nursing Station

Chapter 15   Report

Chapter 16   1st July 1916

Chapter 17   Headquarters

Chapter 18   Mayhem

Chapter 19   The Postman

Chapter 20   Aftermath

Part Three   "Redemption"

Chapter 21   Homecoming

Chapter 22   The Deal

Chapter 23   Requiem

Chapter 24   Balancing the books

Part One

"Lagan"

Chapter 1

Monday morning news

The rain fell at right angles as the wind off Belfast Lough blew across High Street as Danny struggled to open the heavy glass door of River House in Belfast. As he stood in the lift to the 10th floor, he wondered how long it would take his trousers to dry out enough for his meeting with the Senior Partner.

Out of the lift he passed Barbara on reception.

"Wet out there Danny?" she asked as she nudged the signing in sheet without lifting her head.

"How did your weekend go then?" replied Daniel after scrawling his signature on the staff signing in book.

"Ach apart from somebody scraping a shopping trolley right up the side of my car and two ridge tiles blown off with the wind last night, absolutely wonderful," she replied finally raising her head with a pained smile.

"Well, I'm away in to dry off before I see the big man at 9.30," said Danny, looking back over his shoulder as he disappeared from Barbara's view as he headed down the corridor out of her sight.

Barbara had been in Coopers for twenty years, was in her late forties, and had seen many like Danny come and go. She knew what Danny did not know, because nothing happened in Coopers that Barbara did not know.

Danny had recently successfully completed his Chartered Accountant exams and was unaware William Chambers was about to promote him to audit manager.

At 9.30 Danny knocked the door and slowly strolled into Chambers' office. William looked up at him from his desk and nodded for him to take a seat. Danny did what he was told and sat down, giving the impression of being relaxed, while at the same time acutely awake.

William had tapped him on the arm as they had left the elevator to head home on the previous Friday evening and had quietly asked him to call in to see him Monday morning at 9.30. Danny had all his defence systems on red alert.

After all, this was William, legend of Coopers and the Belfast accountancy world. Eighteen stone rugby front row player. Sharp as a razor, a wicked sense of humour, and a proud member of the Orange Order. Unusual for senior members of the accountancy world, but William Chambers was never going to sell his soul for political correctness. What you saw was what you got. North Armagh, Portadown, Huguenot[1] farming stock and despite his

---

[1] Huguenot, French and Dutch migrants to Ireland in the 17th century who had fled from Catholic persecution and became the backbone of the early linen and farming stock of Ulster for the next three hundred years.

accountancy success, kept a few head of cattle. It was still in his blood.

"Right Danny, I'll get to the point. You've served your time here, got your exams a while back, and I'm sure you are checking out your options, but I'm offering you a promotion to an audit manager and every opportunity to end up a partner in the future, if you can hack it."

Inside, Danny's adrenalin surged, but true to form he relaxed back in his chair and looked at the desk in front of him for several seconds.

"Sounds good to me. I'm all ears," Danny replied, almost too casually.

I'm all ears, was his way of saying, what's the benefits, the perks, salary, and the responsibilities attached. Chambers told him what he wanted to know. Danny accepted the offer.

That sorted, William passed him over the list of clients he would now be responsible for and the team of juniors, semi seniors and seniors he would have below him.

Danny scanned his eye down the list. William gave him a pep talk, none of which he heard a word off. His brain took in the client list, but his eyes locked onto one name. Belfast District Orange Lodge.

"Can you handle them ok?" asked Chambers, with a slight almost concealed grin.

Danny decided not to react or comment. He knew William was watching for a reaction to the list and he wasn't going to give him the pleasure.

"Ok William, when does this all take effect?" said Danny.

"Now," replied William. "Take a few juniors and get all that stuff out of the room at the end of the corridor on the 11th floor and get yourself set up for tomorrow morning."

Danny walked, or more accurately, floated on air towards the door and just as he went to turn down the corridor, Chambers shouted after him.

'Would you phone Norman Johnston at the Lodge office today and agree when you are going up to do their audit. He needs it done ASAP."

"Frig you William," Danny thought to himself. "You had to have a laugh to yourself. When it comes to humour, you are one sick bastard, albeit a very likeable one."

Danny went off to gather up two juniors to sort his room and then made two phone calls, the second was to Norman Johnston of The Grand Lodge. The first was to Siobhan, the most important thing in his life. They could now get a mortgage on a good semi in South Belfast. Not too far from Bredagh Gaelic Athletic Club[2] and say goodbye to the flat on the Ormeau Road.

---

[2] Bredagh Gaelic Athletic Club for Gaelic Football, Hurling and Camogie based in South Belfast, a Nationalist Organisation by its Constitution.

The second most important thing to Danny was Bredagh GAC who rented facilities at Deramore Park on the Malone Road. The club played at the grounds and used the facilities with the goodwill of Belfast Harlequins Rugby Club.[3] Both clubs had intelligently played the cross community ace card and been handsomely rewarded with an abundance of Community Peace Building funding. Bredagh, Harlequins and Danny all lived in the real world.

---

[3] Belfast Harlequins Rugby Club, Middle class predominantly Protestant stalwart of Ulster Rugby.

Chapter Two

The Dutch Blue Guard

On Wednesday morning Danny sat in the reception of the Grand Lodge, passing the time of day with Sandra the receptionist, mass of flame red hair, early twenties, who made a big effort with the cosmetics and who, called everyone love. Not a bad creature, thought Danny, but one he would have preferred not to get the wrong side of. Still, she made a good cup of tea, and she gave him a KitKat out of her handbag.

As Danny sat waiting in the large wood panel walls in reception, he scanned the flags, photos and covenants hung around the walls. They all radiated from the photograph of the Queen and Prince Phillip, or Phil the Greek as he was known in his household, on their wedding day. The icons in his household were of the Saints and Mary.

Trying to blank out Sandra's voice talking on the phone to her mate about her latest "fella," he got up and took a closer look at some of the pictures and covenants. As he did, one picture, a painting with a memorial text framed below in a brass edging caught his attention. The painting depicted a scene, not surprisingly in the Grand Lodge office, of King William III

[4]crossing the Boyne.[5] What did surprise and confuse him was the banner carried by a soldier in a blue tunic as he waded chest high in the water.

Below the painting engraved on a brass plaque was written

"See you on the other side."
In memory of Joseph Shannon, 1st July 1916.

Just as his brain began trying to untangle this information a voice interrupted his thoughts.

"Hello Danny, sorry to keep you, stuck on a call there."

It was Norman Johnston as he strode purposefully from the corridor, stretching out a short stumpy hand and shaking Danny's gregariously.

Norman was not a big man, standing about five foot seven inches but his thick set build, shock of thinning sandy hair and direct manner suggested that this was a man who deserved respect. A man who did things up front. A man who you would know where you stood with. Traits which Danny would soon understand were inherent.

"Come on in my office and I'll show you all the books and stuff," he said with a smile.

---

[4] King William III, Dutch, Protestant, Ruled England and Ireland with his wife Queen Mary, daughter of the deposed Catholic King James II. Known as King William of Orange.

[5] The River Boyne. Flows from the west through Drogheda. Site of the Battle of the Boyne in 1690.

As they walked down the dimly lit corridor to Norman's office, Norman turned and looked at Danny.

"You were having a hard look at the walls there Danny. Something caught your attention?" grinned Norman, as Danny's mind raced to find the most diplomatic way to ask,

"What the hell was a Papal banner doing being dragged across the Boyne River? Never mind what is a memorial to a fellow Catholic doing on the wall of the District Orange Lodge in East Belfast, the Cregagh Road to be exact?"

Once in Norman's office, they stood in front of a large round table about the size and not unlike, the one Lord Carson[6] signed the Ulster Covenant. Danny at least knew this because he had seen the real one on a school trip to Belfast City Hall.

Before them, piled on the desk were ledgers, bank statement folders, binders full of invoices and reports and minutes taken by the twenty lodges in the District.

Danny estimated it would take him the rest of the morning to get an overview of what needed done and he would send a junior and semi senior to the lodge office the next day to do the spade work of bank reconciliations, cheque journals and trial balances completed.

---

[6] Lord Edward Carson (1854 -1935) Barrister, Judge, Leader of the Ulster Unionist Party 1910 - 1921

"Why is there a Papal banner on that painting crossing the Boyne?" asked Danny incredulously.

"William was right. He said you don't miss much," laughed Norman.

"You are the first man or woman who ever set foot in this place who has asked that question."

Norman looked at Danny with a sideways glance and expression bordering on mischievousness.

"Then again you're probably the first man to set foot in here to know what a Papal banner looks like," he retorted slightly nervously.

"Aye, well we both have William Chambers to thank for that. He does enjoy putting people on the spot. Out of their comfort zone," laughed Danny.

"You don't have to tell me about William Chambers," laughed Norman.

"Smiling sadist, him. Used to like nothing better than hammer me up and down the rugby pitch, laughing as he did it, but he'd always help me off and buy me a pint after."

There was a silence for about thirty seconds as Danny surveyed the pile.

'Well, I'll leave you to it," said Norman breaking the silence.

"I get my lunch round at Belvoir Golf Club. Give you a shout about one. Best golfers' fry in the city. How does that sound?"

"That's dead on, thanks, appreciate that," replied Danny.

10

"Great and I'll tell you about the Papal banner over lunch and the memorial to Joe you were paying so much attention."

He paused for a few seconds and laughed quietly, almost grunting.

"The memorial is not always appreciated by some of our brethren, but that memorial will never come down. Anyhow, see you at lunch and all will be revealed, Danny boy."

Norman chuckled as he closed the door on his way out.

Danny began his process of scanning the papers available, planning what part of the job to delegate to whom. After about an hour into his assessment he was running his eye down the cheque journal of the Edenderry Lodge he noticed an entry.

"St Claire de Passion Hospice. Amount £100.00."

Danny lost his flow of concentration again. He muttered to himself under his breath.

"What is going on here? This is more curious than Alice in Wonderland, complete with the bloody Hatters."

Norman's lunch was going to be some tea party explaining this one. It would be some source of amusement at Bredagh GAC if his professional standards would have allowed it.

"Here lads have you heard about the Orange Lodge, a Papal banner, memorial to a Taig, and a £100 cheque to a convent?"

'Aye Danny, haven't heard that one, give us the craic."

'No lads I'm serious, it's true bill."

Aye Danny, away and!"

Two hours later at 12.45 Norman ambled into the room.

"Ok Danny, feeding time, let's go."

Within ten minutes they were both entering the bar at Belvoir and looking at the bar snack menu. Two Golfers Fries ordered; tea and a coffee were on the way.

"Well then Danny, I'll put you out of suspense. I'll start with the easy one. The painting of the soldier carrying the papal banner across the Boyne was because that was what happened.

"King William's best and favourite unit was the Dutch Blue Guards. Mostly Catholic to a man. They led the attack across the Boyne River. Flintlock muskets above their heads. Chest high in the river, as it flowed in a strong current down to Drogheda and the Irish Sea. They were sitting ducks until they got across.

"Why there is a painting on the wall of the Lodge Headquarters, you'll understand soon enough.

"The Dutch weren't some super Prod nation intent on wiping out Catholics. King William was primarily interested in defending Holland and Britain from the French. The fact he found it necessary to come over here and sort out the Jacobites,[7] mostly Catholic, some Anglican and native Irish, was more about Prod good fortune than a Williamite quest of Protestant control for the next three hundred years in this neck of the woods."

Danny nodded his head.

---

[7] Jacobites. The forces loyal to the deposed King James II

"That makes sense to me because I had heard my schoolteacher say The Battle of the Boyne was a European battle fought in Ireland, but to be honest, never thought much of it. The Boyne was never a hot topic of conversation in our house."

"I'd have been surprised if it was Danny," chuckled Norman, as he leant back in his chair to let the waitress set the significant plates of bacon, sausage, two eggs and several pieces of soda and potato bread nestle on the table before them. Both offered thanks to the server and as they eagerly tucked in, Norman, between digesting half a sausage, continued.

The Blue Guard in the painting is also linked to the name Joe Shannon. The easy bit of the story, as I said earlier, is why the papal banner is on the painting.

Why it's linked with Joe Shannon is a much longer tale and it's all linked to the £100 to the Hospice in France, which no doubt your keen eye will have noticed."

"I've a feeling it is going to take a bit longer than lunch hour," smiled Danny as he munched on his fry.

"Aye it will that," replied Norman, "but I think you'll find it worth the wait."

At that point, the aroma and taste of the meal took control and they concentrated on using their jaws on eating.

As they worked through reducing the pile on their plates, Norman began his tale, but even then, the name Joseph Shannon, started to rattle around the back of Danny's brain until it began to haunt him.

In the meantime, Norman began a tale that would take several lunch hours over the next few weeks to complete.

Chapter Three

Lagan Days

On a Spring Sunday morning in 1915 the fresh smell of a changing season rose from the hog weed and rushes of the Lagan canal beside the cottage at the locks at Newforge.[8] The steady and purposeful sound of a blacksmith's hammer shaping metal on an anvil pierced the still air. Tom Gibson was working on a set of shoes for the steady flow of barge horses that trod the towpath between Aghalee[9] to Belfast docks. The tone and speed of the hammering sound changed as he exchanged hammers to suit the need, always working fast while the metal kept glowing.

"Where are you off to Davy?" he asked, not lifting his head, or changing his expression.

"I'm away down to Stranmillis,[10] meeting up with Joe and a few mates," replied Davy.

"Well make sure you're not back as late as last night," replied Tom, still not raising his head, or changing expression. He had to take care his cigarette would not fall from his lips.

---

[8] Newforge. An area just a few hundred yards north of Shaw's Bridge on the outskirts of South Belfast, about 4 miles from Belfast.

[9] Aghalee. On the Southeast Corner of Lough Neagh, near where the Lagan Canal meets the Lough.

[10] Stranmillis. An area of South Belfast which runs along the west bank of the Lagan north of Shaws Bridge and two miles from Belfast city centre.

"Don't worry Da, I'm not afraid of the dark anymore. I'm nineteen, not five."

Tom paused, set down the hammer, took the cigarette out of his mouth, holding it between his brown stained thumb and forefinger.

"Don't be clever with me son, remember I've taught you everything you know and forgotten more moves than you know. Sir James has been strutting about in a bad mood because he's losing too much game to poachers. Your mates are top of his list."

''I wasn't poaching last night," replied Davy with the best innocent expression he could muster.

"I know you weren't, but you had enough feathers and fur on your trouser turn ups to tell me you gutted and cleaned their kill for them," said Tom, head cocked slightly to one side, staring straight faced at Davy.

Davy pause, and said apologetically, "Bill gave me a few pence for doing them; only took me half an hour."

"'Aye well at least you'd the sense not to bring any here. Sir James is too close for comfort. That few pence could get you and me both out on the hedgerows. He's our landlord and we are his tenants as he regularly likes to tell me," advised Tom, as he raised himself upright, striking hammer in his right hand hanging by his side and giving Davy a determined stare.

"Yes Da, but it's hard to say No. The boys don't like it if they think you're letting them down."

"Look son, if we lost the roof over our heads do you think your mates would club together and buy us a home? No, not bloody likely!" sneered Tom, with a tone of frustration as he took the butt of his Woodbine and flicked it in the bucket of water at the side of the anvil.

Davy gave an apologetic look at Tom as he left the forge and promised he would be back for eleven that evening.

Tom smiled to himself. He knew Davy was going hunting that afternoon and knew it was birds, but not the feathered variety. Like father like son, he thought to himself and stopped to have a wistful slow draw on his cigarette and laughed a jealous laugh to himself.

Davy jumped on to the lighter, a canal barge that was being towed downstream by a steady paced weary horse, to the first lock at Stranmillis and on to The Gasworks Quay.[11]

It was a Sunday, the morning rain had been replaced by a fresh sunny afternoon, the air filled with the fine smells of Spring, as the lighter reached the lock at the Stranmillis Boat Club. Joe Shannon was leaning against the wall of the factory that was opposite the lock gates. Davy jumped off the lighter and walked in the direction of Joe who straightened himself up from the wall as he finished his cigarette.

---

[11] Gasworks Quay, Cromac St "Markets" area of inner Belfast which exists on the West bank of the Lagan, below Stranmillis.

As Davy came alongside him, they both started walking side by side in the direction of Stranmillis village.

The lads were in good form joking about the prospects of the odds of success at the dance at St Bridget's on the Malone Road where they were destined.

Davy had struck it lucky. Being an Ulster Protestant, he and all his mates had to endure Sunday. No games, no work, no enjoying yourself. Just secretive games of cards and chatting up the local girls if you could get away with it.

Joe on the other hand was a Roman Catholic. He only had to turn up for morning mass and the rest of the day was his to enjoy.

Davy had known Joe for about a year. Joe worked as a drover from Belfast Markets for the cattle moved from farms and the railway.

Davy was a butcher, just completed his apprenticeship and they became good mates since the day they had to capture a spirited bullock that had no desire to take the boat to England. Davy did a bit of drover work for local farmers on summer evenings to earn a bit extra.

Davy was both excited and apprehensive about going to the dance at St Bridget's on Derryvolgie Avenue on the Malone Road.[12] It was best he just told his father he was going to Stranmillis. He hadn't lied to him, just left out the finer detail. Stranmillis was off the Malone Road and, he was going to a

---

[12] St Bridget's Chapel, Derryvolgie Avenue, Malone Road, South Belfast

dance at St Bridget's Parochial Halls on the Malone Road about a mile out of Belfast City, but if he'd told his father, it was St Bridget's he'd have got an ear bashing.

The thing was, all the young Catholic girls from rural Ulster, who had come to find employment in the big houses in South Belfast, descended on the parish hall like a swarm of bees when they got time off from their long hours of domestic servitude, which was still a lot better than twelve hour shifts, bare foot, on the wet floors of the mills.

Davy had turned down previous invitations to go to the dance by Joe despite the impressive descriptions of the standard of young ladies available. His reluctance was born out of a fear of his mates finding out he went anywhere near a chapel, not to mention his father's advice that Catholic girls chase Protestant boys just to get them under the grip of Rome; not to mention the twelve children, scary stuff.

Anyhow, due to the distinct lack of eligible young ladies up to Davy's standards around Shaw's Bridge,[13] he thought he'd give it a go just to break the boredom of an Ulster Sunday.

As they entered the doors of the parish hall the sound of laughter, music and good spirits did not reduce Davy's sense of unease. Would he be struck down by lightning or grabbed by a

---

[13] Shaw's Bridge, Bridge across the Lagan since the 17th Century at Newforge on the southern edge of Belfast, below Edenderry village.

dozen Irish harpies and taken to a monastery in the West never to see the light of day again?

After a few dances Joe came over to Davy with a real looker attached to his arm.

Joe introduced her as Kathleen 'Kitty' Breslin.

As they laughed and joked for ten minutes, it was clear Joe and Kitty had a spark between them. Davy held no disappointment or jealously to Joe as she was out of his comfort zone. He resolved to do his best to help Joe out by spending the rest of the afternoon entertaining Kitty's not so impressive friend. "The things you do for your mates," thought Davy.

As the dance came to an end Kitty said a lingering goodbye to Joe and they agreed to meet the following Sunday. Davy said a friendly and polite goodbye to Kitty's mate.

Davy and Joe headed back over to the locks at the Boat Club for Joe to cadge a lift back down to the Gasworks quay at the Markets.

It was shorter for Joe to walk from the Malone Road direct to the Markets than back over to the Boat Club Locks[14] but it would have meant negotiating Sandy Row[15] or Donegal Pass[16] where, being a Catholic, he would not have gotten a friendly welcome as he passed through. Lions' den wouldn't have been in it. Much

---

[14] Belfast Boat Club on side of Lagan canal, Stranmillis, South Belfast

[15] Sandy Row, working class, protestant, loyalist areas in South Belfast city side of Stranmillis, Malone and Lisburn Roads near Shaftesbury Square.

[16] Donegall Pass, same as Sandy Row.

safer to retrace their steps to the Boat Club locks, cadge a lift down the Lagan, and slip off at the Gasworks in the Markets area deep in his own Catholic territory where a Protestant would get a similarly unfriendly reception.

As Davy and Joe walked back over Broomhill[17] to the locks at the Boat Club on Stranmillis, Joe was on a high after his afternoon with Kitty.

She lived and worked in one of the big houses up near Drumbeg.[18] He smiled in anticipation. It would mean there would be no problem seeing her again. He could even get a lighter up to Drumbeg or meet her at Shaw's Bridge.

"Did you get the name of the big house?" asked Davy, trying to sound only vaguely interested.

It's one of them ones just past Dunmurry Lane. Sir James somebody or other," replied Joe.

Davy looked at him out of the corner of his eye. "Sir James Arthur, Ballydrain House," and laughed in a snort of irony.

"Seems you know the man, Davy," said Joe.

"Know him probably isn't the right term," replied Davy, not lifting his gaze at the ground as he walked.

---

[17] Broomhill, South of Belfast on the Malone Road city side of Newforge and Shaw's Bridge.

[18] Drumbeg Further out of Belfast on the upper Malone Road beyond Ballydrain House. (Now Malone Golf Club)

They continued in silence for about ten seconds before Joe, gathered pace, walked slightly ahead of Davy, half turned, and gave him a taunting grin.

"Something tells me you've more to tell than what you're telling," smirked Joe.

"All you need to know Joe, all you need to know," replied Davy, still not letting his eyes leave the ground, but his face could not conceal the angst in his head.

Joe gave Davy another long stare, but Davy wasn't falling for it and remained silent, drawing on his cigarette. The lads walked on and as the lock gates and the Boat Club came in sight, Davy finally broke the silence that had befallen them on their walk.

"Sir James Arthur," sighed Davy. "Big linen merchant, landowner, rents half the houses in South Belfast, probably owns yours; finger in every pie. Where there's money to be made; Sir James won't miss it."

Davy resumed his silence.

As they reached the Boat Club, Joe broke the awkward silence again.

"Something tells me you've more, Davy," said Joe with a sly glance at Davy.

Joe laughed delighted that he had wound Davy up, which was not easy.

"Sir James Arthur, father of Anna Arthur," sighed Davy, unable to contain his thoughts any further and not wanting to end the day with any bad feelings with Joe.

"Ah, nice one!" laughed Joe.

As Joe was about to start on Davy again, Davy pointed up the canal at the lighter barge and horse coming into view.

"There's your lift Joe. You'd be best getting it if you don't want to swim down the Lagan," said Davy with a smile on his face and chuckling at the same time.

"Right Davy, I'm away here, but I need the full low down before the match Tuesday evening," shouted Joe, half turning as he ran alongside the lighter and jumped on. As Davy ambled up the tow path in the other direction, he could hear Joe singing at the top of his voice the name Anna Arthur to the tune of some Irish ballad that only a Taig would know.

Davy began his walk back up the tow path on the twenty minutes journey it would take him to reach home, his head full of Anna Arthur. He had tried to keep her deep in the back of his mind, denying her existence, like denying a ghost. Anna surely haunted him, but this was a ghost he could not exorcise.

Anna, the girl he had first seen when they were both fourteen years old, playing in the meadows on her father's estate which ran down to the west bank of the tow path. He lived in the blacksmith's cottage at the lock gates at Newforge, just below Shaw's Bridge on the River Lagan, about a mile downstream towards Belfast on the Lagan tow path from the meadows that edged Sir James extensive estate.

The same Anna Arthur whom, when they were both fourteen, fate had it they would meet on a summer day. They had spent it on the riverbank of her father's meadow, catching roach, watching for a Kingfisher, joking, and teasing each other. They continued to meet at the riverbank at the edge of the estate for several unforgettable weeks, until one evening Tom told him in no uncertain terms that he was never to have anything to do with her again.

The same day that Sir James marked the end of Anna playing down at the meadow that ran down to the riverside.

Social division in Belfast wasn't just religious, it was divided by class just as much.

Not long after, Anna had been sent to an expensive boarding school for young ladies in the Cotswolds in England, and then when she was eighteen, sent to Switzerland for a year to learn the art of being Lady of the Manor in high society. Sir James Arthur had it all set out for her. A life of luxury, status, and power.

Until recently she had hardly ever been seen, but now she was back. He had seen her from a distance. It had resurfaced all the memories he had forced to the back of his mind for the last five years. Those days, which seemed so many years ago to a youth of now nineteen, had never left him. Since those days Davy had never sensed such a feeling of ease, compassion, oneness, for anyone. Those days never left his head or his heart. Her smile, her laughter, the way she moved, her mind, her very soul.

Now five years later, Davy had caught sight of her a few weeks earlier as he passed the edge of Sir James's estate that ran down to the Lagan as he walked up to Lambeg to help slaughter a few head of cattle at Crawford's farm.

Several young ladies, all dressed in the best of riding clothes, were trotting their ponies in the field beside the towpath, in the Arthur estate. He did not pay much attention until he heard laughter. It was a laugh he had not heard in five years. He stopped in an instant and stared.

At the same time the girl spotted Davy on the towpath. She turned the horse to face him from higher up the hill in the field and allowed the mount to amble slowly towards the fence separating the estate from the canal tow path. About ten yards from the fence, she halted the horse and stared across at Davy, patting the animal at the same time. He could still not be sure it was Anna, her riding cap pulled well down over her face.

Davy shook himself out of his trance and keep his grin slight and wistful. Anna took off her riding cap and shook her long dark hair loose, just like it was the days they spent years before in the meadow.

Davy was consumed, but he kept his stance. He casually raised his hand and waved at her, dropping his hands to his hips, and got lost in the moment that seemed like a lifetime. It was only broken by Anna turning the horse round, giving him a short regal type of wave at the same time.

As the horse and rider trotted back to the other riders, Davy just stared and wondered what might have been. Then just as he was about to turn and continue up the tow path, Anna twisted in the saddle, glanced over her shoulder, and smiled. What Davy saw before him was an image he would never forget until his eyes would close for the very last time.

Anna was no longer the cute rich girl who liked to play and laugh in the Lagan's evening sun. Before him now was a beautiful young lady. Long dark flowing hair, high cheek bones, perfect mouth, eyes as bright as the stars. She rode the pony with ease. Her tight dainty figure flowing in tune with the movement of the animal below her. She was wearing riding britches and not side saddle as becoming of most young ladies of the time.

The past year or more in Switzerland had given her the poise and presence of a French countess. Not to mention a bit of spirit, and no shortage of confidence.

"Jesus," he thought to himself, "some young toff is going to be one lucky sod."

As Davy walked back up the towpath to the cottage and dragged himself from his memories and the sense of loss, he shook his head and cursed his misfortune. He had not seen her since that day two weeks earlier and had tried unsuccessfully to put her in the back of his mind, and now Joe was chasing one of her father's maid servants who lived up at the mansion. Davy shook his head, staring at the ground as he retraced his steps back home.

Chapter Four

The Match

The football match on Tuesday night between Edenderry and Lambeg[19] at Shaw's Bridge would be tight, local rivals, mates becoming enemies for ninety minutes.

Edenderry against Lambeg was the local derby. Both teams primarily from the two linen mills, only a few miles from each other, all Protestants to a man and boy, except for Joe. He played for Edenderry courtesy of a twist of fate. A few months earlier their goalkeeper, Sammy McCabe, had let them down at the last minute because he had to take the Liverpool boat due to an irate father of a young lady, three months with child as they said in those days.

Davy knew Joe played Gaelic Football, which led him to presume he could catch a ball better than any Protestant and coaxed him to turn up at Edenderry and help them out. Joe, more than a little apprehensively, took up the invitation, more out of loyalty to Davy than anything else.

---

[19] Edenderry and Lambeg, two mill villages on the Lagan a few miles from Shaws Bridge and Ballydrain.

Joe jumped off the lighter that evening at Davy's cottage and the pair hiked up the lane to the pitch beside the bleaching green at the mill.

As the boys saw Davy and Joe approach, they were assessing Joe before he got up to them. He was big enough for a goalkeeper, walked in a purposeful manner and had a large pair of hands. It seemed Davy had kept his word when he said he thought he could find them a replacement.

Bill Johnston was the first to raise his head and make a comment.

"Thank fuck you brought someone. Didn't think you'd manage it Davy," he grunted with no sign of a smile just a slow questioning stare.

"What's your name big lad?" looking at Joe, who like Davy, was a good six foot tall, not that common in 1915.

"Joe," was the reply with a similar blank expression.

"Joe who?" quipped Bill.

"Shannon," replied Joe.

"Joe Shannon sounds like a Fenian name," grunted Bill staring at Joe and taking a deep drag of his Woodbine cigarette at the same time.

"Ten out of ten for observation, mate," snorted Joe.

Bill turned to Davy, still with a straight face. "For fuck sake Davy, you said you'd bring a keeper. You didn't say you'd bring a rebel."

As he spoke, he threw a green goalkeeper's jersey at Joe.

"There you are Joe, even got the right colour for you. A good Fenian green," said Bill, as a thinly guarded grin crossed his face.

Bill turned to the rest of the boys. "Well lads this is Joe, Fenian Joe, and he better have a good game, for your sake, Davy."

Joe made no reaction because Davy had already warned him about Bill's sense of humour.

As they trotted on to the pitch, Bill came up beside Joe.

"See out on this pitch, you are Jim, ok."

"My name's Joe," he grunted back at Bill.

"Aye, so it is, but if those boys from Lambeg catch on to you being a Fenian, this will turn into a kicking match, and you'll come off even worse than the rest of us."

The match progressed with the usual late challenges, a few fists flying, but most importantly, Joe was at his best, dealt with crosses, got down to the low shots despite his height, and showed no fear in diving among flying boots.

As they came off at the end, having won 4 – 1, they were in good mood. Dessie Clarke, the left back, looked sideways at Joe and said, "Did a good job out there, Joe."

As he said it, one of the Lambeg boys had cocked his ears and shouted over to his mates. "Hey lads the Edenderry boys are a bunch of Fenian lovers."

Bill Johnston turned and stepped towards the Lambeg mouthpiece and said, "Hey boy you got a problem!"

"No, you've got the problem. Did you Fenian lovers get a drop of holy water before you started?" was the reply.

Bill stepped forward right into the player's face.

"Aye we've got a Fenian in our team. Joe, Fenian Joe, to his mates and he's our fucking Fenian. Got that! Now take yourself off back to Lambeg."

To a man the Edenderry boys gathered on Bill's shoulder.

"Bit touchy, Bill," laughed the Lambeg lad as he walked away.

"Davy wasn't far wrong when he said Bill was sound," thought Joe, as he puffed on his Woodbine.

"Bill looked after his own."

As the boys walked off together the talk was full of the news about Edward Carson[20] and James Craig[21] wanting an army to fight the Hun and saving Ulster from the Pope. Joe kept out of the conversation and now and again gave Davy a wry look, still puffing his Woodbine slowly. Joe learnt more about the Young Citizens Volunteers[22] than he ever knew existed, as they walked back down to Shaw's Bridge and the lads dispersed at corners and lanes that led to each of their homes.

---

[20] Edward Carson, (1854 – 1935) barrister, judge, leader of the Ulster Unionist Party 1910 – 1921)

[21] James Craig (1871 – 1940) Leader of the Ulster Unionist Party 1921 – 1940. Wealthy Belfast millionaire and owner of Dunville Distillery.

[22] Young Citizens Volunteers (see next page)

Life should have been simple for the boys of the Laganvale. Go to work, play football, bit of poaching and chasing the girls. Life is however rarely simple. Complications always arise and always will. In the Ireland of 1915 complications came in more than its fair share. The Home Rule Bill[23] and the War with Germany saw to it.

Most of the lads worked for, or close to, Sir James either as staff on his estate or as workers at one of his three mills that ran the length of the Lagan between the Locks at the Stranmillis Boat Club[24] up to Hilden near Lisburn. They were all members of the Belfast Young Citizens Volunteers, an organisation which had existed before the War started. It was full of middle class and a few local gentry lads of sixteen to twenty-one. Many Boy Scouts and Young Lads groups, who had blended into a group whose ideas were to contribute to society in a positive way and enjoy it in the process. Saving Ulster was not their original intent. Most of the Edenderry boys would not have fitted into this social group but their close links with Sir James Arthur, who had sponsored the YCV in the area, had drawn then into it.

Roger Arthur, Sir James's son, was two years older than most of the lads and he knew them. He got on well with them. He was much more likeable than his father. Their camps resembled boy

---

[23] Home Rule Bill, draft of British parliamentary intent to give Ireland Independence.

[24] Stranmillis Boat Club – Rowing and tennis club on the banks of the Lagan at Stranmillis, active since the 19th century.

scout activities, encouraged comradeship, and all was well with the world.

Unfortunately for the lads, the YCV were offered to the Irish Rifles as the 14th Battalion of the 36th Ulster Division by a local man of importance by the name of Robert James McMordie. He came up with the wonderful idea that they would be doing their civic duty by going to war to defend Ulster and the Empire.

By 1915 they had been sent to training camps on numerous weekends to Clandeboye and Randalstown Estates and had not particularly enjoyed the experience. The harsh realities of army training did not fit easy for most of these middle-class youths compared to the rank and file of the other Belfast Battalions, mostly working class, who coped better with the training and taking orders, despite their natural instincts to find some way of outwitting the system at every opportunity possible.

Chapter Five

Home to Roost

On the Sunday afternoon following Joe's success with Kitty, Davy was brushing a lighter horse, which was watering at the lock gate, when he saw Joe walking up the towpath with a purposeful stride.

"One guess where you are headed Joe," said Davy.

Joe just shrugged.

"Don't blame you mate, that Kitty girl is well worth a shot. Is she waiting for you up at Shaw's Bridge?"

Joe broke his silence and replied hesitantly.

"Ach knowing my luck she probably won't turn up, but a man has got to do, what a man's got to do!"

"Well, if she doesn't show, drop back in on the way down and there's some barley water my Da found just floating up the canal," said Davy with a smile.

Samples of local contraband regularly dropped off the lighters for Tom Gibson to find for favours rendered to the lighter men.

"You need to come up with me Davy, because she got a message down to me, says she'd bring another friend from the big house," said Joe.

33

"What would be the point? It'll be one of the other maids from the house. It'll be a Bridie or Geraldine, or a Mary, and you know how far that will go," said Davy apologetically.

"Jesus, Davy, I'm not asking you to marry the girl. I just need you to keep the other one occupied so I can concentrate on Kitty. You'd be doing me a favour mate," said Joe.

"Well, if I do, you owe me twice now. I did this last week. I can think of better ways to spend my Sundays than riding shotgun for you again," laughed Davy.

"Give me a few minutes, I'll clean up and catch you at the Bridge. Keep them talking, but if the other one's a bit rough looking give me a wave with your left hand when you see me coming so I can dodge it."

"Don't think that's likely to happen, Davy, don't get yourself excited," laughed Joe as he walked on up the path, turning as he spoke."

Ten minutes later, as Davy got within distance of the bridge, he could see Joe talking to the two girls. One was Kitty, the other had her back to him, so he had no idea what she looked like, but Joe had made no gesture to escape. The two young ladies were both dressed in the mansion maids best Sunday clothes.

As he got within about twenty feet of the three of them the other maid turned as Kitty and Joe greeted him. Davy was good at appearing calm and collected when chatting up the girls, but he had been totally unprepared for what was happening.

Anna Arthur was smiling from ear to ear directly in front of him.

"Still catching a few roach, David? Must be good at it by now," giggled Anna, tilting her head to one side as she spoke.

Davy tried to think of something to say but he was unusually speechless. Only the smile and glint in his eye told Anna that he was more than glad to see her and that she was not going to be made to look foolish.

"Did you know it would be Anna?" asked Davy turning to Joe.

"No mate, Kitty just said if you turned up you wouldn't be disappointed," smiled Joe, as Davy nodded his head in approval, flashing a glance at Anna.

The two couples started to walk from the bridge up the winding tree covered lane that linked up to the Malone Road which led towards South Belfast.

Joe in deep conversation with Kitty, and Davy with Anna. Davy and Anna updated each other on their lives in the past five years.

Davy had completed his apprenticeship as a butcher working for Jack Graham at Shaftesbury Square, beyond the bottom of the Malone Road in the direction of Belfast city centre. Graham's had been the main butchers shop frequented by the upper and middle classes of South Belfast's Malone Road, and the big houses of Drumbeg, the Arthurs' being one.

Davy had been taught by the best, Jack Graham. As gruff a man you could find, but a man who knew his trade better than anyone in the land. Davy had been a good learner.

Davy, trying to impress Anna, told of the day he was cutting chops at the cutting board when a distinguished looking man stood watching him cut through the meat and bone before he broke his silent contemplation.

"Young man," he said," if you had had an education, you would make a surgeon. None of my chaps can cut like that, more's the pity."

He introduced himself as Senior Surgeon of the Royal Victoria Hospital, took his parcel, which Davy had handed to him, and left without another word.

Davy, added for good measure, that he would own his own shop someday, in a further clumsy attempt to impress. Aside of that Davy had nothing special or exciting to tell Anna, except that he never forgotten that summer five years earlier.

Anna's four of the last five years had been spent at a top boarding school in the Cotswolds and the fifth at a Swiss finishing school for young ladies of the upper class to hone their skills in the social graces of high society, enhancing their opportunities for a good marriage. During holidays she had spent little time at home, making regular visits to friends and family. Sir James had been keen to make sure Anna did not waste her time with the local population. He intended her to mix with the top layer of society, which would be in her best interests.

Anna was the apple of his eye, and he wanted the best for her even if she did not appreciate it. She would understand it someday.

Anna talked lovingly of the summer five years earlier. By the time they had drawn breath and a silence fell on their conversation, a few hours had passed. They had reached the gate house at the entrance to the Botanical Gardens opposite Methodist College, almost three miles from their rendezvous at Shaw's Bridge on the edge of Belfast city.

Anna looked up at the clock on the small tower of the gate house and saw it was almost five o 'clock.

"That's not the time is it Kitty? We had better get back home quick!" said Anna in a panic.

"Time flies when you're enjoying yourself, Anna, ma'am," teased Kitty.

"We need to get back before my mother finds Mary asleep in my bed," gasped Anna.

Anna had left the mansion house in what could best be described as secretively. Being aware questions would be asked where she was going that afternoon, she had contrived with Mary, another maid, to pretend to be each other.

Anna had feigned a migraine and said she would be in bed the rest of the day and did not want to be disturbed. Mary had provided Anna with her Sunday best which she wore to chapel and was more than happy to be able to spend the day curled up in a soft bed with beautiful sheets, the sun light splitting through the curtains through the big window that overlooked the lake. Big change from her hard, boarded bunk and rough linen sheets, in the attic along with three other house servants. Not to mention the three pence Anna had slipped into her hand as she left.

Anna had needed to play out this ruse because the rendezvous with Davy and Joe would have been nipped in the bud by Sir James and Lady May. When Anna heard from Kitty what Joe had told her, she had to find some way of meeting Davy.

For the last five years, one way or another, the family had managed to direct her attentions elsewhere but now she was nineteen, a confident, beautiful young women who, like many other young ladies of her status, thought there was more to life than being a good hostess at evening dinners. Anna had a strong spirit and a good heart, and more importantly, she longed for the days of five years earlier. She just had to see Davy and find out if her youthful passions might now be something else.

She was delighted that there was a spark between her and Davy that had not died. It smouldered like a fire slacked overnight. Like slack lifted by the poker in the morning, it had returned into a warm blaze.

That having been said, if she didn't get back by about six o'clock there was every chance that her mother might arrive in the bedroom to check how she was doing. Mary would be sacked immediately, and Anna would have been whisked off to relatives in England, or her cousins' estate at Dungannon, for the rest of the summer, to cool her courage and give her father time to organize her future.

As it happened, Lady May did check the welfare of her daughter, but Mary had pulled the covers up round her so only the top of her hair was visible. She made a good impression of being sound asleep, while being frozen with fear at the prospect of being caught.

When Anna and Kitty got back to Shaw's Bridge, they walked on up the tow path a short distance. They climbed the wall over the back of the estate and sneaked back to the servants' quarters. Anna waited her moment and slipped back to her room. She thanked Mary and promised never to put her in that position again. Mary returned up to the top of the house two steps at a time, eager to hear every detail from Kitty.

Anna, alone in her room, paced up and down, occasionally stopping at the window staring out over the lake. She would have to find some other way of discreetly keeping contact with Davy. By the evening she had hatched a plan.

Later that evening, as the sun sank below the trees, Davy sat on the bench at the lock beside his cottage, Joe alongside him. He drew on his Woodbine, saying nothing.

"Told you that you wouldn't be disappointed," said Joe who was sitting silently beside him, also drawing on his Woodbine.

"I'll give you that Joe," chuckled Davy, "but I don't know what's next with this. It probably will end in tears, mate."

"Take it as it comes Davy. Sure, she said she'll see you tomorrow evening," reassured Joe.

"Aye, but she didn't say where or when. Her confidence, her presence, her beauty, scares me. Somewhere down the line it will end. I don't know if I want to go through all that," sighed Davy.

"Didn't see you as being chicken, Davy. You've passed through the Markets too many times driving cattle and you've stood up for me when I've been in the wrong places for a Catholic and now, you're crapping yourself about a girl," scoffed Joe without a hint of sympathy.

Davy said nothing in reply, he just stared at the ground, slowly smoking his cigarette down to the butt until his fingers started to burn. He let the butt fall to the ground, squashing it with his boot as he got up from the bench.

"There's old Reid's lighter. He's going to the coal key. He'll stop at the Gasworks, nearly at your door, mate," sighed Davy quietly.

"Right Davy, I'm away, see you at the football Wednesday," said Joe as he jumped on to the lighter. As he found himself a spot to sit, he shouted to Davy.

"Maybe you should be like Kitty and me. Us Catholics have a bit of faith. You should try it sometime."

Davy walked along the path keeping pace with the lighter.

"Wise up Joe, the Lord can't help on this one, especially not your sort of Lord," said Davy with more than a sense of frustration.

"Faith in Anna, Davy," shouted Joe, with a degree of frustration in his voice as the lighter slipped on down the canal.

"She planned today. When she heard Kitty mention you being at the dance, Kitty said she never saw her face light up as much as when your name was mentioned. That one's made of strong stuff. Give her the benefit of the doubt, or you might regret it all your days."

Davy grinned and shouted at the slowly disappearing Joe. "Never saw you as the romantic type!"

As Davy stood alone and silent on the canal bank, his mind was jumping in all directions. He could hear his father talking to someone in the cottage and then McCracken, Sir James's Head Groom, left waving Tom a farewell. His thoughts were interrupted by the sound of his father.

"Davy, before you come in, would you stack me a pile of horseshoes and nails by the forge. McCracken is sending down a few of Ballydrain's horses for new shoes tomorrow. Short notice, they weren't done that long ago. Told him so, but somebody up there has decided they are needed. They'll be here in the morning to be collected in the evening."

Davy stood silent; thought for a few seconds.

41

"I'll help you rub the horses down before they get collected tomorrow evening," replied Davy with a level of interest Tom did not expect.

Davy spoke to himself under his breath.

"Anna Arthur, maybe Joe knows you better than me."

Chapter Six

The Grand Entrance

By Monday evening eight of Sir James's horses were all attired with new footwear. They were tethered outside the forge, as Tom and Davy gave them a good brush down. It was not part of the deal but Tom new that it would save the grooms a bit of work and the goodwill was worth the bother. As Davy surveyed the horses, he noticed the one that he had seen Anna canter in the fields a few weeks earlier.

As he ambled over to the animal, he nodded to Tom.

"I'll do this one Da."

"Thought you might son," chuckled Tom.

Davy decided not to respond to his father and a silence descended.

After a minute, Tom, still rubbing down the next horse, and without taking his eyes off the brush on the mare's back said,

"Beautiful filly that one, well bred, spirited, just be careful how you handle her."

Davy still didn't react and kept his gaze on the horse's flanks.

By eight in the evening Sir James's groom and three assistants, including one of Davy's pals, Jonty Price, came down the path to the forge. Jonty was a small lad only about five feet four in height and as thin as a whippet. He was a stable lad who fancied himself as a budding jockey for Sir James's racehorses. His small stature was more than compensated by his big personality. Jonty was never short of a word. His cutting wit made many a lad twice his size recoil.

Four men and one girl in riding gear went over to inspect the horses. Tom emerged from the forge doorway wiping his hands with a cloth.

The girl, rather than the Groom, walked over to Tom and introduced herself.

"Good evening Mr Gibson, my father is at a meeting in Belfast this evening so I thought I would call and collect the horses on his behalf."

She handed Tom a cloth bag of coins that made up the five shillings to pay for the work done.

As the staff gathered up the horses to take them back up the towpath, Davy was deliberately still brushing her horse needlessly. Anna walked over to Davy.

"Hello Davy, you've done a good job there, you really didn't need to," smiled Anna.

"It's a pleasure. Does she do much eventing? asked Davy.

"Not as much as she might be doing in the future," said Anna with a cheeky smile.

Davy tried to hold back a smile.

As Tom engaged in a conversation with the Head Groom, Davy listened to Anna explain the problems getting back to replace Mary, which resulted in muffled giggles that could be heard by all present.

Like the previous day, they had been so engrossed in each other they had not noticed, or at least Davy had not noticed, that the groom and three staff had already headed up the towpath back to the mansion house.

When Davy finally turned to look up the path the group had disappeared out of sight.

"Oh dear," teased Anna "they've left me behind. You will have to walk me back up to the House. It's not safe for a young lady to ride alone when it's getting dark."

"Joe was right about you," laughed Davy.

"Oh, and why is that?" asked Anna as she continued teasing.

"I do hope it was nothing terrible. I thought he was a gentleman."

"No Anna, nothing bad. He's a good friend to both of us and Kitty is too for that matter," said Davy, dropping all chat up tone and showing a seriousness Anna had not seen up to now, but it was a seriousness she enjoyed. At least now she knew that Davy was not just a lightweight womaniser.

Davy had not disappointed her. He was still the honest, handsome, if a little too serious, boy she had spent the best summer of her very privileged young life. There was still the unexplainable sense of affection for him which had not been worn out by time or circumstance in the intervening five years.

45

They walked up the tow path to Shaw's Bridge. As they reached it, Davy walked beside Anna as she walked her horse. He started to go under the bridge to continue up the towpath in the direction of the back entrance of Ballydrain House on the Lagan bank.

"No Davy we aren't going that way. We are going up through the Dub[25] and in the front entrance," said Anna.

"But it's the long way around and your father will see us coming all the way up to your door," spluttered Davy.

Anna stopped the horse, turned to Davy, and with a look of certainty he had never seen before, but would see time and time again.

"That's exactly what is going to happen, unless I embarrass you, in which case I will see myself home."

"Embarrassed by you?" blurted Davy in a mixture of panic and disbelief.

"Embarrassed by you. How could I be embarrassed by you? I've thought about you for five years and cursed my luck at not being one of the spoilt, posh, hooray Henrys that are in your circle."

Davy could not believe what he had just said to Anna. Men did not expose their feelings to women that easy. He reached into his pocket for a cigarette, fumbling with the matches, while he thought what to say next, dreading that he had messed everything

---

[25] The Dub, local term for the Upper Malone Road, the original Dublin Road which passed the entrance to Ballydrain House.

up once and for all. Maybe his father was right five years ago. Getting involved with the upper classes only ends in tears.

To make matters worse, Anna stared at him, motionless and expressionless, deep into his eyes.

After what seemed a lifetime, Anna finally broke the silence.

"Well, I'm glad we got that clear," smiled Anna.

Davy's mind was still reeling. He was well out of his comfort zone. Any communication with girls up to now had been shallow, frivolous, certainly not this serious.

"The light's starting to fade. It'll be pitch dark at this rate and the only ones to see our great entrance will be the badgers," laughed Davy, hoping he had retrieved some sense of control of the situation.

As he started to stride forward purposefully in the direction of the Malone Road, Anna stepped across him, reached up, put her arms round his neck and pressed her lips and her slim waist hard and close to him.

The kiss was like no other Davy had felt before. This was not the usual entertaining snog which only proved he had achieved his aim for the night. That kiss was the real thing. Their souls seemed to meet somewhere from the back of the brain. It was a sensation of ultimate sex, excitement, unity of souls and thought Davy, "So this was love, was it?"

As they stood back from each other, Anna turned to the horse, asked Davy for a hitch up, and told him to get on behind her explaining this was the only way to make sure their grand entrance would be in daylight.

The horse and riders trotted up as far as the junction of Dunmurry Lane just before the entrance to Sir James's gates on the left, Davy dismounted. Anna trotted, head held high, and Davy jogged alongside the two hundred yards walk from the gates, along the elm tree lined driveway towards the courtyard at the back of the house.

Curtains moved in the drawing room and the attic.

In the drawing room, Sir James stopped puffing his pipe. Lady May, on seeing James set down his paper and stand up at the window, stopped her embroidery. Neither spoke.

Up in the attic Kitty and Mary sat mouths open, glancing between each other and the pair in the driveway.

"Sweet mother of Jesus, Kitty, she did it. She fecking did it!" whispered Mary in her Sligo brogue.

"Aye she did Mary. Let's hope it doesn't go down too badly with Sir James and Lady May, or you and me could be out of here and in the workhouse or even worse!" whispered Kitty.

'What in the mother of God is she playing at Kitty," asked Mary in a panic.

'She's setting her stall out. Letting Sir James know what she's about. Testing his resolve. Trying to make him play his hand so she can back him into a corner. So that he has to run with it," whispered Kitty not taking her eyes off the pair deep in conversation in the courtyard below.

"'Get the better of Sir James? That would be a first," chuckled Mary in a panic.

"Well, we'll just have to wait and find out. At least you won't have to risk standing in for Anna again. She's gone past that stage in no uncertain manner."

"Go back to sleep Mary," said Kitty, still looking out the window.

"I think tomorrow morning could be interesting."

Chapter Seven

Late back my dear

The next morning, breakfast at the House was as normal. Lady May arrived first, maintaining a discerning glance at preparations as Kitty flitted in and out of the side door to the kitchen. Lady May noticed that Kitty was not making eye contact with her which she though a bit strange. Kitty usually greeted Lady May with a smile and a few words. This morning she just got a head down, quick exit to the kitchen and a barely audible "Morning Mam."

"Interesting," thought Lady May.

Next Sir James entered, wearing his best business suit, strolled over to the French windows and surveyed his substantial gardens.

"Didn't seem to sleep too well my dear. Tossed and turned all night," said Lady May, as she rose from the breakfast table, stopping, as she stood beside him, staring out at the same view.

"Yes, my dear, I have an important meeting at Hilden. Chap from the Government wants to know how much more we can increase linen production. This war that was supposed to be over by Christmas, might take a bit longer, reading between the lines," mused Sir James.

"You are such a worrier James. It may never come to it," said May, not really believing what she had said but trying to maintain the supportive role of a good wife of the upper class. She could never appear to be anything but calm, collected and slightly superior. Anything less would not really be appropriate.

"But if it does, Roger will be sent to France or Belgium and be in the thick of it. Second Lieutenants are prime targets. I know from the Boer Wars. Saw a few old friends never come home. There's no glory in war, it's just a horrible mess," sighed Sir James, with a fixed gaze over the garden.

"My poor dear, it will all work out for the best," reassured May.

Sir James put his arm around her shoulder and gave her a slight hug with one arm, while still gazing out of the French window.

As they turned to sit at the breakfast table, Roger, their only son, heir to the Arthur empire, entered the room. Roger was two years older than Anna, a fresh faced lad, who looked younger than his age. He was in his second year at Queens University Belfast studying Law, because Sir James thought it would stand him in good stead when he would one day take over the business. Roger for his part enjoyed law, as it suited him. He was an honourable lad, liked to read, think, plan, make good decisions. He had no interest in horses like his father or his sister Anna, but he loved nature, wildlife and loved to paint. Playing rugby, football, were things he had to do as a matter of comradeship, but it didn't really interest him.

He had enjoyed the Young Citizens Volunteers for several years. Going camping, living off the land and the whole sense of comradeship amongst the other young men of better off parts of South Belfast and the Lagan Valley. Roger often racked his brain at the huge wealth that his father had accumulated while he watched men and women grow older than their years at his father's mills. Someday when he was in control, he would like to change things.

"Morning father, morning mother," said Roger, as he pulled back the dining chair.

"Meeting that Ministry chap this morning father?" continued Roger.

"Yes Roger," replied Sir James.

"The war in France seems to be intensifying, not ending, and with McMordie turning the Young Citizens Volunteers into the 14th Battalion it's looking that way," said Roger, as Kitty came through the door with jugs of water.

"Let's not talk of war at the breakfast table, ghastly topic at the best of times," interrupted Lady May to stop Sir James taking up the conversation further.

Anna, with a noticeably determined stride and expression, was the last to enter the room. Roger, who had missed the whole grand entrance of the previous evening, caught her eye with a quizzical look, to which she responded with an expressionless stare back.

"Morning father, morning mother, morning Roger," greeted Anna to all seated.

"Good morning to you Anna," replied Sir James, as he lifted the jug of water.

"Took the scenic route home last night?" His face staring at the plate Kitty had just set before him.

"Yes father. It was getting dark and thought it was safer than up the tow path. David Gibson, the blacksmith's son kindly walked with me, he insisted," replied Anna.

"I'm sure that was a great sacrifice for him," replied Sir James, not raising his eyes.

"You seemed to take a long time thanking him before he left the stables," retorted Sir James. This time lifting his gaze directly to Anna from four foot across the table. Anna looked back at her father, staring him straight in the eye, face expressionless.

"Yes father, David was most kind in seeing me safely home. It was only good manners to express my gratitude and we had plenty to talk about between here and the Forge, making up for four years, seven months and twenty-one days."

A brief silence was interrupted by Roger almost choking on his first sip of water.

Anna looked at him as if she wished he had choked.

"You have learnt your lesson to get back in the daylight with the rest of the group?" asked Sir James.

"Oh yes father, but David said he would escort me back up if it happened again."

"And would it happen again, Anna, that is the question?" said Sir James.

"It might if I am seeing David and it gets dark early."

"So, you intend seeing this David Gibson again?" asked Sir James

"Yes father, next Sunday afternoon," replied Anna confidently and without hesitation.

"I see," said Sir James, as he cut into his gammon.

"Well, I'll have to send one of the grooms down to the forge to explain that you will not be able to attend as you will be away to your uncle and aunts at the Dungannon estate for the next month. They invited you up to their hunt week. Just got word yesterday and you know how much they would be disappointed if you did not go," pressed Sir James.

"Well, I'm sorry Father, I cannot go to Dungannon because I have other arrangements made that have to take precedence," replied Anna.

At this point Kitty entered the room carrying the tea pot.

As she walked behind Sir James, she gave Anna a look that suggested Anna was in mortal danger.

"I have joined the Nursing Auxiliaries at the UVF[26] hospital in Belfast. It is the only way we can help our men in this ghastly war. I must attend training and it starts next week. I do not have the option. Some of my friends are joining as well, so you see I will have to decline uncle's invitation. I am sure he will understand," replied Anna, apologetically.

"I'll be working in Belfast most days of the week so I cannot leave home and certainly not go to Dungannon."

Sir James said no more, ate his breakfast with difficulty, and left to attend his meeting.

"This damn war is going to be the ruination of this family," he thought to himself.

---

[26] UVF Ulster Volunteer Force, the name given to the volunteer divisions of 36th Ulster Division.

Chapter eight

Young Citizens Volunteers

For the rest of the summer of 1915 Anna, Kitty, Joe and. Davy spent many evenings and Sundays together.

Romance bloomed for all four. By the Autumn, the beauty of that summer would turn to darker days.

The Young Citizens Volunteers nicknamed "Chocolate Soldiers" by the other Battalions of the Irish Rifles, being mostly middle class and a bit more privileged, free thinking and gentler natured than the boys from the tough streets of inner Belfast, and who did not respond well to orders at the weekend training camps in the Randalstown and Clandeboye Estates.

Davy, Bill Johnston, Rab Tate, Dessie Clarke, Jonty Price, Peter Liggett and the Bamford twins, Allen and Adam from the football team were all YCV members. Boy Scouts since before the war ever started and had enjoyed every minute of it. That was until they were all landed into the British Army to fight for God, King and Country.

As they gathered at Great Victoria St Station on a damp grey autumn morning to be transported to Clandeboye Estate for initial weekend training, their thoughts were a mixture of excitement and apprehension.

As they started to line up for the train, Bill noticed Joe heading towards them.

"Hey Joe, coming to wave us off?" bantered Bill.

"Not exactly," replied Joe with a grunt filled with irony.

"What the hell, you're not coming with us?

Are you mad, this isn't your war mate, better keeping out of it?" implored Bill.

"They're lining up in droves from the Falls, Markets and Short Strand to join the Connaught Rangers and the Dublin Fusiliers. All Irishmen have a common enemy is what they are saying," said Joe.

"So why aren't you away with them?" asked Bill.

"Aye that's another story," said Joe, turning his head away trying to signal he didn't want to discuss it.

As the lads travelled down to Bangor station, Davy got the chance to get Joe by himself.

"Ok Joe, you've got me confused. We've talked about this war before and you know I'm not keen on dying for Ulster, or anyone else, but I'm stuck on a hook with the YCV and my pals. You, you can give it a bye ball," advised Davy as he handed Joe a Woodbine.

"Not as simple as that, Davy. The 16th Irish are entering on the basis that your government told Ireland it'll get independence, which is a good idea by my thinking. As well as that the pay is a lot better than a drover's wages. I went up to Donegall Street and joined the queue for the Connaught Rangers. There's me standing in the line at the enlisting office in Belfast minding my own business and some bastards knew me and started slagging me off. Calling me a Prod lover because I spend my time with you boys in South Belfast. One cheeky sod called me a Carson lick. I'm telling you Davy; it got a bit scary. Nearly as bad as that day we played up in Woodvale Park. I'm standing there about as popular as a fox in a chicken run, and I thought to myself, the pay's the same in the 14th Battalion, 36th Irish Rifles as it is in the Connaughts. They are both British Army at the end of the day and if I'm going to join up, I'd rather do it with my mates. So that's it," explained Joe making sure no one else heard his words.

Davy sighed and shook his head, "Joe, I didn't think you were a mad bastard. What does Kitty think about it?"

"Haven't told her yet. Reckoned I'd leave it until I see her next Sunday."

"More likely to scare her half to death," replied Davy.

"Not if I ask her to marry me and explain to her. I can send my army pay home. It'll pay for the boat for both of us to go to Canada when this is all over. Get a job on the Canadian Railways. No bigots holding us back, sorted. It's the only way I can earn good money to get us off to a decent start," stressed Joe.

Davy let out a long slow puff of smoke from his mouth and nostrils, stared and said nothing; just shook his head slowly.

"Kitty would marry you if you hadn't two pence. You don't need to risk your life and limb to convince her," said Davy.

"That might be Davy, but I owe it to her to have a good start," replied Joe.

"That's twice you've shown your romantic side, you're starting to make a habit of it," joked Davy.

Joe stared at Davy with an expression of frustration and said,

"You're one to talk about romance. You're running around with Lady Anna like a lap dog. She loves you to bits and you haven't the guts to ask her to marry you."

"But Joe, you know I haven't a pup's chance of marrying her. The family won't allow it. They'll shift her off to some ponce in the Home Counties if it comes to it and I'll be a sad memory,'' replied Davy with a large degree of angst.

"So why are you still knocking around with her, if it's not going anywhere?" mocked Joe.

"Because I can't stop seeing her but I'm just waiting for the moment she'll be gone," sighed Davy.

Joe laughed quietly and drew on his cigarette.

"And you think I'm a mad bastard. See you, you're a thick mad bastard! Have you not caught on by now that Anna is interested in no one else? She could take the pick of the young bucks of local big noises, but she spends her time with you, no other bastard. Don't you worry about the family. From what I've heard from Kitty, Anna is one step ahead of her father up to now.

"Faith Davy, I told you that Sunday, Kitty arranged Shaw's Bridge that day. Have Faith, faith in the future, and faith in Anna," advised Joe, as the train pulled in at Bangor Station for the march to Conlig and the Clandeboye Estate.

Davy smiled and quietly laughed. "Maybe a few Hail Mary's wouldn't go a miss then Joe."

"Take it as done Davy."

Chapter nine

Morning Service

The following Sunday morning, Davy made an uneasy walk up to St Patrick's Church of Ireland at Drumbeg.[27] He sat on the wall of Drumbeg Bridge twenty-five yards from the lichgate that led up the slope to the entrance of the church.

It was about half past ten in the morning. He had been there since ten. Taking in the beauty of the river and the Autumn, watching for the blue flash of the kingfisher dip below the bridge and out the other side, to land on an overhanging willow branch. Even with this idyllic atmosphere he felt uneasy. He had walked up from Newforge, not taking the chance of a lighter up to the bridge, because he was in his Sunday best, and didn't want to risk the coal dust of the lighter, even if he did sit up at the tiller.

For the half hour it had taken him to walk up to Drum Bridge his mind was in turmoil. When he had got back late on Saturday night from Clandeboye training there was a note from Anna that she had left down to the cottage with Tom.

The sight of the note had frozen him with fear. He thought it might be a goodbye letter, until he opened it, to find it was not

---

[27] Drumbeg, Townland near Ballydrain House Upper Malone.

the inevitable ending of relations but a strange request to be outside the front of the church on" Sunday morning.

He wasn't a church goer. Tom had never given him any encouragement, for his father still resented God for not helping his wife, Davy's mother. She had died when Davy was only four years old. A frosty morning, slippery well steps, three hours lying in freezing water at the bottom of the well, concussion, followed by pneumonia and death. Not once had God stepped in to do anything. Tom didn't owe the Lord a thing.

"Outside St Patrick's Drumbeg for morning service?" thought Davy to himself.

"What was wrong with the usual two o'clock outside the bottom gate or Anna arriving down at the cottage on horseback? Anna Arthur, what are you up to? Your whole family will be there. They don't want me near and you're putting me right in the lions' den. Big change from nipping out dressed as a kitchen maid." mused Davy.

"Well Anna Arthur, I'd jump in that river with stones attached if you wanted, so I'll just run with this and see how it goes. Hope Joe is right about faith," he said under his breath.

It wasn't just faith in Anna, it was complicated blind faith, love complete and utter," thought Davy to himself.

His thoughts were broken by the chatter and vision of the family complete with the Church of Ireland members of staff who lived at the mansion, walking down the road from the entrance of the estate some two hundred yards north of the bridge and the church.

It was the usual ceremonial family stroll to church if the weather allowed, and this was a fine Autumn morning. The sun glinting through the trees that lined each side of the road which had been part of the old coach road leading south out of Belfast since medieval times, in the direction of Lisburn, Newry and Dublin far south since the seventeenth century and earlier.

Davy only occasionally looked up towards them, keeping his eyes gazing over the river below, his back to the road.

He was relieved that he could see Anna had at least turned up. She was walking alongside Roger directly behind Sir James and Lady May. Roger and Anna seemed to be having a brother sister type of conversation, the sort where the older brother is teasing the younger sister. They seemed to be whispering to each other, heads tilted inwards. Then Anna nudged him with her elbow and gave him a playful slap on his arm, the effect of which was for Roger to stifle a laugh.

'No prizes for who they are talking about," laughed Davy to himself.

Sir James sensing the antics of Roger and Anna, half turned to them quizzically.

"James, leave them alone and take that pipe out before you reach the bridge. You can't go to church with that hanging out of your mouth," said Lady May, with a smile that said right now or there will be repercussions later.

On seeing Sir James start to stub out his pipe, Davy instinctively removed his cigarette from his mouth and flicked it over the bridge into the river, only for an opportunistic moorhen to dart from the reed bank and gobble it up within a second.

"Here goes nothing, stay calm. Speak when you are spoken to. Be especially courteous to Lady May," was the sum of the advice his father had given earlier that morning as they sat at breakfast.

Tom had always told Davy not to get involved with Anna or any of her kind because he knew it would come to nothing and only leave Davy broken.

Sir James and Davy made eye contact at the same time as the family reached the bridge. They were about ten yards apart.

It was obvious from Sir James's glare that he had not been told Davy would be there. Davy dropped his gaze first and Sir James without turning his head, quietly growled.

"Anna, up here, now!"

He paused, half turned, and proceeded to inspect a wild rose sticking out amongst the hedgerow.

"Yes father, what is it?" asked Anna, as she also inspected the beauty of the wild rose, copying her father's feigned interest in the plant.

'Whatever it is you are cultivating, my dear, I suggest you nip it in the bud. This flower is surely a thing of fleeting beauty. It stands out in this mass of weed and thistle, but it will soon be overcome by them because it does not have the breeding to withstand them," said Sir James, as he snapped the rose, breaking it from its stem, and tossing it in the river where it started to float downstream.

"I allowed you your little moment of glory parading your bit of rough up the drive, all but humiliating me, but this has to stop, if not now, very soon!"

Anna wanted to reproach him for destroying the beautiful flower but bit her lip as her mind raced.

As the brief ten second confrontation took place the servants turned their faces half to one side and spoke between each other with an air of complete detachment. None of them, especially the maids, could wait to let Kitty know about this one.

As the party moved on and passed Davy, Sir James turned to him and said politely,

"Good morning young man, Fine morning," with the air of the factory boss confronting a worker, who had failed to clock in on time.

"Good morning Sir James, Lady May," replied Davy as he gave a courteous bow to Lady May. "A lovely morning it is too Sir, Mam," continued Davy.

Sir and Lady Arthur walked towards the lichgate and up to the church entrance, Roger, closely behind, fixing his gaze mostly to the sky. He smiled through gritted teeth saying to himself,

"Don't do this little sister. He is running out of patience. Do not push him too far."

Anna for her part, had not continued to walk with her father, but had held back feigning failed attempts to find another rose, while inwardly trying to unravel the next move.

As she moved alongside Davy, she put her arm under his arm and proceeded to walk him towards the church entrance.

As they locked arms the servants passed them by and Jonty, the stable lad, never short of a wise crack, started to quietly, but not quietly enough, sing.

"Onward Christian soldiers. Marching off to, Och!"

Big Martha Watson, one of the kitchen maids dug her elbow deep into his ribs so hard he thought he'd been kicked by a stallion.

"Jesus, Martha what was that for?" squealed Jonty.

"For getting in the way of true love, which you wouldn't recognise, even if you got your ribs broke," scoffed Martha.

Anna and Davy heard this spat. She smiled and quietly gave Martha her approval.

"I think you enjoyed that, Martha."

"Aye and he'll get more if he doesn't watch himself," whispered Martha out of side of her mouth. Martha was large boned, with a head of ginger curls, freckles to match, much the same age as Anna and Davy and standing a good six inches taller than the diminutive Jonty.

Still trying to remain calm and collected Davy whispered to Anna.

"What are you playing at Anna? Because whatever it is, it doesn't seem to be working."

"Davy, do you love me?" asked Anna, as they walked more quickly trying to catch up with the rest of the family.

"You know I do. I told you enough times," replied Davy in exasperation.

"Well then just leave this to me and don't waiver. Just stay beside me no matter what," whispered Anna.

As the family proceeded up the centre isle and took up their seats on the front row on the righthand side, the staff slid into the pews at the back of the church.

Anna walked arm in arm with Davy up to the family front pews and surveyed the row. As she proceeded to enter the row, Sir James quietly leaned over and whispered.

"Anna, this is the Arthur Family row; has been for generations. There is one space left and that is yours my dear."

Anna looked at her father, giving him a look of pity and disappointment.

"Very well father we will find two more seats. I will see you after."

Sir James returned his gaze to the pulpit and muttered to himself, "You can be sure of that young madam."

Anna and Davy started to walk back down the centre isle of the church, Anna scanning her eyes for two spaces.

Davy was in complete confusion. He was out of his comfort zone, not just being in church, but being in the direct line of Sir James Arthur's wrath was a whole different level.

Other parishioners, keen not to cross Sir James, quickly spread themselves a bit so that no spaces were available.

As Anna and Davy reached near the back of the church, almost level with the servants, Martha leaned forward along the row.

"Mam, Anna, there is room for two here," whispered Martha, sitting beside Jonty.

Davy gave Jonty a stare. There seemed little enough space for one never mind two.

"There is now," whispered Martha, as she half stood up, moved sideways towards Jonty, and for the better part, sat on him.

"There you go Miss Anna, plenty of room now for you and your man!" grinned Martha.

Davy did as he promised and went along with it all. The Sunday service seemed to take a lifetime to Davy. The only bits that Davy appreciated was one of the readings when the vicar had said something about, 'and wherever you go, I will go also,' stuck in his brain.

Afterwards outside in the church grounds the parishioners milled around. Discreetly polite conversations were about one topic only. All eyes were focused on Sir James and young Anna.

Anna, with Davy still rigidly grasping her arm, walked into the middle of the family group, straight to Sir James,

"Father you need not have worried, we were able to find two seats further back. Lovely sermon this morning. Very appropriate, about love for one's fellow man and all that.

This is David Gibson, the young gentleman who left me back safely those months ago. You never did get the chance to thank him father."

David looked at Sir James and kept his face straight as his own father had told him.

"Yes of course David, very gallant of you, most considerate." responded Sir James; concealing gritted teeth.

"I must reward you with your kindness. I do not want to be in your debt," as he reached into his pocket.

"No Sir James. it was a pleasure to see your daughter back safely."

"But I insist, David," replied Sir James.

"Father don't embarrass him any further, David is my friend, my best friend, not an employee," laughed Anna trying to disarm Sir James with charm. A skill she had been taught almost daily at the Swiss finishing School in Basle.

"Now father, you will have to excuse us, as I have been invited to David's cottage for lunch, so we will have to be going on. Don't worry about me, David will bring me back home safely," reassured Anna.

As they disappeared out of the church yard over the Drumbeg Bridge, Davy whispered to Anna.

"When did my Da organize lunch? He never mentioned it this morning."

Anna squeezed his arm, kept walking, quickening the pace as if to get away as soon as possible, beyond the view of the onlooking church goers.

"He didn't," giggled Anna.

"You are a witch Anna Arthur, and you know what happened to them," laughed Davy, quietly.

They kept walking down the Malone Road in the direction of Belfast and cut across Bladon Meadows until they could see the Stranmillis Boat Club tennis courts in the distance. By the time they reached a canal bench outside the Club, Anna had explained to him what she was playing at with Sir James. The whole grand entrance down the driveway, the church gathering, were intended to present Sir James with a fate accompli that he felt obliged to accept. He would give in to Anna's friendship with Davy once he saw it really meant so much to her, but she admitted to Davy in exasperation it was not working out.

70

As they sat on the wall opposite the watering trough, the adrenalin rush of the battle of wills between Anna and Sir James decreased, Davy sat quietly, slowly dragging on his cigarette. Anna was equally deep in her thoughts.

As they sat beside each other, leaning closely rapped in each other's arms, Davy could feel slow, but steadily increasing, slight jolts coming from Anna's shoulder and arm.

As usual with matters of women and matters of the heart, Davy was slow to catch on.

Davy turned his face to Anna's cheek and felt the moist salted taste of tears on her face that ran down to her mouth and down towards her neck dampening the high silk ruff collar.

Davy looked at her full in the face. He had never seen her like this, before. Gone was the confident, quick witted, beautiful young woman he looked up to like a goddess. He saw instead a fragile, distraught beyond compare, young girl. One who needed his love, his reassurance, his support, his protection. One that he never wanted to see unhappy, one he wanted to be with until his last breath.

As he sat on his haunches in front of this frightened girl he said,

'Hey girl, it'll be all right. We'll just have to try another way." said Davy, not having a clue what that would be.

"How could he be so horrible to us, Davy?" sobbed Anna whose face was reddened and contorted in an outburst of cries.

Davy put his hands on each side of her face and brushed her hair up on each side of her head until it stood out like pigtails and leant forward and kissed each cheek, then her lips slowly, repeatedly, gently at first, then more strongly as he felt her mouth respond. They kissed and caressing each other's backs for what seemed to never end.

"No one, not even Sir James, will ever make you cry again, if it's anything to do with me," whispered Davy.

"As long as I breathe, I will never stop caring for you."

"Will you Davy?" sobbed Anna.

'Till the day I die," sighed Davy almost quivering himself.

They hugged and kissed, hardly saying anything, until they were interrupted by the clopping hooves of a barge horse passing.

"Hey girl, I think we'd best go back to the cottage and get you cleaned up. Don't want your Da saying I left you in this state."

As they walked arm in arm back up the tow path, holding each other round the shoulders, patting each other reassuringly, the mood changed to occasional laughter and whispers, heads almost stuck together.

When they reached the cottage, Tom was sitting on his armchair which he had dragged outside of the cottage, smoking his pipe, looking into the sky.

"Wondered when you two would show up. Thought you were coming for lunch?" he asked, still looking up at the sky.

Davy and Anna, exchanged surprised glances.

"Don't look at me all innocent," continued Tom, now looking at the pair of them with a barely concealed smile on his face.

"The lunch you were coming here for, after you rubbed Sir James's nose in it, in front of half of the townland," grunted Tom.

"How did you know that Da?" asked Davy.

"How did I know that he says," with a chuckle sprinkled with irony.

"Because half of the country has taken to having a Sunday afternoon stroll past here in the hope that they'd see Lady Anna sitting eating her dinner off a tin plate and a tin mug at our busted table. I've heard the full story, before church, in the church, after the church and even you two wrapped round each other's arms all afternoon down at the Boat Club. You must have it bad. Word has it you pair wouldn't have noticed the 12th Parade[28] walk by you this afternoon."

He stared at them both and the contained smile turned to deep concern.

"I am sorry Mr Gibson," said Anna politely.

"It was all my fault. Davy didn't know about it. I thought I could outwit father and force him into accepting Davy, but it all went horribly wrong. I feel such a stupid fool."

Her eyes started to fill up again. Davy interrupted the moment trying to change the mood.

---

[28] 12th Parade" The Orange Order Annual Parade through Belfast.

Davy led Anna to the entrance of the cottage and pointed to the jaw box sink and a bar of coarse carbolic soap, as he raced back out to collect a clean towel that was hanging on the washing line out the back.

After he left it in with Anna, he sat on the ground, his back against the cottage wall close beside Tom, still sitting in his chair.

"I told you son, many times, don't get involved with the big boys and girls. It will only end in tears. Told you find your own level, but no you wouldn't listen," sighed Tom.

"I know Da, but it is, what it is. I can't keep her out of my head. I don't know how to sort this out. We love each other and I'll just have to think of some way that I can deal with Sir James so that Anna is fine."

Tom took his pipe from his mouth and sighed.

"Seems like you intend sticking with this one son. Can't blame you for that. Beautiful, rich, intelligent, good heart; but you are punching above your weight, son.

"Problem is Sir James knows that and thinks you are interested in your own ends. Problem is also you cannot give her what he thinks is best for her, wealth, luxury, position," sighed Tom, as he sucked on his pipe, inhaled deeply, and stared at the ground.

"But if you love someone what has the rest got to do with it?" asked Davy in frustration, as he kicked at a large weed just in reach of his right boot.

Tom tapped his pipe against his own boot.

74

"Sir James is a businessman. Everything is about profit and loss. Making a loss is not in his scheme of things, son. You, as he sees it, are a loss to him and Anna, pure and simple. He has invested in Anna her entire life to become a beautiful, happy, carefree spirit, in the land of affluence. He is protecting his investment.

"Anna doing what she wants and not what he thinks best for her, gives the impression he is not in control of his household.

"Sir James must be seen to be the man in charge. The man in the big picture, otherwise, his power and status crumbles. Solve all that and you are home in a boat," sighed Tom again.

"And how do I do that?" asked Davy, turning half sided to Tom, expecting a revelation that would solve the problem in one fell swoop.

"Damned if I know son, damned if I know," replied Tom, putting his pipe back in his mouth, watching the smoke rise slowly into the autumn sky.

"That son is what you are up against," sighed Tom as he tapped his ash from his pipe.

After a few minutes of silence, Anna reappeared at the cottage door, hair fixed, face, only showing the remnants of earlier grief.

"Well, you two, it's time her ladyship here got back home safe. You seem to be making a habit of staying out when it's getting dark," said Tom.

'Ok Da, we'll go up the towpath and go the short cut in the back way," said Davy, as he rose to his feet.

"No Davy, you stay where you are son. Sir James has seen enough of you for one day. I'll walk your young lady back home this evening. Might be best," said Tom, in a tone suggesting this was not open to debate.

As Davy was about to reply, Anna grabbed him by the arm.

'Your father is right Davy. I have messed things up enough for one day. I'll have to fix it."

She stood on her toes and kissed him on the lips and whispered.

"Nothing will separate us, Davy."

In the meantime, Tom retrieved his coat from the cottage and with it a shawl that had been folded neatly away.

"Here girl, put this over your shoulders, that pretty dress of yours won't do you any favours on these nights. Don't want you catching pneumonia.

"Right Davy, you have everything closed down by the time I get back," instructed Tom.

As Davy watched the unlikely pair walk briskly up the lane into the distance, he noticed that Tom was deep in conversation with Anna, who for a change, was doing the listening.

As he tidied up the outside of the cottage a thought occurred to him which made him smile slowly. The shawl Tom had brought out for Anna was his mother's. From he was a child he had watched his father rap himself in that shawl on a winter's night. No one, not even himself, when he had fevers in winter ever got using that shawl.

"Ah Da, if only Anna could win her father over as easy as you," thought Davy.

By the time Tom and Anna had reached Shaw's Bridge and they cut up the section of towpath to the back entrance on the Lagan bank, Tom had spent the time in polite conversation, trying to settle Anna's mood so she could recover enough composure to at least face her father. By the time they reached the grand house steps Anna had regained her composure. As she entered the heavy double door, she turned and thanked Tom before she disappeared inside. The inside door closed behind Anna, but the outside doors remained open.

Tom walked back to the top step, bent his knees, hitched his trousers legs, and slowly sat on the step. He took out his pipe, rummaged for his tobacco and match, lit up, looked over the front lawn in the direction of the lake and waited.

After about five minutes the inside door slowly opened behind him. As it did, Tom, with his pipe still between his teeth and without turning around said,

"It would appear we have a mutual concern Sir James."

Sir James walked past Tom down the steps and without turning around, also brought his tobacco from his leather pouch, lit up, and still looking in the direction of the lake at the front of the mansion, eventually replied, as he raised his head slightly upwards looking into the night sky.

"Speak your mind Gibson, but make it quick, I've just left a warm fire in the drawing room."

"Short and simple it is then, Sir James.

"Miss Anna and my lad Davy are making life complicated for themselves, and we aren't making it any easier. She is a strong willed, young lady and Davy just thinks the world shines out of her ....."

Tom paused before he pushed his luck too far.

"Get to the point man," replied Sir James.

" The pair of them are beyond taking either your direction or mine. I've told Davy since he was a wean[29] that your kind were to be avoided because you would eat him up and spit him out and you've made it plain that you don't approve of Anna being anywhere near him.

"If we don't tread carefully on this, we'll lose the pair of them, and I don't think either of us want that Sir James."

---

[29] Wean, an Ulster Scot term for a young child.

Tom stood up, still chewing, rather than smoking his pipe, and still slightly behind Sir James, just off his left shoulder. Sir James was still looking out across the lake, judging when turning to face Tom would have maximum effect.

Both men sent pillars of smoke into the damp Autumn air, neither speaking for what seemed an eternity. Sir James was using the established strategy he used in serious meetings of saying little, creating long silences, forcing the other parties to speak more and show their hand.

Tom knew this might happen. He had played too many hands of poker on winters nights in Molly Ward's Inn. Never show your hand first was the rule, so he waited until Sir James was forced, out of exasperation, to turn and face him.

Both men were of a similar height, both about five foot nine inches. It had the effect that neither held any physical advantage when it came to a standoff.

As James looked into Tom's face, two sets of eyes met each other on equal terms; both meaning business.

"You are keeping me from a glass of Craig's finest Dunville whiskey, which I have been looking forward to ending my Sunday evening, but sadly, like everything else this day, nothing has worked out as I planned. Apart from that," he sighed,

"No two fathers should have to talk about their off springs' welfare standing out in the cold air. I apologise for my bad manners and not thanking you in for returning my erstwhile daughter home safely. Please come in and we will share a glass before you journey home."

Sir James had moved on to business strategy second option, if the opposition does not respond to coercion, try the softening up approach.

Tom, fully aware of Sir James's ruse, held his tongue and politely accepted his offer.

Sir James led Tom into the reading room and opened a Tyrone crystal decanter of Dunville Special and poured two generous measures into two matching crystal classes. A bit different to the illicit brews Tom was used to drinking from the enamel cup.

After a few minutes of sipping the Dunville and discussing the merits of brands of whiskey.

"Well then Thomas," said Sir James, deliberately dropping his Sir name in the hope of mellowing Tom.

"What is your solution to this mutual dilemma?"

Sir James had forced Tom to show his hand, he thought, but in fact it was not so. Tom had always wanted to tell him his thoughts, but the problem was to get Sir James to listen. Sitting in the reading room of the big house with a glass of whiskey in a crystal glass meant Sir James was listening.

"They are both nineteen years old. Both, think they are in love and neither of us, for different reasons perhaps, think it is in their best interests," said Tom, looking Sir James straight in the face, not threateningly, but with a look of concern.

80

"I am not in favour of it any more than you because in the long term your lot would make my Davy's life a misery. Treat him like a poor relative and nothing he could do would be good enough. Now my Davy is a good lad. He'll maybe have his own butcher's shop in years to come. Find the right girl and get himself a house on the Lisburn Road and he'll be content, not having to meet expectations all the time. Your crowd would eventually destroy him and no man or woman's going to do that to him as long as I breathe.

"Now your young lady, on the other hand, from the little I know of her and my wee[30] chat with her tonight, tells me she would live with Davy in the hedge rows, and that's not what either of us want.

As I said, they are nineteen. Every man and woman at nineteen have their heads turned with romance. By the time they are a few years older, sad realities of life, changes most of us.

We've a war on and Davy's going off to it. I believe your Roger is, as well, and Anna's down at the UVF hospital in Belfast. If that doesn't change their attitudes nothing will."

A silence fell for about twenty seconds as both men tasted the whiskey and drained the rest of their glasses, a subconscious sign that both had talked as much as they wanted to for the evening.

"Well Tom, so what is your suggestion," asked Sir James.

---

[30] Wee – Ulster Scot term for small.

Tom leaned forward in the comfortable leather chair and as he did, said,

"You're a rugby man Sir James. When do you kick for touch?"

"When I'm under pressure and want to push the opposition back, give the team the chance to regroup, change the emphasis," replied Sir James, slightly surprised by Tom's understanding of the game of rugby football.

"We both step aside from it. We stop getting in their way but coax them both to leave things as they are, until this bloody war is over. That way we won't lose either of them. They'll be a few years older, and a lot of water will be under Shaw's Bridge by then and at worst you can offer me another of these Dunville's and work out plan B."

Tom rose to his feet, looked Sir James in the eye, nodded his head and said,

"Thank you for the malt, Sir James. I'll be off now. Morning will come soon enough."

As Tom turned to shake Sir James's hand. Sir James paused and with a sigh of genuine regret and concern, said,

"I really shouldn't be telling you this, but as you have been forthright with me, I do not consider it right, not to divulge it to you, but Roger has received news of his posting as 2nd Lieutenant and that the Battalion will be leaving these shores in two weeks.

That means Roger, David and all the other young men of the 14th Battalion will be going to England, then on to France. It would seem events have rather pre-empted your suggestion, shrewd as it is. We must both trust in God that we are able to face the dilemma of Anna and David's little tryst when our sons return," advised Sir James, in a tone of barely concealed irony.

Tom stared briefly at Sir James, but did not speak, just nodded and as he turned away, said,

"Thank you again for the malt, Sir James, let's hope we can celebrate with another on the boys' return."

"Seems like a grand idea. We will look forward to it," replied Sir James.

As Tom walked purposefully down the driveway out of the estate, his temper swelled.

"You are one arrogant, greedy bastard Sir James Arthur! It would suit you if Davy never got back. Your little problem solved. If it happens, I'll be back up here to ram your finest Dunville right down your throat and happily swing for it!"

Tom swore to himself.

Chapter Ten

Departure

During the next two weeks the mood in Belfast and throughout Ulster was part excitement and part total dread. Since Carson and Craig had offered up their sons of Ulster to take part in a war of glory that would be over by Christmas the mood by Autumn 1915 was changing. The idea that the war would be over quickly, was long gone.

In the few days coming up to the departures from Donegall Quay in Belfast, the mood was one of excitement and camaraderie for the Volunteers, proud support from loved ones, but below the facade, pure dread.

During the week before leaving, Sir James walked Roger down to the lakeside and recounted some of the military actions that he had found himself in during his time in South Africa, in the Boer Wars. As they walked back up to the mansion forecourt, they saw Lady May and Anna walking around the Italian Garden that had been so perfectly kept by the gardening staff. Sir James and Roger could see that their mood was serious as the two women walked slowly but with their heads facing the ground, occasionally stopping to face each other to emphasis a point.

"I wonder what those pair are up to, Roger?" said Sir James sucking on his pipe, pointing in their direction.

"I believe father we shall soon find out, by the look of things," replied Roger with a guffaw, trying to make light of everything.

Sir James half turned to Roger as they walked nearer to the women.

"I see you are developing a basic skill required by an officer. Never let your men know what you are really thinking. Keeping a calm exterior, even if you are totally lost."

Roger gave his father a contained smile, but it was a smile his father would never erase from his mind.

"Well Roger, looks like we are both about to learn another lesson in women management. A hell of a lot harder than managing a battalion. It's hard enough dealing with one on a mission, but two of them is nigh impossible," whispered Sir James under his breath, trying to make it appear he was not uttering a word.

"Well, my dears, taking in the flowers, what's left of them. The Autumn air is taking its toll," asked Sir James, trying to test the mood.

"Damn the bloody flowers!" barked Lady May to Sir James.

Sir James looked at Roger who just kept his eyes to the ground. It had been years since he had either heard his mother curse or even show any facade other than complete calm, despite Sir James's many quirks and outbursts of displeasure over the years.

"Ask that young lady!" snapped Lady May, as she turned and rushed back in the direction of the mansion steps.

"My God Anna, what have you said to her? You really are tempting my patience this last while," said Sir James in consternation.

"I'm going to France, father," said Anna. "I'll be more use there than cutting bandages in Belfast."

"Don't be stupid young lady, there aren't any female soldiers to my knowledge. Who do you think you are, Joan of Arc?" sneered Sir James.

"No Father, they need nurses who can work on the front line. They need girls like me who can ride a horse, handle a gun if needed, speak French and German."

"Anna, I totally forbid it. It is enough that Roger is going. There is no reason for you to go as well. We are all proud of you doing what you can in Belfast,' replied Sir James almost pleading.

"I agree with father, little sister," blurted Roger, a little too condescendingly for Anna's liking.

"Don't you little sister me, big brother!" sneered Anna.

"Anna, why would you want to do such a hair brained act, charging off to France, by yourself, on a whim?" said Sir James, in frustration and fear.

"I'm not going alone. Kitty is coming with me, and it is no whim. I am not a stupid child anymore. Thanks to you dragging me along to your pheasant shoots I can handle a gun. I ride a horse better than most of the men around here. I can speak good French and German thanks to you sending me to Switzerland to keep me away from David," said Anna, still maintaining her determined tone.

"Ah, so now we are getting to the point. David Gibson, the lad who drinks out of an enamel cup. The lad who is handy with a knife and has a fine chat up line with the young ladies. The young man who will never be able to keep you in the manner you have been accustomed," mused Sir James, as he looked up to the sky laden with mares' tails clouds. A sign of a storm brewing.

"Yes, it is about David, it is about Joseph, it is about Roger, it is about all the other Joes, Rogers and Davys that are going off to this stupid, pointless war. Well, somebody has to help clear up the mess," replied Anna in a tone that suggested she had nothing more to say.

"But Anna," said Sir James, as he was abruptly stopped, mid-sentence, by Roger who grabbed his father's arm, quietly but firmly, said,

"Leave it father, leave it."

Sir James surprisingly did leave it.

Anna catching the mood, turned on her heels, walked into the house up the stairs and into her room.

Back in the Italian garden Sir James and Roger stood silently, Sir James occasionally dead heading a rose that was long past its best, still sucking his pipe.

Roger just paced up and down slowly nearby, waiting for his father to speak, deep in his own thoughts.

Sir James finally broke the silence.

"Come Roger. I think we had better go inside, though God knows what sort of reception we are going to get. I think I am in for a long night my boy."

As they reached the bottom of the steps Sir James was behind Roger.

"You'll make a fine officer, son. You handled that situation well. Said little but took control of it; did well my son. Someday when this war is behind us all I know the Arthur business will be in safe hands," said Sir James as he patted the back of his son's shoulder.

"I look forward to it father," replied Roger with a smile.

Chapter eleven

The last farewell

The Saturday afternoon before the 14th Battalion of the Royal Irish Rifles were to leave Donegall Quay for England, before being dispatched to France, the Arthur family, always wanting to keep up appearances, held a garden party as a farewell for Roger, who had asked that all the other local lads of the Battalion, Davy, Joe, Bill Johnston, and the rest of the lads from the area to be invited to attend.

He said it would be good for morale and comradeship. Sir James and Lady May, reluctantly agreed, on the condition they were not allowed into the Mansion, The Arthurs did not want the great unwashed to see the luxury and affluence they had obtained, while keeping wages at the minimum in the mills and rents on their properties. That might have an effect on industrial output. mused Sir James.

As the event got underway, the lads all gathered in an unofficial bunch joking amongst themselves. The twins laughed about it being the first time they had been on the estate in day light, referring to their midnight poaching activities. Bill poked fun at Jonty about the attention big Martha had been making to him and suggesting he would need step ladders to tackle the big girl. Jonty denying any romantic liaison with the big girl, which only added to the lads' intense bombardment of Jonty.

Davy and Joe were noticeably quiet, on the basis that their presence at the event was slightly different to the rest of the lads. Joe was permanently on the lookout for Kitty whom he assumed was busy doing her job distributing refreshments for the guests. He could not see her anywhere.

Davy was similarly looking out for Anna, dreading that Sir James would hide her amongst the sons of the other big wigs of Belfast and the surrounding gentry, not wanting to miss the opportunity to divert Anna's attention away from Davy.

As the lads continued their destruction of poor Jonty, who was still manfully rebuffing all attacks on his character and prowess, Joe nudged Davy.

"There she is Davy, Anna's coming out of the front door there now."

"Aye, right enough," replied Davy, "and she's with another girl, must be one of her cousins from Dungannon.

"Well, she's pulled out the stops for you today Davy, best clothes, dolled up to the nines. There's only one man here that's for Davy. I think you owe me big time for setting you up that Sunday afternoon at the Bridge," smiled Joe, shoving Davy's shoulder as he laughed.

"Oh Jesus, its Kitty, holy shit it's Kitty," gasped Davy, trying to contain his surprise.

"Where?" asked Joe, I've been watching out for her since we got here and haven't seen her anywhere. That so and so Arthur probably has her working in the kitchen just to piss me off! "Don't think so," laughed Davy, "quite the opposite," he continued, as he smiled at Joe, nodding in the direction of the two aristocratic beautiful young ladies stepping out of the main front door of the mansion.

Joe looked in the direction of Davy's nod and for a few seconds stared but did not get the message. Then it dawned on him like a hard slap on the back of the head.

"Kitty! It's Kitty, the other one's Kitty! Jesus Davy she's all dolled up like a real lady. Better than any of them," he murmured to Davy, trying not to open his mouth and draw attention to himself.

"Nearly as good as Anna," laughed Davy, returning the dig on the shoulder to Joe.

"In your dreams Davy boy," replied Joe, as they both instinctively walked slowly in the direction of the girls, who by this stage had reached the bottom of the steps.

While this was unfolding, the rest of the lads had also spotted Anna coming out of the mansion door and had also not picked up on Kitty beside her, so they immediately dropped their verbal assault on Jonty and started on Davy.

"Aye, away you go Davy," shouted Bill. "Away and lick up to her ladyship. Fancy yourself as the next Sir James. Yes Anna, No Anna!"

"All the world loves a trier," pitched in Jonty, only too glad to divert the ridicule away from himself.

"Aye. if you're taking her down to the bottom meadow, watch your footing Davy. We've a few traps laid down there last night. Wouldn't want you and Anna tripping over them and getting all covered in leaves, God knows what people would think!" joked Allen, one of the twins.

"Aye and it took us long enough setting them. Don't want to have to fix them again because of your romantic capers!" chipped in Adam, the other twin.

Davy, grinned as he walked away from them, putting one hand behind his back with two fingers extended, and as a final act of defiance to his mates, half turned and said quietly.

"Eat your hearts out lads. Eat your hearts out."

As the boys walked towards the girls, they slowed up as they were being greeted by other guests of local high society. Some of them asked who the young lady, Kitty, was, assuming she was a society friend or relative from the country.

Anna answered with, "Oh this is my good friend Kathleen who is also a member of the Nursing Auxiliaries."

Kitty played along by offering her hand in a regal manner. She knew the drill. She had watched it all from the age of twelve at the mansion's get togethers.

When they got the chance, the lads of the YCV stepped forward towards the girls. Davy was beaming from ear to ear, Joe was unusually speechless and stunned. Davy broke the brief silence, stepping forward to Anna lifting her hand and kissing it

"Lady Anna, what a pleasure to see you on this fine afternoon," knowing he was under the microscope of the entire audience, not to mention Sir James. It was the best he could do in the circumstance. He would have to leave anything more intimate for the rabbit trap ridden meadows later, not too much later he hoped.

"And this must be Lady Kathleen," extending his hand to Kitty's hand as well.

Anna kept up the act and directed Kitty before Joe.

"Lady Kathleen, may I introduce you to my good friend Joseph Shannon, Earl of Cromac.[31]"

Joe's stunned silence changed to a broad grin as he stepped forward, lifting Kitty's hand, kissing it slowly, but not letting go as he did.

He leaned forward to Kitty and whispered in her ear. "I love you."

---

[31] Cromac is the name of the townland within which the Markets area of Belfast is situated.

"I love you," whispered Kitty.

"Never fail with the surprises Anna, never know what you're going to get up to next," joked Davy.

"Jesus, Kitty, you'll be getting the sack strolling around like the aristocracy," sighed Joe.

"Kitty doesn't work for the family anymore Joe," replied Anna with a sense of trepidation.

"What!" replied Joe, waiting a few seconds before shaking his head and saying. "Jeez, this is all too complicated for me. Would somebody please explain to me what's happening here?"

"Kitty and I are going to France next week as frontline Nursing Auxiliaries," replied Anna.

"No Anna, Kitty, no chance, it's far too dangerous!" Both lads replied almost in unison.

"What will your father say Anna?" asked Davy.

"I've already told him. Mamma and he have not spoken to me since I told them two nights ago, but we are going and there is nothing they can do about it," replied Anna.

"Well for once I agree with your father," urged Davy. "You'll not be safe there."

"Nor will any of you if you don't have nurses," replied Anna in frustration.

"We'd both rather be out with you rather than lying awake every night worrying about you," interrupted Kitty, finally breaking her silence.

"We have already signed up to go and it's what is happening," stressed Anna.

"No Anna. I won't have you risking your life," said Davy.

"Nor you Kitty," chipped in Joe.

"You two just don't get it, do you. You two are our lives." pressed Anna in exasperation.

"Wherever you go, I go Joe" coaxed Kitty, looking determinedly into Joe's eyes as she leaned forward to hug him reassuringly.

Anna responded in like manner to Davy, knowing full well that jaws would drop all round the mansion garden.

The act was instinctive and from the heart which always rules the thoughts of young love whether its 1066, 1690 or 2000.

The lads, ten yards away, were quick to spot the tryst, and Jonty, still reeling from his verbal battering, was only too glad to divert attention.

"Haey boys!" he shouted, "leave that for the mead..... Awwh!" as Bill Johnston stuck his elbow into him.

"Shut it or I'll get big Martha to deal with you. Don't think that was just a sly grope. Leave it Jonty, wrong time, definitely wrong place!"

Bill Johnston, always the man to have his act together and could weigh a situation up quicker than most, knew that all was not well at the mansion.

The guests in the immediate vicinity all heard Jonty's shout, that Bill had thankfully cut short, before the essence would have been conveyed to anyone. The sound of Jonty's howl of pain reached the love struck four, enough to break them from their moment of their union of souls.

'We had better mingle," whispered Anna, regally.

"Ok girls, see you later," said Joe.

"No way Joe, you're not leaving me alone with this lot," demanded Kitty as she thrust her arm under his.

Anna, for a change, took her instruction from Kitty, and did the same with Davy.

"Take it you were responsible for Kitty's transformation," whispered Davy to Anna as they slowly walked to the groups of milling guests.

Anna laughed, leaning into Davy's side, tightening her grip on his arm.

"Oh God it wasn't easy. Took me half an hour to get her to even try some of the dresses, but when she knew it would please Joe, she ran with it," pausing as she continued.

"Nearly had to push her through the front door when she saw the crowd outside."

"Well," laughed Davy, "Joe certainly loved it. He didn't even recognise her at first and when he did, he was dumbstruck, speechless."

''Joe Shannon speechless, well that's a first," giggled Anna.

With the whole brief incident of the four's romance at the mansion steps having been missed by no one, including Sir and Lady Arthur, the ensuing rush for guests to speak to the four, particularly Anna and Davy, engulfed the two couples.

Anna had introduced Kitty as Kathleen, her friend she knew since she was a child and deflected the conversation if it headed in the direction of where she was from, by saying that she was from the far side of Dungannon.

Well, Sligo was the far side of Dungannon, about seventy miles, on the Atlantic coast.

Joe was introduced as her boyfriend and Joe was cute enough to bluff his way, laughing to himself at the gullible toffs.

Davy was introduced by Anna as her boyfriend, in full knowledge that the aristocratic ladies of South Belfast and the Lagan Valley had heard the rumours of Anna and the blacksmith's son. They were eager to assess the centre of Anna's attentions.

After about an hour of doing the host routine, David and Joe steered the girls in the direction of the lads of the YCV. They weren't trying to show off to the lads, but they feared the thought of them saying that they were avoiding them. Your mates are your mates.

As they approached the lads, Joe spoke first, "Well lads a fine day it is then don't you think?"

"Certainly, fine for some," laughed Bill.

"Jesus, Kitty, you don't half clean up well for a wee girl from the sticks. Joe's lucky you're a Catholic or he'd have no mission. He'd have me to compete with!"

"Ach, Bill," teased Kitty in response, "I didn't know you cared. Should have told me before I met Joe. You'll never know what you might have missed. Don't worry Joe and me will light a wee candle for you at St Bridget's. Just to show there's no hard feelings."

"Don't waste your time, Kitty, just watch for the traps down in that meadow you're so fond of," laughed Bill with a smile.

"Always the gentleman Bill, always the gentleman," Kitty laughed.

Bill turned his eyes to Davy and Anna and threw them a mischievous grin.

"Well lads, look what we have in our midst. The Princess and the Private."

Davy gave Bill a look that suggested and hoped he would not push his luck, at the same time wishing he had a cigarette to calm his thoughts and appear unconcerned of what Bill's banter might unfold.

Before Bill could continue his verbal torture, Anna stepped forward to Bill and offered the back of her hand towards him saying with a smile and the sort of girlish giggle that melted the hearts of men, Bill included.

98

"So, you are William. You are just what David said you would be like."

"Aye Princess and what would that have been? I'm all ears," as he glanced over her shoulder towards Davy behind her.

Davy stared back at Bill, his life seeming to pass before his eyes.

"You've always too much to say for yourself and you think you're God's gift with the ladies," said Anna continuing to tease Bill.

Davy felt a sinking feeling and thought to himself.

"Please God, get me out of this."

"Aye Princess, well it takes one to know one. That right Davy, or sorry, David?" and laughed heartily, backed by a chorus of laughter from the rest of the lads.

"He also said, along with the rest of you, he couldn't be going to France with a better man. I pray to God he is correct, and you all come back safe; even if father keeps losing pheasants," giving a cheeky glance in the direction of the twins, who failed miserably at keeping their faces straight.

As she was about to separate her hand from Bill, he grabbed it with both hands and leant towards her, and quietly, and unusually for Bill, in serious tone, said,

"We'll keep an eye out for Roger as well Princess. He's an Edenderry boy same as us."

Anna was fazed by this sincerity from such a hardnosed individual like Bill. Instinctively she moved close to him and gave him a hug. The lads gave a cheer having not heard Bill and Anna's brief conversation.

"See that Davy, putty in my hands, but don't worry I'm too much of a gentleman to take her off your hands," Bill shouted to Davy, who nodded in approval.

As Anna and Davy turned to mingle with other guests, Bill could not resist having the last word.

"Anna, I hear you are going out to France soon with the nursing corps. If I get shot, will you tend my wounds and give me a body bath?"

Anna turned around. "A bucket of iced water would be the best cure for you Bill," she mocked.

The lads burst out into fits of laughter at Bill's expense and proceeded to jump all over him, only stopping when it slowly dawned on them that Sir James's garden party was not the time or place for corner boy antics.

They straighten their uniforms, apologising to the toffs near them, blaming the mood of excitement of going to fight for King and country. The toffs shook their hands and wished them a safe return, saddened in their hearts, of the fates that might be ahead of them.

Observing the melee around the Young Volunteers, Roger who had been engaging several of the eligible young ladies of Belfast society, all keen to obtain the attention of the heir of one of Belfast's wealthiest family fortunes, felt it appropriate to stride over to take control of the situation.

As he was their Senior Officer, he courteously made his exit from the bevy of young ladies and promising them he would return once he had spoken to his men. This of course went down well with the young ladies, which was exactly what he had intended. Never a good idea to miss an opportunity, even if wasn't business. As he reached the lads, he instinctively went in the direction of Bill.

"Well then Bill, what's the fuss? Really don't want to be embarrassed in front of the ladies and father in the circumstances. Appreciate it if you would keep them tethered, you didn't get those corporal stripes for nothing," stressed Roger with gritted teeth and a smile.

"It's fine Roger, sorry, Lieutenant Arthur sir," apologised Bill, saluting as he spoke.

"Don't need the officer nonsense here Bill. We aren't on parade. You know I still see us as a bunch of mates in the scouts," winced Roger.

"I know that Roger, but the young ladies over there are watching and it makes you look good. Think they are impressed. Least I could do for causing the melee in the first place," whispered Bill, grinning mischievously.

"I swear you could get yourself out of a barrel of grease if you had to. Hope I don't have to call upon your skills in France," replied Roger, while keeping, a strict stance to give the impression to those out of earshot that he was giving Bill a ticking off.

"I hear Anna and Kitty are heading to France as well, Roger. Can you not stop them? No place for a girl over there. It's going to be no garden party."

Roger turned with a grimace.

"My sister Anna is what one could describe as, strong willed. When she is on a mission you cannot talk to her. I have failed, mother has failed, even father's unable to control her. Problem is him and her are too alike and the year in Switzerland has made her even stronger.

All this nonsense about women should have more of a say, not know their place, has gone to her head. That doesn't help either," sighed Roger.

"Aye and not to mention she is head over heels with Davy, the lucky sod. Don't know how he managed that one," replied Bill.

"It is the perfect storm with those two. They have a meeting of minds. They like the look of each other. They are like two people rolled into one when they are together. They'll survive it if this war doesn't ruin it all," said Roger staring at the ground.

"Well Bill, better get back to the harem. A man has got to do and all that,' sighed Roger, as he strode back to the ladies.

Bill could not resist the last word.

"Tough job sir, but someone's got to do it. I'll give you a hand with any of your rejects."

Chapter Twelve

Come back son

On the evening of the 14th's departure from Donegall Quay, the crowds of the families and loved ones of the 36th Ulster Division stood excitedly waving anything red, white, and blue they could get their hands on. Most of the Lagan boys had someone seeing them off; Davy and Roger did not. Neither Tom nor Sir James could stomach the ceremonial goodbyes. Both preferred a short father and son, 'head-to-head,' at their homes in the afternoon.

Sir James reminded Roger of his responsibility to the men under him and to never show any sign of weakness.

Tom bluntly told Davy the only winner in a war was the one who came home in one piece. Davy and Tom had often shaken their heads in dismay at the nonsense of this war, but their pragmatic view on life meant that they both knew that not joining with the rest of the lads was not an option.

"Remember Davy," said Tom, "the King never did you any favours, your Country even less, and as far as God, he didn't bother his arse when your mother froze to death in that well. So just do the basics. Keep your head down and don't volunteer for anything. The world's full of dead heroes," advised Tom.

After Davy had waved at Tom for the last time as he disappeared round the bend of the canal on a Belfast bound lighter, Tom sat slumped on the bench at the water edge at the front of the cottage. As he pulled out his pipe, placing it in his mouth, he fumbled for his matches. Normally this act was done without thinking, in a smooth instinctive manner, but Tom's hand was shaking as he took the match box from his pocket.

Rage, fear, sorrow engulfed the man who was renowned for his strong, controlled, stoic manner. He knew he had some work to have ready, but he could not even get his head round the tasks. He sat there for a long time, cursing God, King and Country, in between repeating over and over shaking his head.

"Ah Davy, come back son. Come back."

He just sat silent, motionless, slumped. He was empty to his soul. He swore to himself that if Carson or Craig ever walked by his cottage, he would nail them both to the lock and open the gates slowly, very slowly. They would have plenty of time to suffer before they screamed for help and he would flick his pipe ash over them, go back into his cottage, sleep in his bed soundly, and enjoy the view in the morning when he drained the lock.

The following Friday, late afternoon, as the autumn air began to give way to the winter chill, Tom was working on some metal brackets when he heard the steady clip clop of horse's hooves coming down the path towards the cottage. It wasn't the sound of a weary lighter horse, nor the heavy canter of a large hunter favoured by Sir James or the groom. It was the short, clipped sound of a more compact animal. The sort that turned up in show jumps and events. A horse for a young lady.

He knew it was Anna before he heard her dismount and walk to the door of the forge.

"Hello Tom," said Anna respectfully, "I hope I am not calling at a bad time."

"You can call with me any time you want girl. It's like Davy is here," smiled Tom.

"Mother has barely spoken to me since I told her about France," said Anna, not knowing what to say next, as she averted her gaze from Tom and looked at the rough floor of the smithy.

"Well, I can't say as I blame her. She's worried sick about you," consoled Tom.

"I have to go to France. I don't have an option," she sighed.

"You do Anna, you can stay home and give your mother and father someone to distract them from this mess. With Roger gone, if you go as well, they have no one. They'll be worried sick about the pair of you. They need you here to give them hope and some comfort in their souls," urged Tom.

Anna looked at Tom, the same look that melted Davy from the first day he saw her those five years earlier.

"Well Thomas Gibson, you are a deep one, but I have to go. Mother and father will deal with it in their own way," replied Anna.

"I can't sit at home tending the flowers and embroidering cushions when Roger, David and Joseph are out there. If anything were to happen, I could not live with myself knowing I could have done more," said Anna adamantly.

A silence came over them both as they walked into the cottage. Anna, hoping Tom would not pursue the topic any further. Tom trying to find the words to enforce his view.

In the silence, Tom lifted a china cup and saucer from the shelf, set them down on the table and lifted the teapot. He noticed Anna's eyes smile quizzically at the cup and saucer.

"Well, I couldn't have you drinking out of the tin mug. Not proper for a young lady. Thought I might have it ready for your royal visits and all that," sighed Tom.

"Was hoping you would have been calling in to visit while Davy's away," continued Tom.

Anna sat and watched Tom prepare the tea, letting it brew in the pot and finally pour it in to the cup first and then his battered tin mug. She forced herself to remain silent.

Anna had learnt well from watching how her father could get around people and she had strengthened this by the charm tactics she had learnt. Anna was a raw but fast learning member of the new high society young ladies of 1915, who would no longer know their place.

As she looked across at Tom, his face staring down at the mug and the table, she saw in front of her, a different Tom Gibson. Gone was the strong, no nonsense, man's man, with a sardonic answer to most things. In front of her she saw a tired, worried, almost fragile shadow of a man. The large shoulders, courtesy of a lifetime wielding blacksmiths' hammers and lifting heavy metal, sagged and seemed to be devoid of strength.

Anna, put both her hands across the table and rested them on Tom's forearms.

"I have to go, Tom. There are thousands of Davys, Rogers, and Joes out there and they need help. Thinking about them from the lake side at Ballydrain won't tend their wounds, stem the bleeding or hold their hands as they pass away."

"Leave it for someone else to do it girl," demanded Tom almost begging.

Another silence descended, although much shorter, before Anna gripped his arms as strong as she could.

"I'm going, Tom, and I'll bring Davy back to you," and added, "We'll both be twenty-one by then."

Tom lifted his eyes and looked at her with an embarrassed expression.

"Yes Tom, I heard every word of your conversation with father that night when he agreed your plan to let it sit until the war was over. My bedroom window is above the porch, close enough to smell the tobacco and hear every word in the still evening air." After another short pause, Anna continued,

"I am leaving tomorrow for the South Coast of England, then on to France after a few months training. Kitty is going also. She feels the same as me."

Tom opened his mouth to speak, but before he could make a sound, Anna placed a hand across his lips and said,

"Could we just sit by the fire and say nothing and just imagine Davy is here in the room with us, please?" said Anna.

The pair moved to the two chairs either side of the fire, Anna sitting in Davy's chair, caressing the arm rests without realizing it.

Tom sat leaning forward, big hands clasped and stared into the fire, occasionally poking it, and adding more fuel. They sat there not talking, deep in their own thoughts.

As time passed, Tom looked across at Anna. He remembered when his own young wife sat in the same chair. Tom held himself together by drawing on his pipe.

Eventually the silence was broken as Anna stood up.

"I had better head back to Ballydrain. I do not want to make a habit of staying here until it's dark."

As they walked to the door Tom opened a cupboard and pulled out his wife's shawl.

"Take this with you girl," offered Tom.

"I'm fine Tom, I've my riding coat in the saddle bag. I'll be fine thanks very much," said Anna thankfully.

"No, but you'll need it on a winter's night in France. It won't protect you from the Hun, but it'll do a grand job with the cold," said Tom as he pressed the shawl into Anna's arms.

Anna was about to refuse it and tell Tom he would need it himself, but she knew this was a gesture that meant more to him than concerns about the cold.

As they left the door of the cottage Anna turned to Tom grabbing him by the arm again and said quietly.

"Don't worry Tom. Someday we will both be back. Just promise me one thing."

"I'll do my best, what is it?" replied Tom, a bit concerned.

"Get some more cups and saucers so I don't feel as if I'm a guest," smiled Anna.

"I would like to be more than that, Tom."

At that she turned her heels, climbed on to her pony, rapped the shawl round her shoulder and rode off in a quick canter, her eyes so glazed it was fortunate that the steed knew its own way home.

The evening after Anna and Kitty left for England. Tom was sitting beside the lock gates, his thoughts going in all directions. A shadow of someone wearing a large hat cut across his vision. He knew by the shape of the hat made even larger by the evening shadow that it was Sir James.

Without looking around he said,

"You're too early for those saddles. The Groom wasn't expected 'till the morning,'" said Tom dryly.

"Ah, Thomas Gibson, blacksmith of this Parish will you for once in your life drop your guard man," replied Sir James in an exasperated tone.

"Any space on that bench for another one?" he continued.

Tom begrudgingly moved along. He was not in the mood for a conversation with Sir James, especially as he would have been a likely candidate to be the third man nailed to the lock side if there had been enough space.

"It is never a good day saying goodbye to your son, knowing you might never see him again," continued Sir James.

They sat in silence as Tom was still not in the mood for conversation.

After a few minutes, as both men sat in contemplation, Tom got up from his seat and walked slowly, shoulders down, unlike his usual straight-backed amble, into the cottage and returned several seconds later with two tin mugs and a dark brown cone shaped bottle with no label. He sat down on the bench again and handed Sir James the better of the two mugs, not looking directly into his face.

"Can't return the compliment with the crystal glass but this stuff might make up for it," said Tom as he handed Sir James the cup and started unscrewing the top of the bottle.

"Don't mind if I do. The pleasure is mine," replied Sir James in a slow depressed tone, most unlike Sir James. The confidence, the arrogance was nowhere to be seen, just a man racked with foreboding.

"This isn't Dunville's finest, it's far better. Best of Armagh poteen, apple based, slides down beautifully, then hits' the back of the neck like one of my hammers. Best thing I can offer," said Tom in a similarly depressed tone, adding a slow sigh.

Tom poured a good measure in the mug, Davy's mug, and offered it to Sir James, and did the same in his own. They chunked mugs, bade each other their health and slugged.

"Aye Sir James, it's never a good day to see your son go to war, but your daughter," sighed Tom, "that's something else man."

"You'd heard," winced Sir James, looking out of the side of his eye at Tom.

"Davy," Tom shock his head as he paused, "He's worried sick about it. Tried to talk her out of it, but you know your daughter, wasting his breath like the rest of us."

"It would seem your little plan that the war might separate them isn't a runner Thomas," said Sir James with more than a touch of irony.

The two men sat for a few minutes just sipping the taste of the illicit brew before Sir James broke the silence again.

"At the garden party, I watched the pair of them. They were like two peas in a pod. She was all but Lady of the Manor. That finishing school in Basle taught her well and David strolled around on her shoulder, like he was born to it," reflected Sir James.

"Aye Sir James, I did bring him up to watch his P's and Q's," said Tom, still looking over the river.

"No, I don't mean his manner, Thomas. He was born to be with Anna," sighed Sir James, not with a sigh of dismay, but of acceptance.

"I have to admit, to my shame, that when you suggested the war might separate them, that David not coming back would end the matter. I will have to live with that terrible thought. I hope you will forgive me Thomas," replied Sir James, shaking his head ruefully as he sighed.

"Can't say I didn't curse you high and low walking back home that night. Seems like we both got it wrong. Dark days, dark thoughts, Sir James," replied Tom, as he unscrewed the bottle and topped up both mugs.

They both took a swig and Sir James let out a grunt of awe.

"My God this stuff does sneak up on you. Armagh, do you say it's from?

If any more falls off a lighter and rolls to your doorstep, you must keep me a bottle."

"Take it as done," grinned Tom. He would have laughed but in this situation, it felt somehow disrespectful, not to Sir James, but their children, all three.

"I've caused this mess Thomas. She has gone to France because I would not countenance their friendship. If I had just let them have their romance of youth, it would have either burnt out or she would have stayed at home and waited for his return. Sort of, live to fight another day.

I should have realised that she is too much like myself. Played it all wrong. If I conducted my business as badly, I would be in the workhouse," said Sir James shaking his head slowly.

Tom made a similar gesture and replied.

"You're not the only one Sir James. Maybe I should have had more faith in Davy. I wasn't happy about their friendship either. I thought Davy couldn't handle your lot, but it seems that with a bit of looking after by Anna, he might well be up to it."

Sir James, staring at the ground nodded in agreement.

"Aye,' continued Tom, "The Lord made them. The Lord matches them," raising his mug to Sir James, who responded likewise.

Sir James sighed.

"Anna and Kitty will be in Northern France, long before Roger and David. The YCV do more training in England for a few months. Something to do with the fact the 36th, apart from the Inniskillings, are not up to scratch. The local training was inappropriate to the needs of the front. We trained for a civil war, local skirmishes, small groups, not conforming to a big plan. The big brass were aghast at the low level of discipline and not sticking to the plan."

Both men shook their heads in dismay once again.

"I just hope it's not lambs to the slaughter, Thomas," mused Sir James, staring out over the canal like Tom.

"Well Davy is used to doing the slaughtering in his trade, so let's hope he's good enough to get both boys back Sir James," sighed Tom, trying rather awkwardly to lighten the mood; not believing a word of it.

Good boning knife against a Maxim or a German shell was not good odds, he thought to himself.

By the time mugs had been topped up beyond the point of counting, the brew had started to take centre stage in both men's brains. Sir James more so, because Tom had many years of experience sipping the brew on a cold winter's night in front of the warm fire. A good fire was never a problem for a blacksmith working alongside the lighter barge full of coal passing his door on a regular basis.

It had long gone dark by the time the two men had exhausted themselves in conversation. Tom was feeling a bit hazy, Sir James had fallen asleep at the bench, shoulders back against the cottage wall, head to one side, mug still clasped in his hand, tilted at right angles, remnants of the brew staining his best breaches.

Tom stood up, bent his knees to get the circulation going and stood in the evening chill, breathing deeply, trying to work out what to do about Sir James. He couldn't leave him lying against the wall all night, and he was sure he himself was in no fit state to get him back up to the big house.

Only option was to prop him up and get him in to the cottage and dump him down on Davy's bed, which, with great difficulty, he achieved and threw a sheet over him.

Having managed that he slumped on to his own bed and was asleep in seconds.

By what seemed like the middle of the night, Tom was retrieved from sleep by the sound of the cottage door opening slowly.

He could see a shadow at the entrance framed by the moonlight casting in at an angle against the interior of the dwelling.

It was McCracken, Sir James's head groom.

"Tom, I've been sent out by Lady May to find Sir James. Thank God he's here. Had an idea he might but he didn't say anything to me when he left the stables. Seemed in a world of his own. Thought it best not to ask," whispered the groom.

As Tom rubbed his eyes and scratched his arm pits. "Well, don't fancy your chances of getting him back up in that state, never mind trying to wake him. Best get yourself back home. Tell Lady May he's safe and call back in the morning when he's sober," advised Tom.

"Sounds good to me Tom." I'll put Wellington in your stable for the night. He's standing out there looking a bit abandoned," chuckled the groom, as he turned back to quietly retrace his steps out the door.

"Best leave it to when everyone's away to work and the less know about this evening the better. Bring his working suit with you so no one sees him heading back home in that state. Wouldn't do much for his image and tongues would wag from here to the Cave Hill," suggested Tom.

The groom laughed quietly and gave Tom a nod of approval.

"Lady May is going to love this," were the groom's last words, as he disappeared into the dark night.

In the morning, Sir James was awoken by the strains on his bladder crying out to get rid of the previous evening's 80% proof Armagh's best. As he staggered out of the cottage and relieved himself, precariously close to the clump of nettles at the side of the cottage, the cool morning air hit his head and the pain intensified.

"Morning your Lordship."

He could hear a voice out in the haze of his brain. He turned in the direction of the sound and saw Tom, pipe in hand, with a grin from ear to ear.

As he gathered his senses, he tried to reply but it was a struggle.

"Ah Thomas, last time I woke like this it was after an officers' dinner in Natal. Young enough to handle it a bit better. Not handling ones' drink, disgraceful, not the behaviour of a gentleman. My apologies Thomas," said Sir James sheepishly,

"So, it's back to Thomas, is it?" laughed Tom. "Last night it was Tom and Tommy once you loosened up, Ahh, I suppose all good things come to an end."

As Sir James turned to sit at the bench. Tom stepped into the cottage and came out again with the same over used mug full of steaming black tea; black enough to polish your boots.

"Here Sir James, get that in you. It'll put a bit of lining in your stomach," tormented Tom.

As Sir James sipped the tea and began slowly breathing in the morning air, his brain started to fill in most of the gaps of the previous evening.

"Where's Wellington?" he asked

"He's fine, Sir James; up in the field behind the cottage. I've just let him out of the stable to stretch his legs," assured Tom.

"Better get back up to the estate and face the music," sighed Sir James.

'Just sit there and I'll stick you on some breakfast. The groom won't be down for a while yet," said Tom.

"The groom?" asked Sir James.

"Aye, he was down here about midnight looking for you. Told him to come back in the morning with a change of clothes. Not a great idea you seen in that state, first thing in the morning.

Discretion is the better part of valour and all that Sir James," laughed Tom.

"I trust David has your skills of endurance and fortitude Thomas, Tom," replied Sir James more than slightly embarrassed.

"Well, I've tried. Time will tell if it works," replied Tom.

"Well, he's shaping up that way, he hasn't shown much weakness in front of me," approved Sir James.

"Away in and get yourself sorted before the groom gets here.

Use my shaving stick and razor, carbolic soap beside the jaw box. Should be warm water in the kettle by the range," said Tom supportively.

Sir James just nodded and walked stiffly inside.

By the time Sir James had negotiated the breakfast supplied to him, he could hear the trap drawing closer to the cottage. The groom had arrived earlier than anticipated and the carriage cover was up to hide the identity of its returning passenger.

Sir James came silently out of the cottage door, not looking the groom directly in the eye.

"At least," thought Sir James, "he has the good sense not to turn up in the Rolls Royce. The trap was a lot less conspicuous."

"Ah hood up, good thinking, McCracken," he muttered.

"Well Thomas, your hospitality was timely, let us say. I trust you will do me the honour of allowing me to return the compliment," said Sir James, shaking Tom's hand solemnly.

"I appreciate your offer, Sir James, but no disrespect, that Dunville stuff wouldn't do that much damage," grinned Tom, gripping Sir James's hand.

'Never mind, we'll have to test your theory out all the same," retorted Sir James, as the groom looked on, not quite believing his ears or eyes at the mood between Sir James and Tom.

The groom cast a puzzled look at Tom over the shoulder of his employer.

Tom managed to make no facial response by sticking his pipe in his mouth. His way of letting the groom know he was saying nothing.

"Best get up to the house as soon as possible. Need to get to Ballydrain before I meet a Ministry of Defence chap about a big order of linen. He is calling at Lambeg mill at lunch time," instructed Sir James.

"Yes, Sir James that's why I came a bit earlier," replied the groom with a sense of superiority.

Sir James gave the groom a look, that he had had his fun, but not to push it. The trap disappeared round the bend up to Shaw's Bridge and back to Ballydrain House.

Part two

The Somme

Chapter Thirteen

Poacher Raids

By early Spring of 1916, the YCV had been mostly assigned to support duties rather than direct combat.

Bill Johnston was the only one with any loyal fervour, wearing his Orange Order sash at every opportunity. Singing British marching songs while they moved from one venue to another. The twins spent every spare moment planning some ruse that would bring them in some contraband or local game they could get Davy to clean and then sell off around the line to be heartily consumed by all and sundry. It was best policy to give a good deal to the Sergeant if the process were to operate. The officers turned a blind eye as they thought it was good for moral and best left to flourish.

Davy had taken the trouble to pack his two best boning knives and sharpener, knowing full well that the twins would be up to something that would need his expertise.

Joe spent his time not saying much, just working out how much pay he could set aside and daydreaming about Kitty. Sometimes romantic thoughts. sometimes more carnal. Certainly not ones for the Division's priest when he had time for confession.

As there were only about fifty or sixty of his fellow Roman Catholics in the 14th Irish Rifles, the priest was not overly busy and spent much of his time helping the Church of Ireland Padre with what they called Pastoral Support.

Big Rab Tate spent many an hour, head buried in his Bible, reading passages, laying his head back, closing his eyes and thinking. Davy sat many times in awe of Rab's perseverance, dedication, and observance. Davy did not understand it.

He admired Rab's single mindedness, but most of all the fact he kept it to himself. Davy detested the evangelical firebrand types. If Rab had been like one of them, he would have kept well out of his way. Instead, his demeanour intrigued him and often made him feel envious of the big lad's focus and tranquility. Not that he would ever tell him.

Roger, when he wasn't in his corner underground writing up reports, would lighten his worries by sketching anything that took his fancy. Sketches of the men or cartoons with witty catchphrases, sometimes downright cruel, went down a treat with the group and many a nickname started and stuck for a lifetime, as a result, of these artistic gems.

The twins got Stoat and Badger, Rab, the Vicar, Jonty, the Mouse on account of his small stature and nimble movement, making him invaluable as the messenger scurrying between trenches. Joe got The Rebel, and Davy got The Knife, Bill, the General. That nickname was started by officers who were fully aware that Bill had more respect and loyalty than Maitland,

Nugent, or any other Brigadiers. The Edenderry Boys did nothing without the say of one William Johnston.

The Knife, which Davy hated, arose from the time the boys had their first serious combat with the Hun.

It was constantly a nagging question amongst the mid rank officers, "What do we do with the 14th Battalion?"

Eventually someone came up with the bright idea of attaching the 14th Battalion Young Citizens Volunteers to the Inniskilling Fusiliers, in particular the 10th Battalion. The idea being that the Inniskillings would be able to control them better than the other Irish volunteer brigades. The Inniskillings would use them as their support soldiers, taking up the rear of any Inniskilling manoeuvres.

The Inniskillings had been a proud and honoured regiment since their origins back in the Spanish Campaigns, serving with Wellington, played a key role in the victory at Waterloo and just about any major conflict of British military history. The Inniskillings were professional, career soldiers, experienced and very capable, a different bunch to the inexperienced volunteers from the streets of Belfast and the villages of rural Ulster.

On an evening in April 1916, Roger sat in the dugout come shed, deep below the trench with another 2nd Lieutenant and their captain.

"Well chaps, this is the word from the gentlemen tucked up safely five miles back," started the captain. "The Frogs are getting a tad pissed off with the hammering they are getting down the road at Verdun and they are giving off that we aren't doing enough to distract Gerry."

"It's messing up Haig's plans for a well organised attack this end of September. It's all being brought forward to the end of June. Problem is we are behind on information about what Gerry is at along the whole line. Consequently, this section is under orders to send a party to Gerry's lines to listen, look and report back. The info is all to be sent back to the top brass and they can make good use of it."

Roger and Lieutenant Maxwell from the 10th Inniskillings, sat deep in their thoughts for a few minutes, Roger smoking his pipe trying to look calm and casual. The Inniskilling Lieutenant taking a cigarette, nodding as he did so, to the captain, also an Inniskilling.

'Right," said the Inniskilling junior officer, as he took an extra draw on his cigarette. "I'll get Sergeant Quinn to organise a sortie after dark and we'll see what we can find. I'll go out over with them. Know a bit of German. Try and glean what I can."

The captain, nodded his head in approval, drawing on his cigarette at the same time.

As they all shuffled through their papers trying to sort other issues to be dealt with, Roger broke his silence.

"I've another idea, if you don't mind me putting in my penny's worth, gentlemen," still gripping his pipe between his mouth.

Roger was all of twenty-two and no fighting man by nature, but he had learned from his father that image, confidence, and an air of cool candour was vital in any business deal and after all war was a form of business. Moves, planning, investment in stock, albeit the stock on a battlefield was human flesh, and souls.

He raised himself up from his makeshift armchair and in as commanding a tone as he could manage, pointed to the map of the Thiepval Woods, the Schwaben Redoubt, and the river.

"I think a change of personnel for this little exercise."

'Do speak, Lt Arthur, we are all ears," said the captain as his eyebrows disappeared under his cap, slightly sarcastically, thinking to himself, "what does this mild mannered, decent but privileged lad know about real fighting?"

"The woods, the Redoubt, the river here are virtually identical to my estate at home. We have trained in these conditions, mostly for small engagements for a civil war back home. Some of my chaps can do this one if you would give them the chance.

This mission does not need expert soldiers. It needs stealth and believe me I know the very team that can do that better than any of the Inniskillings' best." explained Roger quietly but confidently.

The Inniskilling Lieutenant almost choked on his cigarette as he inhaled.

"You are jesting Roger. We appreciate your intent, but we couldn't take the risk," sighed the Inniskilling Lieutenant condescendingly.

Roger not being in a mood to be scorned, continued.

"The Bamford twins are the best poachers in the whole of the Lagan Valley. I should know, they have tormented my father and the game keeper for years. We can never catch them. They have slipped through more attempts than we have eaten tins of bully beef since we got here. They can see in the dark like nobody I know, silent as the mist, and the Mouse can get himself about quick as lightning. You never see him until he's on your shoulder. Stealth, silence, is vital. We do not want carbines and mills bombs clanking about. Send Gibson, Shannon and Johnston as guard," explained Roger, doing his best to contain his frustration at the others' lack of confidence.

"Why Gibson, Shannon, and Johnston?" asked the captain, who was beginning to show a reluctant interest in what Roger had to say.

"I've seen Davy Gibson slaughter an angry bull in a shed. Just him and the beast. Pole in one hand, slaughter knife in the other. One crack on the head with one hand, throat slit right through with the other, bull collapsed. Not a sound, other than a few hundred pounds of prime steak hitting the floor. Knife got wiped and the next unfortunate beast was sent in. Whole business was not pretty, but he's as much a professional killer as your lot."

"Ahh," grunted the captain, "one thing to kill an animal that's coming at you, another a human being. How sure are you he could do that, Roger?"

"Because he wants to survive this war, go home and spend the rest of his life with my sister and believe me if that is what it takes for David to get back, he will do it," assured Roger.

"Shannon and Johnston?" asked the captain, continuing to draw on his cigarette.

Shannon is very, as they say, street wise, misses nothing, reads situations well and is a good scrapper if it comes to hand to hand. Johnston back home is the leader. He is the rock that binds them. They just aren't a team without him."

Roger stood in silence, as did the Inniskilling junior officer waiting for the captain to reply.

The captain turned to the map of their sector, made movements of his finger up and down the map, drew a lot on his cigarette and then looked at the ground.

"Get me Sergeant Quinn in here immediately," he instructed the Inniskilling officer, who immediately left the dugout to retrieve Quinn.

The captain looked sternly at Roger.

"Lieutenant Arthur, I am prepared to run with this scheme as long as you understand that it will be down to you, that boys were sent to their deaths doing a man's job and that if I have to send out Inniskillings another night it will be all the more difficult with the Hun watching out for them."

"I'll send Lt Maxwell with them to add some sort of expertise to this exercise," continued the captain.

"No sir, with respect, I need to be the officer in charge of this one," replied Roger, with determination.

"God give me strength, Lieutenant Arthur. I can't send a sortie out consisting of a bunch of amateurs and no expertise!" exclaimed the captain, running out of patience.

"How good is Maxwell's German?" asked Roger.

"Not great but enough to get the gist," replied the captain.

"It's not as good as mine," said Roger in an Arthur superior tone. "I have been taught German at school for nearly fifteen years and correspond with my father's German business associates, both written and verbally at meetings. Attended a few social events with German merchants. even know a few rude German drinking songs. I'll bring back more details than Maxwell for all his attributes," reassured Roger.

"The German language bit probably will not matter that much. You're unlikely to get that close." replied the captain without lifting his head from the floor.

128

"We will get right amongst them, Captain. Do not worry about that," assured Roger, staring directly at the top of the captain's head until he lifted it to look at Roger's face.

The stare of the young lieutenant said more than words to convince the captain this just might work.

Shortly, after Maxwell returned with Quinn at his shoulder, the captain explained the situation to the sergeant. He looked just as bemused as the others had earlier but being a soldier of fifteen years of service in Africa and India, knew his function was to carry out orders and only give an opinion when asked for it.

"Right Quinn, gather up Corporal Johnston, Lance Corporals Shannon and Gibson and Privates Bamford, both of them, Private Price and get them in here," ordered the captain with a heavy sigh.

By the time Quinn meandered up the zig zag trench line and retrieved the worried bunch, it took about ten minutes for them to appear in the underground office.

The Sergeant had told them nothing.

The lads thought they were in for a rollicking over their antics while back on the reserve line the previous week. Jonty had the, not so clever, idea, of chucking a grenade in to the river to save wasting all day fishing. Half a dozen fish floated to the surface, the lads rolled around laughing on the bank, Jonty felt very clever, Davy filleted the fish and Bill used his YCV campfire skills to complete a fine day. Almost felt as if, they were back on the Lagan at Minnowburn Beeches.

The captain stood up slowly and gave each of the group, except Quinn, a long slow silent stare.

"Oh shit, this looks serious," thought Joe. "If we get court martialled and kicked out, bang goes my wages and bang goes all my plans, Canada, the lot."

The lads were all doing their best to stand up straight at attention, which in the cramped space was easy for the twins, Bill, and Jonty but Davy and Joe had to bend their necks to avoid the ceiling. This only added physical discomfort to their mental concerns.

"At ease men, find a space to set yourselves down if you can."

The lads' guilty consciences about the fish caper disappeared. They were not about to get a rollicking if they were being asked to take a seat.

"Right gentlemen, I am informed, somewhat surprisingly, that you bunch of happy campers might be finally of some use to this war," continued the captain leading forward in his chair and lifting his pipe from a shelf at his side as he spoke.

"I hear you chaps have skills of a nocturnal nature; honed out of years of playing fast and loose with the local wildlife." The captain paused and brandished the unlit pipe in their direction.

The twins looked at each other, both doing their best to keep their faces straight.

Davy looked to the crumbling roof of the dugout. Joe looked straight ahead relieved his finances were not about to be cut and Jonty moved nervously from one foot to the other.

After a few seconds Bill spoke first.

"Night work, Captain sir, is it then? Bit of poaching? Rations short sir?" asked Bill, straight faced, unable to refrain from his dry wit. It was always his reaction when he was trying to conceal his nervousness.

Davy and Joe knew this and gave each other a glance.

"Poaching, Corporal Johnston, but not for food. Information, intelligence, a quality which I find myself, looking at you lot of chocolate soldiers, I fear might be in short supply," sighed the captain before continuing.

"We need to find out what is going on in Gerry's trenches."

Pausing as he sucked the still unlit pipe.

"I am reliably informed by Lieutenant Arthur that you lot have particular expertise in the dark of night. You will be going over the top tomorrow night to get yourself as near as you can to Gerry. Find out as much as you can and report back. All before the dawn. Think you can handle it?"

The lads looked at each other for assurance, Bill again broke the silence.

"Yes sir, we can do that sir." in as dry a tone as he could muster. "We would need to be filled in on the general lie of the land, so to speak. Couldn't just pop over in the next ten minutes without a bit of head scratching first. If that's all right with you sir."

Captain Montgomery let out a slow sigh of frustration. "Have you not been listening, Johnston.? I have already said tomorrow evening. Lieutenants Maxwell and Arthur will give you all the details we have of the other side and Arthur with be going with you as officer in charge."

Maxwell and Quinn exchanged glances of surprise.

Quinn was the first to break the silence.

"Permission to speak, Sir?" in his staccato sharp style used when on official duty.

"Arthur is going because he speaks better German than Maxwell, pure and simple," explained the captain, assuming Quinn's question in advance.

Maxwell, looking positively shocked, not to say insulted, at being overlooked in favour of Roger, stood with his mouth half open.

"You need not look at me like that, Maxwell!" mocked the captain and nodded to Roger.

Roger looked directly at Maxwell and spoke to him in German for about ten seconds without a pause. Maxwell, taken aback, hesitated, but after a few seconds replied in an accurate but disjointed response. Roger replied again, without a pause, save for breath, for a good minute.

"Kept that to yourself Arthur," grinned Maxwell, secretly glad that Roger was taking this risk instead of him, while his reputation was still intact. His non selection for this mission had nothing to do with his soldiering ability; he was content enough to leave it at that.

"Right then gentlemen, get to work with Maxwell and Arthur on the scenery. Quinn, need a bit of fresh air, stretch the legs and all that. Come with me!" ordered the captain.

As the lads shuffled around the tight space to gather round Maxwell and Roger, Montgomery and Quinn left the relative safety of the dugout and stepped into the cool of the night air.

"Well Sergeant Quinn, thoughts, I know you have them?" asked the captain as he struggled to pull out his cigarettes to offer one to Quinn.

Quinn, fully aware it was never a good idea to tell an officer he was barking mad, answered.

"Risky Sir, those lads might panic when they see the Hun up close and get themselves wiped out. On the other hand, they are such a bunch of chancers they might get out of our sight, sit there for an hour or two, freezing their balls off; if they have any, and come back telling us a load of nonsense just to make life easy for themselves."

He paused as he offered the captain a light.

The sergeant took the cigarette and scratched his jaw.

"The thing is I know our men. They do what they are told, they have respect for the regiment. They can be relied upon. The YCV, particularly that bunch, are loose cannons. Not a soldier amongst them and the other battalions don't have any time for them. That's why we got landed with them."

Quinn took a draw on the Woodbine, waiting for the captain's reply.

"I totally agree on your assessment, Quinn, of that bunch in there, but I am mindful of Lieutenant Arthur's shrewdness and his understanding of them. The Lieutenant has a lot more guile and level headedness than most of the volunteer Lieutenants that sadly all too briefly pass through my command before some Gerry marksman gets them in his sights. My gut tells me this just might work."

Quinn looked at the captain in silence, as they both puffed on the butts left on their lips.

Montgomery broke the silence.

"Here is what I want you to do. When they go over the parapet tomorrow night, I want you to keep offside, give them about fifty yards or so and climb out behind them. Watch what they get up to. Do not let them know you are there. If they try any tricks, countermand, under my authority, Arthur, and get them back here. If they get spotted, do your best to pull them out of it and get them back. Don't risk your own life, the British army would suffer a greater loss if it lost a good sergeant rather than a few hapless souls, God rest them, Quinn."

Another short silence was broken by Quinn as he raised his eyes from the duck board below and looked in the direction of the captain's face.

"Well sir," said Quinn. "I've heard it said that life is an experience. We are certainly getting our full share of it out here. It looks like tomorrow night will be no different!"

"That it will Quinn, that it will," replied the captain.

"Well, if that's all sir, I'm away to check none of the watch have nodded off dreaming of shagging a French barmaid or one of those fine nurses back down the line."

"Goodnight Quinn and keep your naughty nightmares to yourself!" grinned the captain.

"Aye Sir, my naughty nightmare is sitting at home in Ramelton, County Donegal with my four children," he said wistfully, as he looked to the sky and flicked his butt down into the duck board, where it bounced on down into the channel of water, the red end disappearing into the darkness below.

Both men headed off in opposite directions with their thoughts.

The lads, meantime, had gathered round the crumpled, stained, crudely drawn map of the wire systems in no man's land, the lie of the land, the pattern of the German first and second line and the likely sentry and machine gun spots. The two lieutenants explained to them that their mission was to get as near to the trenches as possible, survey everything they could, and in the case of Roger, try and eavesdrop on conversations. Establish the calibre of the troops, numbers, morale, any signs of special activities, be all eyes and ears, get back to report everything, get their heads down for a bit of shut eye and leave the rest for the senior brass to mull over.

After a few minutes one of the twins, Allen Bamford, broke the silence.

"Best heading up our trench line to the woods at Thiepval and crawling out from there," he said in a serious abrupt manner.

"Why is that?" asked Lt Maxwell.

"'Cause them woods are just like his, sorry Sir, like Lt Arthur's woods back home on his estate," pointing at Roger sheepishly.

"Some of us know how to disappear in those conditions and besides it's a shorter distance of open ground in no mans' land. Less distance to make a noise. Sound gets lost in trees behind us. The wind carries sounds of the trees into open land and filters out a lot of noise by the time it reached the Huns trenches."

"They won't see our shadows against the backdrop of the woods, like they would against open land with nothing but sky behind it," chipped in Adam.

"We'll be right among them, sir, and they won't even know it."

Lt Maxwell raised his eyebrows slightly and slowly nodded his approval. At the same time, he sensed that Bill was itching to add his tuppence worth.

136

'Something to add, Corporal Johnston?" he asked Bill in a slightly condescending tone.

"Be best to leave our rifles behind, Sir," suggested Bill, half drawing himself to an upright stance, trying to emphasis the certainty of the comment.

At this point Roger tapped his pencil against the map and looking at Lt Maxwell, said,

"Because when they are culling my father's game, they don't have guns with them. They are cumbersome, noisy. The lads don't kill by shooting. Wakens up the whole neighbourhood for miles around. Slip in, slip out. Don't overdo it, right lads?" explained Roger, almost taunting them.

"But what happens if you are spotted, and you need to fight your way back? I'm not sending you on a suicide mission." snapped Lt Maxwell.

"Aye," shrugged Bill. "If we get spotted our rifles aren't going to do much when the whole trench opens up."

Bill nodded over at Davy who was standing at the shoulder of Lt Maxwell.

"He's our best option if we get spotted," assured Bill confidently.

"If we are seen," continued Bill, "we'll likely be spotted by one, maybe two, and we'll be close to them. Best chance is sorting it quickly and quietly and no one knows. One shot fired and we are fucked, Sir!"

"I see and that is where you come in Lance Corporal Gibson, I understand from Lieutenant Arthur," added Lt Maxwell, as he lifted his gaze in the direction of Davy, sighing with an air of frustration.

"One thing slaughtering a few dumb animals; another a human being, Lance Corporal. Do you think you have got what it takes? One thing firing a rifle from one hundred yards, even if you see your hit, he is too far away for it to get personal. Close in with a knife, smelling his breath, seeing his fear, and watching his life ebb away; very different. Not to mention he'll be coming at you with a rifle with a bayonet on the end of it."

Davy looked disappointedly at Lt Maxwell, did not speak, just drew slowly on his Woodbine.

"He'll not let us down!" came Joe's voice from the darkness of the corner of the makeshift underground office.

"I've slaughtered lots of lambs, Sir," assured Davy finally, with a sense of shame, as he stared at the ground before raising his eyes to the Lieutenant.

The Lieutenant laughed in Davy's face.

"My God man, lambs, real lambs. What a true man of steel we have amongst us gentlemen. You'll all be safe as houses with the Lance Corporal then," as he continued to laugh in Davy's face.

"Lambs," replied Davy, ignoring Lt Maxwell's, sarcasm. "Lambs, sir, are the hardest to kill. They are innocent, aren't aggressive, look cute, walk up to you totally trusting and then!" Davy made a horizontal cutting movement with his hand.

"Hated killing every one of them; detested it the first few times I had to do it, when I was learning the trade, only just turned twelve years old. I don't mind telling you I cried walking back from farms on a dark night. Nobody about to see me."

Davy drew again on his Woodbine and continued,

"Bulls, cattle on the other hand, no problem, choice is easy. You are in a small shed not much bigger than this space and he's not in good form being pushed around. He's coming at you head down. The decision is easy. Short pole to stun him in one hand and slaughter knife in the other. Needs done quick. No time for the luxury of emotion or even fear."

Davy drew on his Woodbine again.

"Any German who gets in our way will be no different to them bulls sir. Don't like doing any of it, not even the bulls, but old Jack Graham taught me well. If the job's done right, they'll not suffer, because they'll not know anything about it. Hate it when the job's done badly by amateurs. I'm a professional, I'm trained for working with a knife. It's what I do. It's the only skill I have, sir," sighed Davy.

The Lieutenant, slightly taken aback by the cold assured answer of this gangly youth, and feeling the need to regain the upper hand, retorted still with a snigger in his voice.

"And what, pray tell, happens when you lose this great Excalibur of yours? How do you cope with that then, our silent assassin?"

At this point Davy looked over to Roger who had sat silently sucking on his pipe.

Roger caught Davy's stare and looked up at him, trying to contain a grin.

Roger gave him the slightest of nods that was made in the second that Lt Maxwell had looked down to relight his pipe.

Joe who had caught on what was coming next and the part he would have to play, moved unnoticed round the side of the wall of the dugout until he was a few feet behind Lt Maxwell.

Roger, in the meantime, tilted his pipe in a slight downwards movement, responding to Davy, effectively giving him permission for the next act.

Joe scratched the back wall with the edge of his helmet, Lt Maxwell turned his head round to identify the source of the noise and as he did, Davy stretched his hand out to the side of Lt Maxwell's neck, pressing two fingers against a spot on the veins. The Lieutenant crumpled immediately, legs went from under him, his eyes rolled in his head and all his senses left him.

Bill and Joe grabbed hold of Lt Maxwell before he could hit the ground or do himself damage on the edge of the metal makeshift desk and let him slump into his makeshift chair.

After about ten minutes Lt Maxwell started to come around, safe, and well, except for a blinding headache as the blood tried frantically to return to his brain. As he leant forward head in hands, Roger laughed quietly, trying to set the tone in the cramped space.

"Sorry about that, Maxy old chap, but a practical example was better than words in the circumstances."

"Point taken," croaked Lt Maxwell. "I assume that was Gibson's doing," he spluttered in embarrassment.

"Pressure points, Sir. Just gave you a short jab in the right spot. That's what I do if the knife fails or there's a lot of sheep to be killed. Saves being up to your ankles in the red stuff." explained Davy, keeping his face straight, not wanting to cause the officer any further angst.

"If you had been one of the Hun, he'd have kept the pressure on a few seconds longer or broke your neck as easy sir. Either way you'd be gone. You don't know the half of it, sir," added Bill, not wanting to appear a side act in this performance.

"That's nothing compared to what he could have done with both hands."

Maxwell, maintaining the posture of an unflappable officer of His Majesty's British Army, dragged himself upright and giving a poorly focused stare at the trench map, said without averting his gaze.

"Remind me chaps, never to stand near Gibson again!"

The team of officers and soldiers continued to talk amongst each other on a more equal footing. the Lieutenants, mainly

Maxwell pointing out the potential hazards, requirements, and advice for about two hours before the lads were dismissed and told they were to keep themselves to themselves until 21.30 hours the next evening and not to take part in any other duties in between. Sergeant Quinn was told they were to be exempt for "Special Operations." This delighted the lads as they were fed up getting all the dirty jobs from their Inniskilling minders and had no doubt they could complete the task.

At 22.00 hours, they gathered at the northern end of the trench system near Thiepval Wood leaving all weapons with the captain, so they could not be accused of lying down their arms, leaving them open to claims of desertion.

The captain gave the signal as they each slipped over the parapet, and out into the darkness. It was fortunately a dark night as thick cloud covered the moon and the stars which could light up the skies on many a night. The twins went first, then Jonty and Bill, followed by Joe, Davy and finally Roger.

The gap between them and the first line was only a few hundred yards at the narrowest point of the zigzag German trenches. About fifty yards out, the twins signalled to the rest to stay low while they found the gaps in the German wire always left for German sorties.

This done, they got back to the rest of the lads.

Once back, they gave hand signals for Davy and Joe to follow Adam through the wire and then Allen, Jonty, and Bill.

Roger tapped a twin on the shoulder and indicated his confusion at not being given any direction.

"Roger, sir," he whispered, "suggest you lay there and tell the 'eedjit' [32]who's following us to clear off and stop making such a racket. You'd hear him in Berlin. If he gets any nearer the Hun will hear him as well and we are all fucked. When you've sent him packing, we'll be laying in front of the gap in the wire hundred yards just left of centre."

The boys quietly melted in to the dark one at a time while Roger waited.

It was about another thirty seconds by the time Quinn reached a point a few yards left of Roger. He had not seen Roger as he was too focused on trying to follow the errant spies ahead. Roger tossed a small stone at the sergeant's back as he crawled by him. The stone rolled slowly down the sergeant's side and landed silently on the half dry earth of no man's land.

The Inniskilling looked in surprise and saw Roger, finger at his lips, gesturing the sergeant to get back to his trench.

The sergeant gestured back at him by placing three fingers on his shoulder, nodding back at their trench. He tapped his shoulder again with three fingers and then nodded in the direction of the German trench. The sergeant had indicated to Roger, that the captain, three pips on his shoulder, had told him to keep an eye

---

[32] "Eedjit" Irish term for idiot.

on them. Roger fumed inside, both because of the problems the sergeant would cause but also because the captain didn't have enough faith in him not to need a nurse maid.

Roger sighed, and as he gave the sergeant a disdainful glare, nodded for him to follow him. As he did, he pointed to the pips on his shoulder and then directed his finger in the face of the sergeant, making it clear that out here he, Roger, was in charge of this operation and the sergeant was to do exactly what he was ordered and not by anyone back in the relative safety of the trench behind them.

When Roger and the sergeant caught up with the rest, Bill looked at Roger and mouthed what all the rest were thinking.

"What the fuck's he doing here?"

The twins both instinctively looked at the ground, closing their eyes in exasperation, while trying to adjust their moves to allow for the encumbrance.

One of the twins stared at Roger and pointed at the sergeant, gesturing that Roger should order him to stay there and go no further. Roger passed the instruction to Quinn. At the same time Roger gestured to Bill to keep the sergeant out on no man's land.

When the twins got close enough to the German trench to peer into it, Joe, Davy, and Jonty lay motionless acting as cover. The front line was empty apart from a few sentries thinly spread amongst the trenches. No other Germans were to be seen or heard. The twins had mixed feelings, On the one hand it had made it easier to get right up to the line, even slip into the trench at a pinch, but where the rest of the bastards where, was their greater worry.

One of the twins crawled back to Roger and beckoned him forward while the rest followed behind at intervals, leaving only Bill and Quinn further back in the darkness. Adam and Allen slid into the trench at points in between the sentries which was made easy by the zigzag formations, built to defend against an assault by a platoon of men, but not equipped to stop a lone ferret.

The twins could see a different trench set up compared to the 36th. The Gerry front line did not seem to have the same level of activity, less boot marks, equipment about, or significant supports.

As they lay silently, they could hear a low droning noise, punctuated by the occasional short laugh. As they both sat motionless at different parts of the trench it dawned on them that the main force of Germans was deep below their feet, not a few feet, but way down; fifty foot or more, they reckoned.

Adam noticed some concrete block and bags of cement packed against the side of a small section of the trench wall. He stepped forward a few yards and attempted to inspect further and as he did, he noticed steps leading down to the darkness on the floor of the top level of the trench.

"Jesus, the Hun are deep below ground, halfway to Hell," thought Adam, "and worse still, they are making things comfortable for themselves!"

While the twins completed their surveys, Roger sat listening in a shell hole only a few feet from the trench parapet. Adam signalled to him to slide down into the trench. Roger sat still and listened. The twins moved silently off either side of him.

After a few minutes of surveying the German trench, either side of Roger, the twins re-emerged. They made no sound but gestured to Roger to follow them along the trench pointing to the dark hole in the corner, framed by heavy sandbags. Roger propped himself against the edge of the entrance. The twins crouched at each end of the unguarded zig zag. Roger listened to the hum of noise far below, picking out every comment he could understand. He was able to establish that the sentries were in good humour and talked regularly with reference to the quarters down below. He was able to pick up talk of hardened reinforcements coming in soon. As he lay silently his blood ran cold when he heard sentries laying on bets on the time machine gun crews could set up the fastest. Roger could hear eight and seven minutes mentioned. His mind whirled as he began to doubt his translation. Had he been confused by a regional dialect? Roger knew the normal time was ten minutes. Any less was exceptional, but the sentries were talking eight, even near seven minutes. One voice had reckoned it could come down to near five when one of the crack troop teams arrived.

Roger's information gathering was abruptly interrupted by Adam tossing a small handful of dirt at his shoulder and nodding up at no man's land. He had held his ear close to the duck board and could sense the movement of heavy boots from the next zigzag round the corner.

The twins and Roger slipped along the trench in the opposite direction to the boots and out on the edge over the parapet.

Jonty, Davy, and Joe, still covering out on the edge, could hear a German voice whisper in the darkness between them and Bill and the mistrusting Sergeant Quinn. They stayed silent and still as the twins and Roger crawled back beside them.

Bill was the closest to the three poachers of information. He gestured to the nearest, putting one finger to his mouth and then jabbed it to the darkness to his left.

After about five seconds, which seemed like thirty, the shape of two Germans walking crouched in the black night looking in the direction of Quinn and Bill's position appeared.

Within less than a minute, the two Germans knew exactly where Quinn and Bill where lying, faces down, trying not to breathe, hoping the two enemy might not yet have spotted them. The hope was in vain. They had seen the foe approaching but had opted to attempt to hide, knowing that the sergeant's gunfire or bayonet skills would have alerted the German trench and the young scouts would have been caught in the consequences.

As the larger German raised his rifle a few yards from Quinn's chest, the smaller shape did the same to Bill.

The larger German pulled back the bolt on his rifle to finish Quinn off. The younger, smaller soldier looked at him in despair, anticipating he would be expected to do the same. As the larger

147

German moved his finger to the trigger, he felt a knock on the back of each knee almost simultaneously which caused him to slump on to his knees, but as he did so, he tried instinctively to fire his rifle as a flash of steel came across his windpipe, so deep and quick he knew nothing about it. At the same time the younger soldier was hit from behind and was being held face down by Joe.

"Nein, nein," he tried to mutter as Joe rammed his hand over his mouth trying to keep the incident unheard back in the enemy trench.

The young German had a look of fear Davy and Joe had never seen before. It was not the look of a hard bitten, evil Hun, but a frightened lad, who, like them, didn't really want to be in this bloody war.

Davy crawled forward to the lad, knife, still dripping with the blood of the now departed larger Hun. The young German began to shake in uncontrollable fear.

Davy made two slashing movements, each severing the lad's two Achilles tendons in the space just above the top of his boots. He then pressed his fingers against his neck and the lad passed out.

"That'll stop you getting back to warn your mates before we are long gone," thought Davy to himself.

The young German would waken in half an hour, head splitting, unable to move too far. He would be found by his comrades and get his ticket back home. His war was over. No use to the German war effort with two wrecked Achilles. He would walk again properly after a year or two, Thousands would have taken that one.

The lads all stayed motionless in silence for a minute, just to make sure they had remained unnoticed or in case another pair of lookouts turned up. Then they made a quick but ghost like journey back to their line.

They spotted the marker left by the captain on the top edge of the trench so they would be safe to slide back in and not get shot to bits by uninformed 'colleagues mistaking them for a German raiding party.

As the last man, the sergeant, hit the duck board of the trench, they were ushered off in single file back down the line of trenches straight into the captain's dug out.

Not a word was spoken as they passed through, only nods from soldiers leaning against the trench walls, most seeking solace from a Woodbine. The onlookers sensed that the squad had been in the thick of something. Not just because of the lads' dishevelled state and frozen expressions, as they did their best to avoid contact. It was Sergeant Quinn that gave the game away.

"Holy fuck, did you see the look on the Sarg's face?" mumbled one soldier to his mate as they shared a match.

"Looks like he's seen a ghost."

"Might have been his own by the look of it," replied the other.

"Did you see the tall skinny lad? Someone lost a lot of blood out there and it wasn't his. Better than that, those lads are YCV

"Chocolate Boys!" Whatever they were at, they didn't do much melting."

Back in the 'office' the lads were immediately ushered to set themselves down wherever they could find a space. The captain and Lt Maxwell sat side by side, Maxwell leaned forward and offered cigarettes to them all.

The captain briefly surveyed their faces and gave a respectful nod to Roger. He noticed Quinn was not standing as usual but sitting slumped on his backside like the rest of them, giving him a long, slow, relieved stare.

"Now that just about says it all!" thought the captain.

Quinn, understanding the captain's gaze, dipped his head at a slight angle, signalling they had done well, which was more than he could say for himself, he thought.

"Well then Lt Arthur, what's the state of play with Gerry then?"

"They are dug deep, very deep. A good fifty feet down. Our twenty-five pounders will not do them much damage. Needs the big Howitzers the Frogs are using at Verdun to do any serious damage. They are in good spirits. Most concerning information we got was that they are bringing up crack units. Men that know what they are doing under pressure and," Roger sighed deeply. "They seem to have got resetting a machine gun unit back up after a bombardment down to seven minutes. The best we have manage, up to now, is near ten."

Captain Montgomery remained silent, taking time to fill and light his pipe and let Roger continue.

"I would prefer to lay it all out in my report in the morning, appreciate a few hours to get my head round it all and give you something more coherent, if that is all right with you Sir?" asked Roger respectfully.

Roger looked in the direction of the twins, continued.

"Those two got much deeper in than I did. They are the ones you should hear from as much as myself, sir. I listened to plenty, but they saw even more.

The twins explained all they had seen and heard. The captain listened intently, pausing only to relight his crook shaped pipe.

At the end, he looked round the line of tired faces and asked,

"Well, is that it or is there anything else to add, gentlemen?" The lads looked at each other for a lead and shrugged their shoulders. Montgomery let out a sigh of resignation.

"I would have thought that blood soaking your shirt would warrant an explanation Lance Corporal."

He hesitated as he struggled to remember Davy's name.

"Gibson," Roger's voice intervened.

"It's not mine, so nothing to worry about sir," assured Davy as he sucked slowly on his cigarette.

The captain, laughed wearily, "I know it's not yours, man. If you had lost that amount of blood, you would not be sitting here. I would be organising a burial party."

"Aye and if it wasn't for him and his mate there, the burial party would be for me and Corporal Johnston," added Sergeant Quinn, rather sheepishly, still sitting with his back against the door.

"I'll give you a full report in the morning too, if that is allowed, Sir. It has been quite a night for us all. The lads done well, Sir, even with me making it difficult for them. You've nothing to worry about these lads. Nothing much chocolate about them," as he moved his eyes between the captain's gaze and the floor below him.

"Permission to leave now Sir?" as he dragged himself up from the floor assuming his request would be granted.

"Aye Sergeant, go ahead man and the rest of you, go and get your heads down. Good night's work men, well done," instructed the captain. Then, as they raised themselves, continued,

"None of this evening goes beyond this excuse for an office, gentlemen. None of it, not a word! The rest of the men out there must hear nothing. This goes up the line, not along it. Army rules; need to know basis. If Sergeant Quinn hears of it getting out, the whole lot of you, despite your good work tonight, will be up for court marshalling. Understood?"

All concerned, including Quinn, nodded in approval.

As the lads stepped back into the chill of the night air and headed off back down to their trench position, Joe nudged his shoulder against Davy's.

152

'Well done men," he laughed mockingly. "I'd have preferred if he'd offered us double time for night work!"

"Don't hold your breath Joe," replied Davy as he repaid the shoulder nudge.

"I tell you, after that performance, you've nothing to worry about walking through the Markets[33] when you get back home," laughed Joe, continuing to poke at Davy.

They walked on in silence puffing their Woodbines, as Davy, keeping his stare at the duck board said,

"Problem would be if I had come off with that trick back home, I'd hang for it!" sighed Davy, shaking his head slowly in remorse.

"Take away any notion of feeling bad about it, Davy. That bastard would have got the Sergeant, Bill, maybe me, as well. Don't you think any more about it. Sleep with a clear conscience. I would mate," reassured Joe.

Davy half turned around to Joe and nodded slowly as he sought more solace in his cigarette. Joe may well have been right, but it didn't stop Davy having nightmares about that night before his brain let it drain to the far recesses of his memory only resurfacing on the odd occasion until his eyes would close for the last time.

---

[33] Markets - Irish Nationalist area of Inner Belfast where Joe lived.

The lads did settle down for the night and in the morning, when asked where they had been, they gave the same response. "Ah, just a bit of poaching."

Early the next morning the captain, the two lieutenants and the sergeant studied all the information they had gleaned. At the end of the session the captain leaned back in his makeshift chair and blew smoke from his pipe and said,

"This must go to General Nugent himself, gentlemen. This information goes against the grain of what the top brass are planning. Some of them will not want to hear it, but Nugent is his own man; proved it many times. He does not make a habit of sacrificing men's lives for a lost cause. If the situation is the same as over there, all the way down the line, then the whole of X Corp and its Battalions on the seven miles Somme section could be biting off more than they can chew."

The other three all nodded in agreement.

"Our report will have to go up to headquarters by 14.00 hours at the latest. Get me Private Price to run it back to Headquarters with express instructions that it must go to General Nugent personally. Right into the palm of his hand," insisted the captain. "I do not want it being withheld or diluted by some Major who does not want to rock the party line."

Chapter Fourteen

Nursing station

While this had been the first bad night for the friends, the same could not have been said back at the nursing station. Anna and Kitty had been posted to a frontline nursing station, a few miles back from the front, a full six months earlier.

The early weeks of their nursing experience had the benefit of a lull in action on their section of the line in support of the 36th Division. Their work involved mostly the care of wounded soldiers, awaiting return to England, or patched up, and sent back to the front line. Casualties were steady but manageable. The Matron and her sisters had the station operating in a coordinated fashion, much more capably than the generals on the battlefield. The early spell of quiet did not last for long.

When word of the arrival of any significant number of casualties came in, the Matron would stride in and shout firmly and formidably and with a restrained sigh,

"Girls, to your stations, be strong!"

Anna and Kitty often needed all their reserves of mental and often physical strength to keep it all together. Many times, they caught each other's gaze as they stemmed blood, held the hands of dying soldiers. Their gazes said to each other,

155

"What if one of them was Davy or Joe or Roger?"

On one brief day of rest, they walked in the countryside and sat by a stream in silence.

"God Kitty," said Anna breaking the silence, "I am sorry I brought you to this. You did not have to be here. You should be sitting on the Lagan, waiting for Joe to come home, not in this hell. It is not even your war. I do not deserve your forgiveness."

Kitty lifted her head back and looked at the sky and sighed.

"Anna, I'm here because Joe is here. You didn't force me, and I don't give a damn about Ireland either. I just couldn't have stayed at Ballydrain, waiting for him to return. I need to be near him just as much as you need to be near Davy, and don't give me all that nonsense about 'the men on the front need me' bit that you tried to sell to your father. You are only here for one reason, just the same as me. So here we are, two love struck girls, scared senseless, not knowing what is ahead of us or our men.

Silence overcame them both until Kitty, finally turning on her side to face Anna, looking for a response.

"I wonder what they are up to now, at this moment Kitty?" said Anna after a long silence broken only by a few birds.

Kitty still staring at the sky replied,

"If you close your eyes, you could imagine you are sitting at Minnowburn Beeches.[34] That's as near as we are getting to home for quite a while the way this mess is going."

She paused for a few seconds. "So much for your father's mate Craig, Eh girl? Him and his glory and honour and God and Ulster. Ulster or Ireland isn't much use to you if your man is dead."

Having got that off her chest, Kitty lay back on the riverbank and stared at the sky. Anna, silent, did the same.

Between the Autumn of 1915 and June 1916 Anna, Davy, Kitty and Joe had never managed to be together properly. On one occasion Davy had escorted some walking wounded back to the same nursing post where Kitty and Anna were based, but the best they could manage was to look across the ward as the girls worked at incoming cases.

Even if they had the chance to speak face to face the Matron would have come down on it hard and heavy.

All Davy could do was mouth discreetly across the ward.

"Are you ok? I love you."

Anna mouthed back, saying the words under her breath.

"Fine, I love you forever, keep safe."

---

[34] Minnowburn Beeches – a local beauty spot on the Lagan near Shaw's Bridge Belfast opposite Ballydrain House.

The wounded soldier she was attending heard the words, "I love you forever," and in his state of euphoria, shouted in pain to an unconscious soldier next to him.

"She loves me mate. Fuck me this is worth getting shot for!" as the sharp pain in his chest hammered him again. He lurched, falling back into unconsciousness.

He was lucky, he was able to his tell grandchildren about the beautiful nurse who saved his life by giving him the will to live, even if she didn't keep her promise.

Before Davy had to turn and leave, she nodded her head and mouthed "Joe?" to which Davy nodded back with a smile, a wink, and a nod.

Anna turned her head in the direction of where she had last seen Kitty and met her stare. Kitty had been watching Anna's silent conversation with Davy. She nodded back to Anna with a relieved smile and continued her work, while scanning the room to make sure Matron's discerning eye would not notice their distraction from duty.

Matron's regular pep talk was,

"Remember girls, the soldier you are attending is the only thing that matters. Any nurse whom I find letting their minds wander or seeking a distraction will be a sorry nurse. Men's lives depend on you, stay focused, no matter what. Do I make myself clear!" After a pause there was the almost ceremonial bow of the head by all and a "Yes Matron!"

Anna used to think with embarrassment, "So this is what it's like for Kitty, Mary, Jonty, Martha and the rest back home. God it'll be different when I have my say when I get home."

Chapter Fifteen

The Report

Back at the front, by the middle of June, tensions were rising on the lads' section near Thiepval, directly opposite the Schwaben Redoubt. High rankers were being seen more regularly. Extra supplies had been building up. Joe and Davy both agreed that something big was about to happen.

Back on that morning in April, Jonty had been sent to hand the first report to General Nugent, the message was in Nugent's grip by 12.00 hours.

The outside of the report was addressed for the attention of General Nugent and curiously below the name was added, *"From Captain Montgomery, Lieutenant Arthur (Ballydrain)."*

Inside was a handwritten note which was separate from the report with additional instructions:

"It is requested that Private Price waits to return any further instructions."

When Nugent received the report from Jonty, he started to scan the first few lines and as the content began to spread through his brain, he walked slowly over to his desk and sat in his chair while still reading and puffing on his drop shaped

162

pipe. Nugent perused the report. Jonty, having not been given the order to stand easy, was riveted to attention throughout the General's perusal of the report.

As he completed the last sentence, Nugent looked briefly at Jonty, as he returned his gaze to the report, turned it back to the front page, placed it on his desk, put one finger on the front cover and tapped it slowly as he digested the information.

"Were you one of the soldiers on this mission?" Nugent asked Jonty directly.

"Yes sir, Private Price, sir!" replied Jonty.

"Well Private Price, set yourself down on the bench over there in the corner while I write a note that I want you to take back to Captain Montgomery."

As he wrote the note, he paused, as if trying to write as little as possible, yet making sure the instructions were clear. Every few minutes he sat back and stared at the ceiling, ejecting plumes of blue grey smoke in that direction.

"So, you know the basic content of this report?" he asked Jonty in a casual manner.

"Well, I was at Gerry's trench and sat in the back at the officers' dugout when the other lads and Lieutenant Arthur and Sergeant Quinn gave their accounts. I didn't understand any of the German voices. Roger understood that stuff, I mean Lieutenant Arthur, was picking it up easy enough. I wasn't picked to go because of my language skills. I was there so if it all went badly, I was the one they reckoned could get back to tell the tale, so to speak, General,' replied Jonty.

"I'm the Mouse, that's my nickname. The Mouse sir." Jonty continued quite proudly.

"Are you indeed?" grinned the General over his spectacles.

"And what did you do before you came to this great adventure?" continued Nugent.

"Stable lad at Ballydrain House for Sir James Arthur, Sir."

Nugent stared at a space beyond Jonty's left ear and then leaning back, let out a sigh of understanding.

"Ah, so that's why you said Roger and then Lt Arthur. I went to Campbell College with James, and I meet up with him at most of the Alma Mater dinners that I manage to attend. I heard he had two children Anna and Roger if my memory is correct. Roger is out here with the 14th Battalion," reflected Nugent.

"Yes sir, lot of us from Milltown, Edenderry, Shaw's Bridge are here with him, Sir. It's the Belfast Scouts at the biggest jamboree in the world," replied Jonty, as the nerves of speaking face to face with one of the top Generals; one of the few he had any regard for, got the better of him. The general's record of concern for the safety of his men and record of keeping casualties as low as possible assured him of that respect.

"How is Jimmy these days?" inquired Nugent as he penned a few more words.

"Sir James is Sir James," replied Jonty, sheepishly.

164

"Ha hah!" grunted Nugent. "Still takes no prisoners then. Goes by the rules, doesn't suffer fools gladly, and his way is right."

"That's him, sir, but he runs a good show, doesn't take too many liberties. He's hard, but fair. Takes no prisoners, but there's a lot worse among the big noises in Belfast than Sir James."

"I would wager he is glad at least he has Anna at home," said Nugent. "Empty house without your children."

"Aye well that's not the way it is, sir," replied Jonty.

The General was completing his last line of his note and his curiosity got the better of him.

"Explain, Private Price, what is not the way it is?" asked Nugent, as he signed the note.

"Anna is out here with the nurses, few miles back at one of the frontline posts."

As Nugent rose to his feet and handed the reply letter to Jonty to put in his satchel, he continued,

"So young Anna is a chip off the old block then. Headstrong, like her father. Surprised Jimmy didn't stop her coming out here," replied the General.

"Ah, well sir, she's even more headstrong than her Da, I mean Sir James, Sir. That and she has personal reasons for being here in the form of Davy Gibson. Davy, the same David that's handy with the knife. Reference to him in the report," said Jonty, as he stood up from his chair, adjusted his uniform and placed his helmet back on his head.

"Right!" said General Nugent. "Get yourself back to Captain Montgomery. Keep your head down and I'll see what the rest of the experts here think of this. I know what I think but it's not all down to me, Price."

Jonty saluted. "Yes Sir, do my best sir!"

"I do not doubt it, Price. Akela, we do our best Dib, Dib, Dib and all that," replied Nugent, offering Jonty his left hand, the handshake of a fellow scout.

Jonty just stuck out his left hand in response and said, "Dob, Dob, Dob, Dob sir!"

"Well, Price, I hope that the next time we shake hands it's at a jamboree when this is all history," was the final comment between Jonty and the General.

Jonty left the office and passed down the corridors of the headquarters, as eyes raised from desks followed him every inch of the way until he got out in the fresh air free from the thick smell of stale pipe tobacco in the building and began his journey back to the front line.

Back in his office the General paced up and down, blowing smoke like the train to St Pancras. The general's thoughts of the frontline German trenches filled his brain at the expense of all others.

So, the Germans were dug deep and in concrete. They had recently brought up some of their elite regiments. They were living in good conditions, morale was high, and they were working on getting their machine guns set in seven minutes, not the standard ten.

This indeed did not fit well with the big plan he and his fellow generals had in mind. It would be interesting how the other generals on the section would react to this information, probably, he thought, not to his pleasing.

When Jonty slipped back down the ladder and along the duckboard back into the captain's shelter office, he stood to attention and saluted as he handed the letter from Nugent. Captain Montgomery. Lieutenants Maxwell and Arthur arriving on his shoulder in the candle lit retreat almost immediately.

"Thank you, Price. Take a quick swig of that Bushmills in the corner and get yourself back to your pals. Well done, dismissed. Oh! and yes, Sergeant Quinn will organise you with a stripe, Lance Corporal Price, in the morning." said Captain Montgomery without changing his solemn expression as he started to peruse the first lines of the letter.

"Yes sir, thank you sir," replied Jonty, as he saluted walking backwards out of the makeshift door.

Captain Montgomery read the letter and read it a second time before turning and handing it to the Lieutenants, who had already gotten the gist of the contents as they squinted in the

167

poor light over the shoulders of the captain as he had been reading the contents signed at the bottom by General Nugent. The lines in the letter that caught the eye most were,

"When there is an attack against the German Line, the first wave of troops must already be out in no man's land as far forward as prevailing shelling from our lines will permit, well in advance of the whistle. This action is imperative to counteract any improved timing of German machine gun posts. Furthermore, to counteract the introduction of high calibre reinforcements, the 36th Division attack must be led by the Inniskillings. The other Battalions of the 36th Division are to be used in the second wave."

The final part of the letter instructed,

"This instruction must be adhered to, irrespective of any other future orders given which may attempt to countermand it. Pass this letter to the most senior officer on the front line. Everything is on a 'need to know' basis and an element of surprise is paramount, to avoid the potential for an unthinkable level of losses.
Signed General Nugent.

"Well gentlemen, so there you are, we got his attention. Looks like we might have a problem here. Reading between the lines I do not think senior command want to hear this. It goes against their plans, but Nugent knows, that is all that matters. Nugent wants us out there and on top of the Germans before they know what hits them," said Maxwell with Roger nodding slowly in approval.

"I have a problem now," sighed the captain.

"I have to take this to Major Forsythe and the first thing he will ask is why he was bypassed on this."

"Quite," agreed Lt Maxwell.

"Difficult to tell the Major he was kept in the dark because we didn't trust him to pass the full story back to the top in case the news didn't go down well!"

"We had to do it this way. The General agrees. That's why he replied in the way he did. If we had not, the General might not have gotten the full report and we would not have been given this bit of an edge if hardy comes to hardy, gentlemen." interrupted Roger.

"If you get flack Captain you can blame it on me," suggested Roger. "Tell him, I gave the instruction to the messenger to take it directly to Nugent, without your knowledge. Casually mention my father and Nugent are old pals. The Major, like yourself, is a career soldier. He will not want to come up against any of the senior brass or create any waves. I do not have an Army career to protect."

Captain Montgomery, waved his hand that was not holding his pipe, dismissing Roger's offer of clemency.

"No need, Lt Arthur, you may well have come up with the idea, but I made the decision, which as it turns out was the best solution. If the Major wants to make the air blue, good luck to him. More likely the Major will bite his tongue for fear it might get back to Nugent."

"He might get his revenge by having us digging latrines for the next month. We are in the shit either way!" laughed the captain ruefully.

"It looks gentlemen, that we will just have to work on the basis that our shells close ahead of us as we lay in no mans' land for a few hours is a better bet than running into a wall of machine gun bullets," added Roger.

"Exactly," added Maxwell, "which is just what the General is doing; giving us an edge."

"Well gentlemen," sighed Captain Montgomery, "I'll head down the line and update the Major. The next hour should be character building," he sighed.

"Into the Valley of death rode the one," sighed Maxwell with a slightly sympathetic grin.

"Hopefully, the General's plan will avoid that. Au revoir gentlemen," said Montgomery, as he stood, straightened his tunic, lifted his helmet, and disappeared out into the evening chill, placing his helmet on his head as he orientated his way along the zig zag trench lines to the Major's repost.

Chapter sixteen

1st July 1916

By the 28th of June, the 36th Division, and all the other Divisions of X Corps, were under no doubt they were close to the big push. Bombardment of seven miles of German lines had begun the day before and had not stopped since; a steady rhythm of constant delivery of twenty-five pounder shells had been sailing high above their heads, hammering the German first and second line of defenses. The ground never seemed to remain still. The main thought amongst the men was that they thanked God, and anyone else, that they were not on the receiving end.

Most were happy to accept the notion that the enemy would either be dead or traumatised by such a pounding if it kept up long enough.

The men of the Belfast battalions of the Irish Rifles were to advance in the second wave. They thought they would be going over to German trenches filled only with the dead who could not scramble several miles back to safety.

The Inniskillings, sitting in the forward trenches would have done any mopping up before they even got there.

"Must be simple if they were taking the Chocolate Soldiers of the Belfast Young Citizens with them," they joked amongst themselves.

As suspected by Cpt Montgomery, Lt Maxwell, and Lt Arthur the top brass had not changed their overall plan of attack to allow for the report they had smuggled to General Nugent.

The General had for his part laid the details of the report at the table of the meeting at Headquarters. The attack, however, went ahead as originally planned by General Rawlinson who was the senior of command. The only change was weather conditions postponing it from the 28th of June to the morning of the 1st July 1916.

General Nugent's information on the extent of German strength in personnel and preparations had not fallen on deaf ears, but it was not enough for the top brass to change tactics they had set and planned for months. They were only getting similar reports from sporadic areas of the German lines. Too many sorties to the German lines had been less intrusive than the Edenderry Boys. The generals had relied too heavily on rushed photographs from the air, taken at great risk, under attack from trench gunfire and marauding bi-plane Fokkers. The photographs gave no indication of what was going on fifty feet down below.

Two million casualties at Verdun further down the line, together with their system of keeping troops on the front line for months on end, fuelled the French Generals with the fear their troops might mutiny over the summer months. The British

172

system of a fortnightly rotation between the front and the reserve stations was much better for morale and recovery.

The dice was loaded. The top brass were prepared to convince themselves that a constant bombardment for four days would be enough to take care of the deep defences, if they existed to any extent. Even the best of soldiers would not be anywhere near as quick in resetting positions in less than ten minutes. The Irish must have exaggerated, they assured themselves. It was, some of them scoffed, all very well practicing quicker gun positions in quiet circumstance; simply not realistic when you have been pounded for four days and nights by everything the British Army had to throw at them.

By the evening of the 30th of June 1916, the Edenderry Boys found themselves sitting in the frontline trench watching Quinn, the Captain, Maxwell, and Roger, and occasionally the Major, parading past attempting words of reassurance and readiness. The lads knew there would be no grand whistle, just a nod from the Sergeant or officers to climb up the ladders and crawl out into no man's land.

Sat in a group facing each other, backs against the wall of the trench, there was not much chat out of any of them. Bill Johnston had his Orange Lodge sash in his lap and just stared at it as he wiped it, shone the badges repeatedly and occasionally taking it off, putting it back on again. Then a few minutes later he would wipe and clean it all again. The last time he put it on, he threaded

173

it down the inside of his battle tunic and buttoned it to the neck, putting the largest bronze medal to his lips as he closed the last few buttons, whispering, "No Surrender," to himself.

Every boy and man had his own way of coping with fear.

Jonty flicked a penny until it started to annoy Davy, but he didn't have the heart to say to him. What if the last words he ever said to him were words of anger? Even if he could be a pain in the arse at times, he was still one of the Edenderry Boys and the Edenderry Boys were loyal, especially to each other.

Big Rab, sat reading his Bible. Davy reckoned he must have read it from Genesis to Revelations in the months they had been at war. Nothing new about that, but this evening he seemed to be reading the same thing repeatedly. He flicked between two pages back and forward.

Joe just sat silently, as he often did, with a Woodbine between his lips, thinking of Kitty and cursing his stupidity for thinking this would be an easy way to make a bit of extra money.

"Fucking blood money, his fucking blood," he thought to himself.

Davy sat with his head back, eyes closed, and thought of home and the perfect days and evenings with Anna, his father, and the Lagan. Anna, hair flowing, face turned towards him smiling, laughing, teasing, with that look in her eyes.

"Jesus, God, I'll give you a second chance if you get me through this and let me take Anna home and spend the rest of my natural life with her, no matter what Sir James or my father say."

The twins Allen and Adam sat beside each other throwing dice, competing to the end.

After a long period of silence, Davy's curiosity got the better of him.

"Rab, what's the bit you are reading over and over again? You'd think you'd have understood it by now?" asked Davy, with just the slightest hint of humour while taking care not to offend Rab.

"The 23rd Psalm Davy," replied Rab, with a decidedly tired rueful sigh.

Davy, not having had the pleasure of church, apart from the occasion he had been tricked into attending by Anna, and having no idea what it was about, gave Rab a puzzled stare.

Joe caught Davy's blank look in Rab's direction and laughed quietly.

"You really are a heathen, Davy. Not a bit of Christian spirit in you, sad bastard," goaded Joe, as he looked over at Rab.

"I think you should give him a bit of religious education Rab; no better a time for the 23rd Psalm. Rab, if you would do us the honour?"

Rab gave Joe a look of surprise, mixed with compassion and glanced at Davy, Bill, Jonty, the twins, and Sgt Quinn, who was sitting just beyond Joe checking his rifle, grenades, and kit a dozen times.

"Aye, go ahead Rab, all contributions to survival greatly appreciated," said Bill from the darkness of a corner he had found for himself.

Rab leaned forward, shifting his large frame from the wall of the trench, and stared at the page on the Bible in front of him.

He was staring at the page, but the words came out without reading. He knew the Psalm off by heart. The book in his hands was only a prop, a comforter. This allowed him to say the words without it being cold and stilted. He was able to speak it, in his own way. He caught the mood of the moment and delivered a reading, a sort of homily to Joe, which were the most spiritual words any of the group would ever hear.

"The Lord is my Shepherd. I shall not want.
He makes me lie down in green pastures.
He leads me in the paths of righteous for his name's sake.
Even though I walk through the valley of death, I fear no evil;
for thou are with me.
Thy rod and they staff, they comfort me.
Thou preparest a table before me in the presence of my
enemies
Thou anointest my head with oil, my cup overflows.
Surely goodness and mercy shall follow me all the days of my
life; and I shall dwell in the house of the Lord for ever."

When he had finished the group sat in silence. You could have heard a pin drop. Every man's and boy's thoughts became consumed with Rab's words. Joe stopped smoking throughout.

The twins Allen and Adam dropped the dice and put their arms round each other's shoulders and stared at the ground.

Bill sat hoping the words would be right.

Davy, sat looking up at the sky and thinking, "Well God, this is your last chance, don't let my Da down again, please."

The silence was broken, with the voice of Sgt Quinn from the end of the row.

"Well done, son. Said that better than that pompous git that turns up on Sunday morning telling us about the glory of dying. If you get out of this alive you should take up the cloth, son."

The Sergeant shuffled from his position, stood upright in front of Rab and offered his hand to him. Rab, with an embarrassed glance, stood upright and shook the Sergeant's hand. Then almost immediately remembered the drill and saluted, accompanied with a "Thank you Sergeant."

The rest of the lads followed suit and stood up and thanked the increasingly embarrassed, now flushed, big lad. The scene looked all the part of any vicar bidding goodbye to his flock in the vestibule of the church on Sunday morning.

After a few nervous jokes, the lads went back to their thoughts and rituals they had been engrossed in earlier.

At 04.00 hours, the Captain, Maxwell and Arthur paced the trench line giving last instructions, making sure the exit out of the trench would be seamless and, most importantly, quiet and unnoticed.

As the lads stood in a huddle waiting for the nod, Sgt Quinn walked into the centre of the group.

"Right lads," he whispered, "the YCV are supposed to go out with the Inniskillings and when we take the first trench you lot are also supposed to sit tight and hold it until the second wave of the Belfast units arrive. The Inniskillings, go on to the second line, where the real action will take place. I could do with you lot with me in the second line attack. I'm giving you your choice now. No shame in keeping the head low in the first trench, I'm not ordering you; I'm asking you."

Sergeant Quinn made eye contact with Davy, Joe, Bill, Jonty, Rab and the twins in turn.

'We're with you Sarge," offered Bill, before anyone else could get chance to raise their approval or otherwise.

Davy glanced across to Joe, who just shook his head and had a last puff on his Woodbine before looking over at Quinn.

"Will we get bonus pay, Sarge?"

Quinn gave him a look of exasperation.

"I'll take that as a yes then," sighed Joe as he turned towards the ladder leading to no man's land.

As the Inniskillings and YCV crawled silently from the trench, under the cover of darkness, into no man's land, the ground shook below them as it had done for four solid days. The noise and shuddering seemed louder than when they were down in the relative safety of their trench. When they managed to look up in the direction of the German front line, they could see a constant line of explosions raining down on the first, second, and third lines of German trenches.

Everything was going to plan. The only, and not insignificant worry, was the risk of a few badly aimed shells falling a hundred yards short amongst them, but on the grand scale of things it was a much lesser risk than a solid wall of machine gun bullets. As they lay only a few hundred yards from the German trenches, they did not fear the machine gun posts. Even if they could get their machine guns back up in seven minutes, the Inniskillings would still have five minutes to spare. Enough time to be in the German first line trenches and seal them off or wipe them out in their rat holes deep below.

While the bombardment continued, there was little chance of many being in the first line. The second would still be deep underground and at their mercy.

So it was, when the bombardment stopped after 07.00 hours on the 1st of July 2016, the two battalions of 10th Inniskillings and 14th Irish Rifles, Young Citizens Volunteers raised themselves from the damp dew and charged at the German front trench.

By the time they got to the front trench the resistance was minimal, apart from a few dazed and frightened survivors who had managed to avoid a direct hit from the reinforced front line.

It took little time for the Young Volunteers to fill the vacant first line of trenches and gather up the shell-shocked prisoners. The Volunteers were happy enough to play a low profile in the scheme of things. The Inniskillings, on the other hand, were the professionals and they had a job to do. The Regiment, honour and ability needed to be satisfied.

They were soldiers above all else, for good or bad, rough, or smooth. Their sense of comradeship, duty and valour had to be shown.

The lads had kept close to Bill, who had kept close to Sgt Quinn. Up to that point it had been easy, apart from the occasional fire bursts in the sky above.

"Right lads, all present and correct," rasped Quinn, as he glanced round the group of thoughtful volunteers. All eyes were on the sergeant, Joe looked over at Davy, who stared back, filled his cheeks with air, and blew out. Joe shook his head from side to side and then rolled his eyes to the sky. They knew the next bit might not be so straight forward. Tom's instruction never to volunteer for anything invaded Davy's brain. He contented himself with the thought that he hadn't volunteered. That honour was down to Bill.

As they got about fifty yards from the second German trench, rifle shots were beginning to rake the ground around them sporadically. The sooner they could get amongst them before the machine guns could get set up the better it would be for them. Hiding in shell holes or behind burnt tree stumps would only make them captives of a deadly destiny.

Bravery and valour were not the prime motivation for charging full tilt at the German second line, but basic common sense. Get there before they set up the guns or accept the consequences.

Sgt Quinn, Bill, Joe, Davy, and the twins raced to the German second line, one bullet in the barrel and bayonets attached from the time they left the first German trench. Once in the German second trench, they knew it would be hand to hand, bayonet work. It was hand to hand guerrilla warfare they were trained for in the UVF camps at Randalstown and Clandeboye. Little space, little chance to duck, weave or hide. It had to be quicker and more focused, like the bull in the shed.

They all dropped into the second trench unrestricted, as the Sergeant had dispatched the only unfortunate German who had managed to get to his duckboard first. As they looked around to get their bearings, they could hear voices shouting from the left just below them as they steadied themselves to fire their single shot, the Sgt lobbed a grenade down the entrance of the underground haven, turned tomb.

A silence lasted for a second, replaced by screams and groans.

Davy would never forget the sight of a young German his own age, stagger out of the gap in the trench wall, holding his hands to what was once a face.

How he managed to move without a jaw, nose or eyes was beyond Davy. That was enough for Davy to decide his best chance of survival in these conditions was his slaughtering knife which he had placed carefully down his putties, wrapped between his boots and lower trouser leg. He knew he could defend himself better with it than welding an awkward rifle and bayonet in this cramped space, where speed and agility could be life changing.

The Inniskillings may be expert soldiers, but he was an expert slaughterer. This was as near as he would get to a bull in a shed. He'd feel he was doing any German a favour making it quick and clean and not leaving him like this poor sod.

He disconnected his bayonet, slung his rifle over his shoulder, dropped to his haunches and awaited the imminent sight of a German emerging from the bowels of the earth.

Another sound of panicking German voices could be heard from the right. Sgt Quinn again located the source and lobbed another grenade which had a similar result as the first. This time, after about ten seconds, several volleys of shots flew up from the gap at the base of the trench wall, one of which caught the Sgt a graze on the arm, causing him to wince and curse at the same time. "Ah fucking bastards!" as he lobbed another grenade with his uninjured arm.

This time no shots rang out, the only noise from below was, "We surrender, hands up!" in German as a piece of white cloth emerged on the end of a pole. The Germans below had seen the consequences of trying to exit the two ways to the surface of their dugout and had decided the only chance of survival was surrender and hope the Irish above would be civilised, which he could not know but had no other option.

The young German lieutenant had been relieved that the white sheet protruding from the gap in the trench wall had not been met with another grenade. He extended his other arm out into the daylight showing he was unarmed. Still no grenade or volley of shots. He heard a gruff voice speaking a language he could not understand. His only understanding of English was of small samples of upper-class English on scratchy gramophones. The accent of a gnarled sergeant from Ramelton, Donegal was too much for him to comprehend, but he had to take the chance of sticking his head out to the great unknown. As he emerged fully from the darkness below into the morning light, he blinked nervously. Roger stepped towards him and spoke to him in German,

"Tell your comrades to come out, hands in the air, no weapons. If there is any nonsense," he nodded in Quinn's direction. Quinn, holding up two more grenades, looked to the abyss below. The German, in a tone of panic and pleading, gave the orders for the rest of his disorientated squad to spill out of the bowels of the trench, to which they eagerly complied.

"Right Rab and Jonty, take them back to the first trench and hand them over and get back up here if you can!" ordered the Sergeant.

Within seconds, Jonty led the way, while Rab, delighted in giving the six survivors a regular dig with his rifle or back of his hand if they did not move quickly enough.

"Vengeance is mine saith the Lord, you bunch of Philistines!" laughed the big fellow at regular intervals.

"What now Roger?" shouted Bill as the prisoners disappeared out of sight.

"Stay put until we are given fresh orders. We were ordered to take the second trench and that is what we've done!" shouted Roger as he surveyed the trench.

As the lads gathered their thoughts and their breath, they listened to the noise of the battlefield. The ground had ceased to shudder from the four days of bombardment and now the noise was from the 36th shouting, firing gun shots, and two lines of German conscripts making a failed attempt to hold the line under intensive and brutal bombardment.

Sergeant Quinn was the first to pick up the change. The monotonous sound of machine guns was coming from the right, on down the line. Roger grabbed a trench periscope that was still intact but dislodged from the parapet wall, courtesy of it being demolished by an earlier direct hit.

He surveyed the landscape below and to the right, which was lower than the ground where they had mounted their successful assault.

Roger stared silently through the lens for several seconds, then dropped his face to the ground. He let out a mouthful of air, nodded to the captain and passed the lens to him.

The captain paused, fearing that it might give him sight of what he did not want to see. What he saw was much worse than he had imaged. The doomed Accrington, Preston, Burnley, and Manchester Pals units of the 32nd Division had obediently stepped out of the trench at the sound of the whistle and walked, as ordered, to the German lines. Without the instruction that Nugent gave to the 36"Division, the 32nd Lancashire Division did not stand a chance.

"Seems like the Generals didn't take heed, Captain," grunted Quinn in frustration and irony.

"Well, here is where we are, Sergeant Quinn, and here is where we can't stay. As soon as the Hun gather their senses, they'll have those machine gun bastards in the third line waiting for us. You know as well as I do those machine guns can fire a good mile." whispered the captain, shaking his head slowly.

"Our orders were to take the second trench of the Schwaben Redoubt, we've done that!" snapped Quinn, forgetting his rank, seriously concerned about what might be coming next from the thoughts of the captain.

185

"We need to forge on to the third line, no option. If we stay here and pat ourselves on the back for reaching objectives, Gerry will be down on us with some of their finest. We'll have to try and take the third line before the Hun get set up. It's our best hope."

Sgt Quinn stared at the ground, shoulders down. He didn't want to hear that, but he knew the captain was right. Quinn raised his gaze in the direction of the lads, who by now wished they were in the thick of a football riot between Linfield and Belfast Celtic[35] compared to this caper. The Second Lieutenants negotiated a path up and down their corner of the captured second line, before leading them on through the choking smoke to the third line. Their destiny was again in the hands of surprise.

---

[35] Linfield Football Club. Protestant, Loyalist supported team from Belfast. Belfast Celtic, Catholic Nationalist supported team from Belfast. One of the most "heated" football rivalries in the game at that time. Equal to Glasgow Rangers and Glasgow Celtic today.

Chapter Seventeen

Headquarters

Back at Headquarters news of the catastrophe taking place most of the way down the line of British attack, was filtering through from runners and spotters in high trees with a vantage point of the battlefield. The senior ranks pondered over the options. Some suggested retreat and calling the whole mess off, others demanding the second wave advance and tip the balance by outnumbering the beleaguered German defenses.

Amidst the deliberations, a messenger burst through the door, halting, and straightening himself immediately as the Brigadiers and Generals of the Divisions of the British Army's X Corp had all lifted their respective gazes from maps on the large desk in front of them, looking at him grimly for his disrespectful entrance.

"The 36th Ulster have broken through, taken the first and second lines at the Schwaben Redoubt, and gone to attack the third line!" blurted the messenger in excitement.

The Brigadiers stared back at him, motionless. After a stunned silence, Nugent, spoke in a quiet but determined tone,

"Well, that's it, gentlemen. Redirect the reserve line up there. Flanking movement. Cut Gerry off. Encircle them. Stop reinforcements getting up to them. Their defence will suffocate."

He refrained from saying, "I told you so!" about getting men out on no man's land before the whistle.

General Rawlinson, famous for his caution and sticking to the plan and methodology, senior of commander of X Corp, was the first to respond.

"It cannot be done, Nugent. We would not be able to redirect quickly enough. Let us see how an hour of the reserve line wearing down Gerry goes and take it from there. This is no time for changing plans we have made for weeks with a knee jerk reaction."

"And how many more will be cut down in the next hour because of a plan that's not working? The 36th can hold the third line for as long as it takes. Order the reserve sections to force march, run if they must, to the top of the line. Cut the bastards off!" shouted Nugent.

"Nugent," said Rawlinson, in a tone mixed with condescension and frustration. "This is no time for a cavalier approach. Steadfastly sticking to plan will tip it in our favour. Give it one hour."

The rest of the group said nothing and averted their gaze to the map on the table. None wanting to make eye contact with Nugent or Rawlinson, fearing such a gaze would be either showing support for Nugent or concern about Rawlinson's decision. This was no day for ruining a lifetime army career. If anyone was going to get a bad press it was going to land on Nugent or Rawlinson's head, certainly not theirs.

Chapter Eighteen

Mayhem

Meanwhile back on the third German line the Captain, Maxwell, Arthur, Sgt Quinn, and the lads had all managed to survive due to Captain Montgomery and Sgt Quinn using their experience in finding gaps and soft spots in the third line of German resistance. The surprise early attack by the Inniskillings had left the Germans in their sector decidedly weak.

At the same time the Brigade had ordered the Belfast Battalions of the 36th Division onto the field. As they left the safety of the trenches at 09.00 hours they were in different spirits to Davy and the boys who had crawled stealthily out onto the field, confident that it would all work out well, much earlier in the morning.

The Belfast battalions had been sitting in the exit trenches waiting for the whistle they did not want to hear. They had sat for a good hour listening to the sound of constant machine gun fire and the chilling sound of pain and panic from the ground high beyond the parapet.

Word had been spreading down the trench, whispered between Woodbine filled lips, that it had all gone belly up further down the line. When the whistle did blow the men of the Belfast Battalions did not go over the top in hope of an easy run. They knew full well they were going to drag themselves over the parapet and enter Hell.

The painting in Belfast City Hall, still hanging on the wall one hundred years later, of the officer standing on the edge of the battlefield waving his eager soldiers onwards to victory, was just a painting, artistic license, stretched to and beyond its limits; designed to portray the gallantry of the battalion. It did little to show the raw bravery of men knowing they had probably seen their last sunrise and just hoped it would be clean, quick; not slow and wretched.

While the Inniskillings had taken the first and second German trench lines and on to the third line, the Germans, spirits lifted by their success further down the line in the 32nd Lancashire Division sector south of the 36th Ulster Division, had begun to angle their guns to their right, cutting down the Belfast battalions as they advanced in support of the second wave.

Men from the Shankill, Sandy Row, Ballynafeigh, Ballymacaret and Shore Road were falling like flies; dead, wounded, and disorientated. Meanwhile the lads of Edenderry and their group were now being cut off and relying on the Belfast men who were finding it hard to make much progress in overwhelming the newly set up German defences. As time passed it was looking more likely both sides were going to grind this out at all costs.

191

Back at Headquarters, when the hour had passed, all eyes and ears were on Rawlinson. As a silence came down at the appointed hour, Nugent was the first to speak.

"One hour has now passed, General Rawlinson," he said, head not lifting, in a quiet voice, which failed to hide the sense of frustration, despair and irony.

"I am all too well aware of the time, General Nugent!" replied Rawlinson, also quietly, but with more than an element of annoyance.

He put both hands on the table, staring at the battle plan for what seemed an eternity. The other senior brigade members shifting their feet, looked out the window, sucked their pipes and cigarettes, not wanting to give away their thoughts. This was one huge poker match with the lives of thousands of men, the chips, thrown on the table every time someone raised the stakes. The German machine gunners had 'raised and called.' Rawlinson had to show his hand.

After a few minutes of painful silence, Rawlinson turned from the table and walked slowly to the window, through which the constant gunfire could be heard in the distance. As he stared out of the window in silence, he raised his pipe in the palm of his hand and stuffed more tobacco into it. After he had packed it, he lit the substance and sucked a few times on the pipe, raising his head upwards as he blew blue smoke at the already yellowing ceiling.

"Instruct Artillery to recommence bombardment on the German third line and one hundred yards beyond their second line," he said without a hint of emotion.

Nugent was stunned and slammed his regimental baton, which he had kept tightly under his arm pit, against the table and said nothing.

Rawlinson looked across the table at Nugent.

"Something on your mind Nugent?"

"The 36th, my men, are in German lines first, second and third as you well know. I sent them out to risk getting killed by the Hun, not by us. You, in your infinite wisdom, decided to ignore the reports in April. Now you are going to betray them with our own guns!

"We cannot let our men down like this, it is wrong. It is immoral. It is our duty to protect our men who have placed their trust in us. We are going to..."

Rawlinson shook his head in total disbelief.

"If I don't, Nugent, the whole seven miles of men out there will be massacred. I am sorry, but the 36th will have to take its chance in the interest of the bigger picture. The 36th will take heavy casualties but it should save the complete annihilation of the rest." explained Rawlinson, before continuing.

"Please tell me if you have any better option?"

"The better option is too late now. A forced march, begun an hour ago, would have been with the 36th in another hour. My men could have held the Germans off until then." He shook his head in despair as he continued.

It's too late now," as he put both hands on the table, head bowed, directly opposite Rawlinson.

"So that is it agreed then, Gentlemen," rasped Rawlinson, eyes staring at the officers in the room.

No one made any gesture to the contrary. Rawlinson turned to his adjutant.

The other officers present slowly left the room with the excuse of a breath of air, only Nugent and Rawlinson remained. Nugent continued to stare at the table, refusing to look up and give Rawlinson the opening to speak to him.

Rawlinson knew quite well this was his game and countered it by pointing his own baton at various parts of the board contemplating potential troop movements. After Nugent gathered his thoughts, he raised his head and lifted his hands from the map covered table.

"With permission, General, I wish to extract myself from this command centre and join my men up at Thiepval. I will be of more use to them up there than I am down here. If we are going to use them as sacrificial lambs, I am best with my flock," barked Nugent determinedly.

"Didn't take you as a devoutly religious man Nugent," enquired Rawlinson.

"No more than the next man, Rawlinson," replied Nugent with a sigh. "Today a lot less so. At this rate, the Lord could be up for court martial based on this morning's performance. If the Lord's letting them down, I am damn sure I am not! If it's all right with you I need to be with my men!"

Nugent was already heading to the door as he spoke, irrespective of whether Rawlinson approved or not.

At the same time the boys had slid down and sheltered for cover in the third line at soft spots, picked out by the Captain and Quinn. As they did, they could hear explosions, just beyond the trenches, where they had just found themselves. Only a few at first, then more, and as they increased, they seemed to be coming closer.

"Mother of God, what the fuck's going on now?" shouted Joe to Davy as they sat squatted in the trench, ducking their heads instinctively as each shell started to make the ground move under them throwing sods of French earth like confetti over their shoulders and helmets.

"Germans must be trying to bombard us back but they're falling short," shouted Davy. "Bastards are so messed up by the last four days they can't hold their hand steady for shaking, never mind get the range right," as he ducked every few seconds.

Joe looked at him and just shook his head.

"Don't think so Davy. Listen to the shells as they fly over."

Davy stared up at the sky and tried to focus his eyes and ears.

After a few seconds he dropped his gaze from the sky and looked sideways at Joe. "Those aren't German shells are they Joe? They're our shells." whispered Davy almost in disbelief.

"Go to the top of the class young Gibson," whispered Joe.

Before they could continue to debate the revelation, Sgt Quinn came staggering down the trench towards them.

"Right lads, back to the second line!

"Don't need to tell you to keep your heads down!" he shouted as he approached them.

"What's the craic[36] then Sergeant?" shouted Bill in his gruff voice befitting a man twice his age. "We've only got here!"

As the sergeant passed by them, eager to spread word down the line as best he could, he shouted, as he looked back over his shoulder.

"Our barrage has started up again, trying to stop those machine guns slaughtering further down the line."

"But don't they know we are up here?" shouted Bill, in disbelief as the sergeant reached the bend in the trench system. Before he disappeared beyond view, the Sgt shouted in anguish,

"Oh! they know all right son, they fucking know, but there's less of us up here than the poor bastards all the way down the line. Get back to our lines, keep near the Captain, Maxwell or Arthur," snarled Quinn.

"I'll catch you up on the way. Now get out of here!"

---

[36] Craic. Irish term for talk, gossip, news.

Joe looked at Davy. They both looked at Bill, none spoke. Their gazes were broken by the captain, Roger and Maxwell appearing from the same direction that the sergeant had emerged.

"Right follow me back to the second line!" shouted the captain as he tried to get a grip with his feet on the steep crumbling trench wall to heave himself out of the trench. Roger and Maxwell copied his actions.

As all three scrambled on to the top of the trench they lay on their fronts and offered a hand to the lads to make it easier and quicker to scale the trench wall.

All six had emerged from the trench and lay face down only peering up to survey exit routs back to the Second German line they had taken earlier. Being behind the main German line they had already overrun, they did not have the problem of the wall of machine gun fire, like other regiments, only the intermittent shots from belligerent Germans in isolated pockets of earth, but with increasing numbers of shells falling around them the odds were still not good.

As Joe and Davy lay side by side face down on the battlefield Davy could hear Joe laughing to himself.

"My Dad was right, Davy," laughed Joe, in almost disbelief. "He said never trust the British; turns out he was right. Perfidious Albion, he called them."

Davy did not reply at first, He reckoned this was no time or place for a chat about moral standards.

197

"Joe, I don't give a fuck about King and Country, and it looks like my Dad was right about God. I just want us to get back to the girls and get them out of this hell hole!" shouted Davy, trying to be heard above the increasing ferocity of shells, landing ever closer, as the British artillery found their distance.

As Davy completed his last rebuff to Joe, he tried to get a glimpse of the chance of another route back through the exploding no mans' land. The captain signalled with a finger pointing to a gap between some wire in the direction of their own lines.

As the lads raised themselves to a crouching position, Joe shouted to Davy. "See you on the other side, wherever that is!" and proceeded to head back.

Davy just had the time to shout back at Joe who was a few steps ahead of him.

"Get Anna back home safe if I can't!"

Joe didn't have the luxury to turn and reply but just raised his rifle to the air for a split second.

The small group ducked and weaved their way from shell hole to hollow, through broken debris and broken bodies, finding refuge for a few seconds wherever they could find it.

At one of the larger shell holes all six managed to regroup and assess their next move.

As they lay on the ground in the relative safety of the shell hole, they were facing back in the direction of the third German line they had left, Roger was the first to notice the grey shapes emerging from the south side of them, as they slowly approached from the smoke-filled air.

"Captain?" he whispered, as he glanced in Montgomery's direction and pointed at the shapes gaining ground about twenty-five yards away.

A group of about ten German soldiers were lumbering in their general direction, having just retaken their line in the Lancashire Regiments section and now turning their attention to the retreating Ulstermen. Their gait and movement suggested they were from a crack unit brought up to halt the British attack.

It was too late to dislodge themselves from the shell hole and make a run for it. The only option was to stay low and surprise the enemy with a barrage of rifle fire.

The captain gestured, bayonets set, rifles at the ready and to wait for his signal.

As the Germans, who were spread out a few feet apart in crouching position, got within ten yards of the shell hole, the captain gave the nod. Simultaneously, all six raised themselves just above the edge of the hole and fired at the approaching Hun. Six of the enemy group fell and the rest dived to the ground. The lads looked at each other briefly and smiled at their unexpected success.

Then a German stick grenade sailed through the air.

"Grenade!" shouted Quinn as he was the first to catch sight of it through the battlefield haze.

Joe was the next to focus on it. The stick grenade was heading in his direction and as it began to descend amongst the frozen group, Joe instinctively dived, as if tipping a shot over the bar. With his arm outstretched, he tipped the airborne object on beyond the shell hole and on to the open ground beyond them.

It exploded on the ground behind the lads and showered them with earth and debris as they turned their backs and covered their heads

Before they could move another grenade came through the air. This time it was further away from Joe, but again he kept his eye on the incoming danger, moved across, caught it clean, and in the same motion flung it back in the direction from where it came.

As it landed and exploded a cry of pain and German curses erupted from a dip in the ground ahead of them.

The lads, without waiting for any orders, scrambled out of the shell hole and began to run back to intended safety.

Lieutenant Maxwell led the way followed by Davy, Bill, and Sgt Quinn. As they moved on, the Captain, Roger and Joe were still rising from the shell hole. They were all with their backs to the German line, facing the direction of safe refuge. They did not see two more grenades which were lobbed low and fast into the shell hole.

Both grenades exploded; both right below Joe's feet. He felt the rustle of the ground below him. He looked down at the same time as they both exploded.

The unexpected explosion caused shrapnel and mud to fly in all directions. Some hitting Davy and Sgt Quinn in the back ripping into their battle tunics and cutting into the outer skin, enough to make them winch in pain. As they gathered their senses, they could see that Roger was dead. A large piece of shrapnel had entered the base of his head just behind the ear, below the level of his helmet and was protruding out of the other side of his head near the top of his skull. The captain was unconscious but alive. Davy knew he was alive because blood was pumping from an artery in the remains of his right leg which had been blown clean off above the knee. If the blood was pumping, so was the heart.

Davy scanned the carnage but could not locate Joe.

"Joe, Joe, where are you mate?" At the same moment he felt a shove in the back that made him fall to the ground, face in the mud.

Sgt Quinn falling on top of him, whispered in his ear.

"Joe's gone Davy, and there's at least one of them still out there. Play dead, knife ready, time for your party piece when I say!"

Davy did not speak but removed his boning knife from its sheath in his putty, signifying he had got the message.

The two soldiers lay motionless, Maxwell had received a nod from Quinn and made himself appear dead on the higher ground beyond the shell hole

The shape of a German at the edge of the hole surveying his good work, clambering down into the drop was the time for Maxwell to shout, "Now!"

Quinn swung his rifle butt at the back of the German's knees which made him collapse to the ground. Before he had chance to gather himself a boning knife was plunged deep into the base of his stomach and driven upwards until it passed up through his rib cage and slid out just below his throat. The second stroke slit his throat like the unfortunate German a few months earlier.

"That's from Joe, Fritz, Ya fuckin' bastard!" shouted Davy in a rage, as he sat with his hands on his thighs, knees dug into the earth.

"You've ruined it all, fuckin' bastard!"

"Come on son," shouted Quinn. "Let's get out of here!"

Davy raised his gaze to Quinn. "Kitty, oh Jesus, Kitty, how do I tell her?"

"You'll not be telling anyone anything if you sit there whining. Come on son, let's get out of here!"

As they raised themselves to a crouching position, they passed the captain, unconscious, blood still pumping from the artery.

"What about the Captain?" shouted Davy as Quinn scrambled past him.

"Nothing we can do lad, artery. He'll bleed to death in a few minutes, he's unconscious, he'll never know anything about it.

He's already dead. It's everyman for himself now. Come on lad!" cajoled Quinn.

"Might be able to sort it," shouted Davy, almost talking to himself.

He crawled over to the captain and pulled back the torn remnants of trouser that was sticking to the stump of his thigh bone. As he pulled the cloth back, the artery spilling blood was clearly visible. Davy grabbed the end of the artery pulled and stretched it gently and got enough length on it to make a knot in the end, just as he had done with cattle he butchered when the cut had gone wrong and too much blood was flying.

The flow of blood reduced to a seepage. Quinn and Maxwell stared in amazement.

Davy motioned to carry him, Maxwell scrambled back into the shell hole and the three of them pulled the captain up. Davy and Quinn got an arm over each of their necks and started to struggle with him back out into no mans' land.

Maxwell, Quinn, and Davy had gotten beyond dodging explosions, gun fire and shrapnel and just kept their heads down with a relentless desire to get back to the second line. The captain thankfully was oblivious to it all.

After about ten minutes, "the Good Lord," as Bill would recall years later, with too much drink in him in the Homestead Inn at Drumbo, "finally got his arse in gear."

The four conscious and one seriously unconscious member of the 36th Division slid down into the second line.

As they sank on their knees, gathering their breath, looking at the smoke laden sky and listening to the continuous sound of their own shells over their heads, they caught the stare of the first of the Belfast Battalions Boys who had been fortunate enough to survive the machine guns and shrapnel, dropping with relief into the second line of the taken German second trenches alongside them.

Quinn shouted at them.

"Wasted journey lads!" as he looked at the sets of eyes staring at him. The frustration and anger at his superior officers' treachery had finally overcome the hard-bitten professional who, had always carried out his orders, done his best, and never let his feelings be known. That was up until that moment.

"Get yourselves back if you get the chance lads, never mind what anyone tells you. We've been sent on a fools' errand!" shouted Quinn as he looked at Maxwell and Davy as they inspected the captain's wound and his breathing.

"Right Lieutenant sir, and you Davy, best the pair of you follow me. You know the drill, keep low, follow the lowest points, drop into any hole in the ground you find, short bursts all the way back. If I go down just keep it the same. Right have you got him steady, right!" as he raised his hand and extended one finger, "One," second finger raised, "Two," third finger, "Three, Go!"

As they headed over the top of the trench, holding the captain who was beginning to regain consciousness, two of the Belfast Boys decided it might be a good idea to help the captain back and supported him out of the trench and joined them in retreat.

After ten minutes of doing exactly what Quinn had told them, scrambling in short bursts from shell hole to dip, taking care to do as little damage as possible to the captain, they got back to the first German line where 36th Battalion medics were already gathering to get the wounded off the fields of carnage.

Davy and Bill laid the captain on a stretcher, much to the dismay of the orderly.

"Leave that stretcher, it's for designated wounded!" he shouted.

"Fuck off!" shouted Bill in the soldier's face.

"It's for him!" pointing to the captain, leg blown away, sitting staring into oblivion thanks to the haven of shock.

"But he hasn't been assessed. He has to be assessed before he can be allocated a stretcher!" appealed the orderly.

"Ah! so you only get a stretcher if you get both legs blown off then!" snarled Quinn.

''None of your nonsense, son!" shouted Quinn at the orderly as he tapped his sergeant's stripes that were in tatters from numerous scrapes from flying debris.

"Just you leave that stretcher with me and allocate yourself out of my sight!"

As the orderly pondered his response Quinn looked to Davy. "Explain to him, Corporal!"

Davy at this point was still in a rage at Joe's disintegration before his eyes. He raised himself from bending over the captain, to his full six foot one and stepped towards the orderly, removing his boning knife from his putties.

The orderly's eyes opened wide in fear as Davy stepped towards him menacingly.

"Ok, ok, take it, take it!" he spluttered.

The retreat of Bill, Davy, Quinn, Maxwell, and the delirious Captain back to the 36th Division's trench was less difficult as it was by now virtually behind the advanced lines of the 36th Ulster. They had gotten within about fifty yards of safety when a stray shell, landed just behind Quinn and Davy. After instinctively diving to the ground, they lifted their faces from the grass and soil of the battlefield to see Maxwell, lying motionless face down and Bill on his knees bent forward holding his hands to his ears, minus his helmet which had been dislodged from his head.

Davy stumbled over to Bill, relieved to find he was not about to die, just badly disorientated. Quinn scrambled over to Maxwell and dropped his head in despair to find he was gone. Davy reached over and steadied the now staggering Bill and pulled him down to the relative safety of a shell hole. Shrapnel had imbedded itself in the back of Bill's ear, low enough to miss

206

his brain and high enough to avoid any arteries in the neck. His chest hurt as if he had been kicked by a mule, and the combination of deafness down one side and effect on his balance, rendered Bill incapable of coordinated movement.

Quinn rolled back into the hole alongside the two Belfast lads who were hoping he would have all the answers.

"Nearly home, one more run. Don't stop until you get to the line. Grab the captain, keep low, I'll follow, Go, Go!"

Davy and a disoriented but determined Bill dipped their shoulders below the captain, raised themselves upright, and the captain's remaining leg lifted off the ground. The lads looked at each other, nodded simultaneously, dropped their heads, and charged straight for the safety of the trench they had crawled from earlier that morning.

The confusion in the trench was such that Quinn and the lads didn't trust the safety of their captain to anyone. Quinn gestured for the lads to follow him, and they continued down the trench until they found an exit point to waiting carts, motor vehicles and anything on four legs that could carry maimed and dying men.

Quinn pointed to a military ambulance that was about to leave, they hoped, for the nearest hospital unit. The back door opened to accommodate two walking wounded. Quinn looked at one who seemed to have full use of his legs, ordered him out while grabbing him by the lapels at the same time and told the lads to lay the captain in the freshly available space.

As the ambulance struggled through the debris Davy and Bill jumped on to the duck boards and grabbed hold of the loose canvas tarpaulin that hid the injured men lying inside.

Quinn stayed where he was and watched the lads and the ambulance disappear in the smoke and mayhem.

After another twenty minutes the ambulance arrived at the entrance to the casualty station. Stretcher bearers surrounded the ambulance, pulling out on to the ground at the side of the vehicle, two who had not survived the journey back and pointed to the walking wounded. A long line of scared, confused, blank faces, sitting slumped at one side.

Bill nodded to Davy, letting him know he was joining that line and blew his cheeks as he turned away from him. An orderly pushed Davy out of the way to get the captain and other survivors on stretchers to be taken to the treatment area.

"I have to go with him!" shouted Davy.

"Best leave this to us Corporal, you've done your bit for today. Get in that line with your mate and get that shrapnel out of your back before it goes all bad."

The adrenaline for the last hour had removed any awareness of pain from the splinters of metal and wood that were embedded in Davy's battle dress, skin tissue and shoulder blades,

"I need to keep that leg from opening up again, unless you know how to!" shouted Davy.

The orderly looked at the wound, the reduced bleeding, and the artery.

"You do that, Corporal?" asked the orderly as he continued to stare into the wound.

"Right, no time for inquests. Follow on in with those stretcher bearers until a doctor gets to look at him," urged the orderly as he averted his gaze to the next serious casualty that came into his sight.

Inside the hospital unit the scene was worse than the battlefield. Here the screams and shouts, were not spread over seven miles of battle front, they were close and uncomfortable. Doctors and medics were working systematically, trying to deal with the overwhelming casualties being dragged through the doors. Doctors were moving from bay to bay assessing, making immediate decisions, passing instructions to nurses and auxiliaries, ensuring the quick removal of lost souls to the burial detail zone.

One tired, but totally focused doctor stood over the forlorn captain who was, at this stage conscious, but not too sure of what was happening around him. Shock had removed the sense of pain from his brain.

A nurse was trying to remove some of the remnants of the captain's trouser leg from the shattered stump that was once a leg. The Doctor leaned forward and studied the wound briefly to assess whether it was worth spending any time on it. Instant decisions had to be made. Establish who could be saved; concentrate on them was the rule.

The Doctor's quick survey of the wound confounded him. Normally a wound like this did not get to the unit. The recipient of this type of explosive injury should have died on the battlefield as shock and loss of blood took its toll.

He leant closer to the wound, pulled out his magnifying glass and gazed for a few seconds.

"Who stopped the bleeding on this one?" he gasped in confusion.

The nurse shrugged her shoulders.

They both looked over at Davy, who was standing on the other side of the prostrate captain.

"You do this Corporal?" asked the Doctor impatiently.

"Yes sir, back up at the German second line on the way back from the 3rd line," replied Davy

"How long ago?" asked the Doctor again.

"Happened near the German third line. Probably about an hour ago," replied Davy.

The doctor shook his head in disbelief.

"Where did you learn to do this?" asked the doctor as he continued to survey the treated wound.

"Jack Graham's, Shaftesbury Square."

The Doctor looked up from the wound at Davy, closing and opening his eyes in frustration.

Davy got the message,

"I'm a butcher, sir. Know my way round a carcass. Muscle tissue, bones, veins, and all that. Same principle with people sir," replied Davy, in a matter-of-fact way, which mirrored the doctor's mood.

"Well, you'll be right at home in this butchers' shop Corporal," said the Doctor dryly, as his eyes continued to inspect the wound and make a difficult decision.

"Right, nurse, get this man ready for the operating table. You just might have given your captain a bit of time," snapped the doctor with a restrained look of approval.

The doctor turned to move to the next injury and as he did, he turned back to Davy. He took a pencil and paper from his breast pocket and scribbled on it, handed it to Davy and told him.

"Go over to the top of the light injuries queue, show them this. Get that back cleaned up and be back down as soon as you can. I've work for you here. Go on man, don't hang about!"

Davy did as he was told and got his back cleaned up and pieces of shrapnel removed from outer tissue. As his adrenalin slowed, he became aware of the sensation that he had been attacked by an entire wasps' nest, giant ones.

When Davy returned, the doctor was still moving about, advising, and administering amongst the wounded soldiers, but now he, the nurses and auxiliaries were even more strained looking, their white coats and aprons more red than white.

"Right corporal," ordered the doctor, "See those curtains over the far corner, go through them, down the left and the surgeon has the very job for you."

Davy sensed the urgency and did not reply, just nodded, and headed off in the direction of the surgeon. As he entered the room, he met a sight that would never leave his memory.

Just like Grahams' shop, only, instead of wooden block tables with prime County Down beef carcasses laid out for cutting up, there were about ten soldiers all laid out in various forms of distress and injury.

"Right Corporal, I am told you are handy at cutting bone and tissue. There's the implements, if we tell you to cut, saw, or stitch you will do just that," said a young surgeon in a low, almost whispering, voice in his ear.

"But I'm a butcher not a surgeon, sir!" whispered Davy back to the doctor. "I'm not qualified for this."

"Needs must, as they say, old chap," he responded in a polite condescending tone.

"Rules went out the window at 07.00 hours this morning. Amputations and blood loss needs speeded up or the fatalities will get even worse. Get this apron on and do whatever you are told; now, Corporal!"

As Davy tied the apron, he continued to look at the young surgeon in disbelief. The surgeon gave him a final stare as he turned to assess the latest sorry wretch laid on the slab before him.

"You are a butcher, Corporal. Welcome to the biggest butcher's shop you'll ever have to work in. Get over here and carry out your orders. Now!"

Davy cut, sawed, hacked, held, stitched as he was trained to do until late in the night, when he was replaced by other nursing staff, orderlies and medics who had been sent up from the rear. He was told to take a few hours of sleep and report back at 07.00 hours later that morning, the 2nd July 1916.

He found a dip in the ground outside the centre, sat himself down, covered himself with a spare greatcoat he found, from an unfortunate who would never need it again, and tried to sleep but his brain raced with thoughts of Anna, Kitty, Joe, and Roger. It was a full hour before the luxury of an exhausted sleep overcame him

Just before 07.00 hours he was abruptly awakened by a boot on his rear end as he lay on his side in the sanctuary of sleep.

"Hay mate, you Corporal David Gibson?" said an orderly with a Red Cross band on his arm.

Davy said yes, as he struggled to open his eyes. "You've to be in the centre for 07.00 hours. Sent out to find you, make sure you didn't sleep in."

"Take it breakfast isn't being served then," sighed Davy as he lifted his aching body to a standing position.

As he re-entered the 'butcher's shop' a slight semblance of order had been achieved, thanks to the extra hands that had eventually filtered through to the line medical stations.

He started to search for a white apron and await his orders. A voice from the far end of the room was from the young surgeon he had worked with earlier. He spotted the young surgeon who shook his head from left to right telling him not to find an apron but pointed beyond Davy's shoulder.

Davy turned, and a soldier with the rank of Major was listening intently to a more senior surgeon. The two men noticed Davy staring vaguely at them both.

"I take it you are Gibson, Corporal?" snapped the Major.

Get yourself outside to my staff car. I'll be out there in a minute."

A few minutes later the Major appeared beside the staff car where Davy was sharing a smoke with the driver. The Driver dropped the cigarette, buried it with his heel and stood to attention, saluting as he did, Davy thought it best to do the same.

Beside the Major stood a few other soldiers who had been assisting the Medical Corps.

For his part, the Major had been sent up to assess the situation at the front line and report back, but he had been made aware of Davy and a few other potential recruits.

"Right, you lot, jump in, find a space and I'll tell you what's happening. Chop, Chop! Time is of the essence!"

As the staff car trundled, bounced, and slid its way back from the front line, it was explained to Davy and the others that their abilities were noted and that they would be of more use at the main medical centre five miles back. A decision which, although they could not show it, filled all with a sense of relief.

"Five miles back," thought Davy, "That'll do me nicely, there must be a God after all."

No sooner had this idea crossed his mind than he cursed himself, once his thoughts of the fates of Joe, Roger and the others swept over him.

"I'm sorry Joe, Roger, lads," he whispered to himself. He bowed his head in shame at his thoughts as he listened to the Major.

The crux of the deal was that, based upon the reports to the Major of the previous evening, Davy and the others would be of more use in the medical units than as German target practice. If they did their new jobs adequately, there would be no more dawn raids, gas attacks or bombardments.

The rest of the way back Davy settled his thoughts on one person, Anna Arthur.

Back at the main medical post Kitty and Anna had been receiving tragic numbers of the maimed and dying. All night they worked bandaging, holding down, stemming blood, pretending to be mothers and wives to the dying. Kitty even gave the last rites to some which seemed to settle their tormented souls. Some

215

passed over thinking they were being comforted by the Holy Mother herself.

As they worked, they could tell that all was not going well at the front. The continued machine gun fire and the heavy bombardment starting up again, combined with the casualties flooding in, told them all they needed to know and fear.

As they worked, they scanned around, the large reception triage area they worked in, hoping to see a face they might recognise. Hoping upon hope, that someone would be able to say that they had seen Joe, Davy, and Roger alive and well. A few times they saw stretchers dragged in with wounded that might have been them, but on closer glance were just lookalikes, masked with dirt and blood.

By 08.00 hours on the 2nd of July that morning they had both been ordered by matron to go to their quarters, rest and get back by 14.00 hours. Both girls offered to work on, but the Matron refused, explaining that an exhausted nurse can make fatal mistakes.

As the girls left the medical unit, five miles back from the frontline, picking their way through the groups of walking wounded, on their way to their quarters, a staff car with a Major and a few soldiers slowed up in front of them.

They stepped back to let it pass. As they did, a soldier sitting on the roadside spotted Kitty and shouted to her.

"Hey nurse, love, I've got shrapnel in my bum, you wouldn't mind bandaging it would you?" His fellow walking wounded laughed.

Kitty, never lost for words at the best of times, turned to him and began a bit of repartee with the adoring squaddie, who was doing his best to make himself seem a hardcase, and not the frightened seventeen-year-old he was, that wanted to be held in his mother's arms.

While Kitty was enjoying the banter, Anna looked at the staff car again. As she did, one of the soldiers in the back turned his face upwards. Her heart raced, her body shook, her jaw dropped, but it was long enough for Davy to shake his head and put his fingers to his lips as his eyes looked over Anna's shoulder in the direction of Kitty. Anna just put her hand over her mouth as the initial jubilation turned to gut wrenching despair.

She mouthed, "Joe" at Davy, then looked over at Kitty who was still engrossed in banter with the soldier and was oblivious to Davy or Anna.

Davy, gave her a look of despair, dropped his head again and shook it slowly. The driver in the staff car dropped a gear and accelerated past the nurses and the group of wounded. As it did, Davy kept his head down and his helmet well forward.

Anna tried to gather her composure as Kitty finally broke off from the soldier with the sore backside and smiled to Anna,

"Let's get out of here, I could sleep for a week," sighed Kitty, as she rolled her eyes in embarrassment at the squaddies. Anna forced herself to smile.

Anna feigned tiredness on not wanting to talk anymore and fell into bed face down, thoughts spinning.

Kitty, grasped her rosary beads, mumbled something to herself, part Latin interspersed with the words Hail Mary and Joe's name mentioned. She then also flopped into her bunk and exhaustion overcame them both.

Anna, like Davy earlier, found sleep a lot more difficult. Like Davy, she haunted herself with regret. When sleep did overwhelm her, Anna's sleep was neither peaceful nor contented. Her thoughts had not yet fallen on Roger. That was the first thing that stirred her brain a few hours later.

As Anna woke, she sat on the side of her bunk hands on her thighs, staring at the floor and glancing over at Kitty, face turned against the wall, still sound asleep. What would she say to her? What if she had misread Davy's glances? Best to hold off saying anything until she had managed a conversation with Davy.

As Kitty stirred, Anna did her best to blank the fleeting acknowledgement from Davy and decided to act as if nothing had happened for the time being.

Anna and Kitty made their way back to the medical unit and continued with their duties. Davy in the meantime had reported to the Chief Surgeon and was soon busy performing the same duties he had done the previous evening, only now five miles back.

Near 15.00 hours Davy was ordered to wheel a barrel full of dismembered limbs and entrails out to an area at the back which was closed off from view. As he crossed a communal area to the exit door and the enclosed outside area, Kitty came out of a medical area down the corridor intent on finding fresh linen.

She saw Davy before he saw her. She paused for a moment, trying to take in what he was doing there and why he had a bloodied apron on top of his uniform. The adrenalin rushed through her body.

"Davy, Davy!" she shouted as she ran towards him, still holding the fresh linen she had retrieved. "What are you doing here? Is Joe with you?"

Davy was surprised by Kitty's sudden appearance in front of him. He had run it through his brain all morning how he would speak to her, but now his mind was blank.

He looked at her, bowed his head and shook it from left to right. He could find no words.

"Where is he Davy, Davy, is he alright?" she pleaded. Davy finally spoke. "He's gone Kitty," with a sigh filled with grief and shame. "He's gone."

Davy lifted his eyes to the ceiling as he swallowed hard. His lip quivered as he leaned forward and buried his head down into Kitty's shoulder as he hid his tortured face from view.

Kitty stood rigid, then shook and shoved him away. She screamed.

"No, No, No, No!" at the top of her voice, loudly enough it could be heard above the moans and shouts from the medical units nearby.

The Matron heard the commotion and proceeded to head for the corridor to find out what was going on.

Kitty had dropped involuntarily to her knees and was beating the stone floor with the clenched sides of her hands. Swaying back and forwards as if in a trance.

Davy, and an orderly passing by, leaned forward to try and pick her up and take her aside, but she lashed out and swore at them both.

Davy turned halfway round and looked at the ceiling again, wishing the whole place would fall down around him; ashamed again that he had survived.

Anna heard the screams and was in no doubt it was Kitty. She had been administering a bandage to a soldier burnt down one side of his face from the flash of an explosion and knew he could wait.

"She knows now," she thought to herself, as she thanked her luck at not having to break the news and ran out of the treatment area into the corridor.

Kitty had risen from her knees and was lunging forward at Davy, fists and legs flying, screaming constantly. Davy just stood and let her get on with it. The Matron was the first to grab hold of Kitty, but Kitty swung round and hit the matron full in the face, knocking her straight to the floor.

"Feck off and leave me alone!" she screamed before she broke down in tears on the floor again.

Anna reached out to Kitty and tried to hold her as she rocked uncontrollably on her knees on the hard, cold, stone surface.

Davy began to kneel beside them both, but Anna gave him a look and waved him away.

"Wrong time, Davy, make yourself scarce!"

As Davy straightened up to walk away and return to the sanctuary of the wooden slabs, Anna spoke to him again.

"Roger, what about Roger, Davy?" she said in as calm a voice as she could muster.

Davy turned halfway round to Anna and looked down at her.

"He's with Joe, they're together," sighed Davy, who exhaled heavily as he clasped his hands round the back of his neck, before winching, as the tightening of his shoulders broke open the stitches on his wounds on his upper back.

Anna's face drained in front of his eyes. She was as fragile as the day at the Boat Club that Sunday afternoon. He had promised her he would protect her from ever feeling like that again. He had failed. He had let her down again. He wanted to hold her like a lost child and leaned forward towards her.

She released her grip from Kitty, buried her forehead in the palms of her hands and when Davy's hands touched her shoulders, she pushed him away. Davy knew again, now was not the time. He turned and walked as if he was carrying ten ton on his back and disappeared to bury himself in his duties.

Anna and Kitty buried their faces into each other's shoulders and shook in sorrow.

Matron, turned on her side, pulled herself up and placed her right hand on her swelling eye.

"Nurse Arthur, get nurse Breslin out of my sight and get yourself back to your duties as soon as she has come to her senses. I told you before this started, nothing takes precedence over the soldiers you are dealing with and by God that is the way it will be. I'll see both of you in my office at the end of your shift!"

Anna opened her mouth to reply, but the Matron raised her hand to her swollen face and shouted.

"No, not another word or two can play at this game!" as she drew her arm back making it clear that Anna would get the full force of her hand long before she could get out of the way of it.

Anna and Kitty dragged each other to the far end of the corridor, and out into the open. The girls managed to get themselves away from the queues of walking wounded outside the medical units and walked, without thinking, to the riverbank at the rear of the medical unit. Neither spoke for some time, both just sitting linked in each other's arms, sitting on the riverbank not unlike the Lagan back home.

Anna spoke first when she felt the time was right.

"Roger is with Joe," she said, staring at the sky, afraid to look at Kitty.

Kitty sighed, "Sweet Mary and Joseph, and for what?" she asked as she pressed her hand into Anna's, bowing her head at the same time. "What happened to them? Is Davy sure?"

"What did he tell you Kitty?" asked Anna quietly, looking Kitty straight in the face.

"Nothing Anna. When he got to say Joe is gone, I lost it. Oh Anna, the Matron, poor woman!"

"I'll get to speak to Davy as soon as I get the chance. Seems he has been sent to work in surgical. Don't know how that's happened," said Anna.

"Maybe he's wrong, confused in all that chaos," replied Kitty.

"I'll have to find out. He must be over in the amputation unit. I'll be waiting outside next time he comes out," assured Anna.

They sat together in silence for a few more minutes as they gathered inner strength to exist in the mayhem. They stood up together, brushed the grass from their long, ankle length uniforms, and started to walk back to their unit.

As they got within sight of the medical unit, Kitty pulled on Anna's arm. "I'll have to go and see matron," she said without any sign of concern.

"Do you think that's wise, give her chance to calm down?" advised Anna.

Kitty grabbed Anna by the arm, "Anna, I fear nothing and no one anymore. My greatest nightmare was for real today. Joe was, is, my life, we are both dead. What have I to fear? You go and wait to see Davy. I'll find my fate with Matron."

Kitty entered the ward to search out Matron who she found stroking the head of a dying soldier, no more than sixteen years old, who in those moments, thought he was at home being put to bed by his mother.

As the Private passed away, Matron raised herself from the bed side, intent on moving on to another poor soul. As she turned, she was met by Kitty standing straight faced, close enough to her face she could smell the salt from the tears that were still seeping from the corners of Kitty's eyes.

"I am sorry Matron," as her lip quivered. "But my man has gone." As she burst out in tears again, Matron opened her mouth to speak but paused, giving Kitty time to contain her sobs.

Matron put one hand on her shoulder and in quiet compassion said, "Nurse Breslin, if you can get yourself over to that bed and comfort that young man who will be with your man in another few minutes, we'll put this down to a bitter and painful experience."

Kitty, without being aware, gave a curtsey, and thanked the matron, in the same way she had done back at Ballydrain to Lady May, and went off to the bedside as ordered.

Anna had waited about fifteen minutes outside the surgeons' room, deep in her own thoughts and had started to feel guilty that she could have been attending to a soldier in greater need. She drew in her breath, entered the amputations area, and walked over to one of the young, exhausted doctors and discreetly asked when Corporal Gibson might be off duty. She was told it would not be until at least midnight, but nothing definite.

Anna then walked back to the ward and scanned for the Matron, who had seen her first. Matron waved her away and pointed to a bedside not far from where she was standing and turned her gaze towards Kitty who was helping hold down a soldier writhing in pain.

Anna did as she was told and lost herself in her work until she was relieved and went back to sitting outside the surgical unit.

At 02.00 hours in the morning, Davy appeared, exhausted, from the entrance of the surgeons' area. He didn't see Anna at first, as he came from the brighter lights of the surgery to the gloom of the corridor. He leaned against the wall of the corridor and breathed hard in and out, before catching his raw shoulder wounds once again and winced some more.

As he tried to walk out into the night, Anna came up behind him, linked her arm under his and said in her quiet voice.

"Just keep walking soldier, tell me everything that happened out there."

They found a makeshift bench outside and sat down.

Before Davy started to speak, he fumbled in his pocket for a Woodbine and as he tapped it on the tin and brought it to his lips, Anna snatched it from him.

"Better get yourself one as well," she said, straight faced, as Davy looked at her in surprise.

"When did you start these?" he asked.

"Since now!" she snapped, as she gestured for a light, hand shaking.

"You know these things stunt your growth. Some say they're bad for your health," sighed Davy, straight faced; any emotion was drained from him.

Anna shook her head at the irony of that concern in the circumstances.

"We'll just have to take our chances then," shrugged Anna, in similar fashion.

Davy lit a match, covering it with his hands from the breeze, Anna leaned forward, sucked in the ignited Woodbine, and almost choked. She got the method right on the second attempt.

Davy gave her the background on how it played out from the time they crawled out into no mans' land at 04.00 hours on the morning of the 1st of July. Anna learnt the horrible truth of Joe's demise but was told that Roger had been caught with a sniper's bullet and killed instantly leading his men. He could not tell her that her handsome brother had his brain ripped apart. He did not want her to ever remember him with that image. He explained that the Bamford twins had been twenty yards behind him when a shell exploded and that was the last that he ever saw of them.

Anna sat silently trying to make sense of it all. Trying to rally her inner strength to deal with this nightmare. Finally, she got up from the makeshift bench, straightened her uniform, wiped her face, and looked to the sky.

"It's just you and me now, Davy," said Anna, as she bowed her head.

"I promised Thomas, I would bring you home. I didn't promise my mother and father I would bring Roger home," sighed Anna.

"How could I have been so heartless, so selfish, consumed with us. Oh Roger, dear Roger!" as she rubbed the tips of her fingers against her forehead, trying to settle her tormented soul.

Davy stood up to gathered her in his arms as they embraced for only a few seconds before Anna stepped back releasing his grip.

"Best go now, Davy." whispered Anna as she turned to walk away.

"Anna," said Davy, raising his voice.

"I love you, and when we get back home you can tell your mother and father you love them. Don't torment yourself; they love you as much as I do."

Anna put her hands on her hips, wiped her face with her forearm, shook her head slowly, before she disappeared down the dimly lit passageway back to her unit.

When Anna told Kitty all that Davy had told. Kitty sat silently and listened. No tears, just a hard stare at the ground. Kitty hardly spoke for a week and more. She did her work, making eye contact with no one, cocooned in her sorrow. No conversation, just bandaging, holding, wiping, lifting, void of any emotion, working tirelessly day after day.

At the end of her shift, she would walk back to her bunk, kneel, pray, and say "Goodnight" to Anna and any others present and bury her face in the pillow, thinking of Joe and what it was like for him on the other side. He said he would wait for her if he didn't make it. She knew he would, of that there was no doubt.

One morning, a few weeks after the first day of the Somme, Kitty and Anna woke from an exhausted but uneasy sleep. Kitty was in a world of her own thoughts. Anna in a turmoil of what to say or not to say. The couple's morning ritual, preparing themselves for another shift on the wards, was held in silence. As they left the dormitory Kitty finally broke the silence.

"You go on ahead Anna. I need to see Matron," she said, looking straight ahead without turning to face Anna. Kitty had already quickened her pace and was slightly ahead of her. Anna understood it was Kitty's way of saying that she did not want any discussion about it and just nodded as Kitty disappeared down the dimly lit corridor.

Kitty found Matron talking to a captain surrounded by a group of a dozen medical auxiliaries who were being debriefed before going out to act as triage in no man's land during a lull in the fighting. Kitty stood off side of the group listening to every word. As the Matron and senior officer completed their instructions Kitty drew in her breath and strode forward to Matron's shoulder.

"Matron, I want to be attached to a field recovery unit," asked Kitty without drawing breath and staring Matron purposefully in the eyes. Matron inhaled and stared back at her.

"You are needed here, nurse Breslin. Out there is not the place for you. Now please join your section," replied Matron without any emotion.

"I have to, Matron," replied Kitty almost begging.

"Nurse Breslin, I appreciate your situation, but it has been made clear to me that your young man can regrettably not be retrieved." Matron, in a rare gesture of emotion, placed both her hands onto Kitty's shoulders.

"Now please return to your normal post, my dear."

"I know he's gone Matron but there's a lot of Joes out there. I can bring some Joe back, please Matron," begged Kitty as she failed to hold back the tears.

'I'll be more use than some of those ones going out. Most of them have far less experience than me."

"You will be going out there tramping through wire, unexploded devices, all manner of debris, physical and human, assessing who can be saved and retrieved first. You will have to walk away from the untreatable as they beg you to help them; move on to the those who have a chance. You will have to mark each you find with ribbons, colour coded so the stretcher bearer knows who to lift and who to leave. You will be saint and executioner. You will have to live with that and sleep in your bed at night," explained Matron, with only the slightest hint of concern in her otherwise emotionless voice.

"I need to go out there, Matron," repeated Kitty, still staring through tearful eyes at Matron.

Matron sighed, looked at the ceiling, and back down to Kitty.

"Get yourself over and find a uniform small enough. Report to the captain."

I will allow you to go out today, but no more. It will not be a regular occurrence. Do you understand me? Tomorrow I will expect you in the ward and do not consider asking me the same question again."

While Kitty prepared herself for the open battlefield. Anna's thoughts of her were distracted by a constant intake of wounded. By late evening, Anna, who had still not seen Kitty all day, walked wearily back to her bunk, sat on the edge, untied her nurse's head cap, loosened her hair, and let it fall over her face and shoulders. She placed her hands under her fallen hair, pressed them against her face, leant forward with her elbows on her knees and did not move for about a minute. Deep in her thoughts, which were many.

She was tired but sleep before Kitty returned was out of the question. Anna changed into her nightwear, propped her pillow, sat upright in her bed, with her thoughts, and waited.

Almost two more hours passed by and just as her eyelids began flickering to find the solace of sleep, she heard footsteps quietly entering the darkness of the dormitory. She could see a shape moving in the darkness until it loomed over her and then lowered itself wearily into Kitty's bunk opposite.

Anna straightened herself up from her bed and leant forward towards Kitty, who was now sitting, hands on her knees, as if in a trance, hair fallen around her face.

Anna leaned forward and placed her hands each side of Kitty's head and began stroking her hair and face, like a mother consoles a sad child.

Kitty put her hands around Anna's back. The pair did not speak, just rocked slowly back and forward.

"Joe's not coming back, Anna," sighed Kitty. "I know that now."

Anna just kept caressing Kitty's hair. As she did, she felt it was wet and matted. It took her aback when she realised it was a mixture of blood and mud.

"How bad is it out there?" whispered Anna.

"There's hundreds of them Anna," sighed Kitty. "Some of them thought I was their mother bringing them home. Some even thought I was the Holy Mother herself. Some thought I was an angel taking them to heaven. Some swore and cursed me as I left them, begging me not to leave them."

Kitty just shook her head, staring back at Anna.

Anna still did not speak but just sat and hugged her friend.

After another long silence, Kitty whispered in a tone of acceptance. "I know where he died, Anna," as she shook her head again.

Anna stayed silent, afraid to say something stupid.

Kitty released herself from Anna's arms and put her right hand deep under her tunic top and pulled out a set of rosary beads.

"Found these out there. They're Joe's. A few hundred yards from our line in our boys' sector. A few hundred yards from safety. Davy was right when he said he was gone. They couldn't bring him back. Nothing to bring back!"

Anna waited for a flood of tears. They didn't happen.

Instead, Kitty just said,

"I'm tired, I need to sleep."

She leaned back on her bunk, without making any attempt to remove the bloodstained uniform and fell silent instantly.

Anna leant back over to her bunk, curled herself into a ball and wept silently before sleep finally overcame her.

Chapter Nineteen

The Postman

A few hundred miles away, back at Newforge on a sunny morning in late July, the moorhens were still cackling, the swans dipping and Tom Gibson's hammer still hitting metal against metal, echoing down the water's edge and across the green fields towards the Belmont Estate at Belvoir. Tom was getting his work done as best he could manage but his heart was not in it.

The sense of pride and satisfaction of doing a good job was missing, as, while he got through his work, his thoughts were in France. Word had got back that it had not gone well at the Somme and a steady flow of news of the casualties and death toll was building day by day.

It was nearly four weeks and Tom had still no word about Davy or any of the other lads.

"No news is good news," was the only comfort he could give himself.

As he left the forge and walked out to lift a few metal rods lying against the outside wall he saw the postman cycling on his bicycle, bag over his back. Martin usually whistled as he rode his bicycle. This morning there wasn't a sound, his peddling was slower and more thoughtful than usual.

"Oh no, please God, no. I don't like the look of this," thought Tom as he stared at the weary figure cycling before him.

"Morning Martin," hailed Tom, in the same manner as he greeted the postman every morning as he would pass on his way to his deliveries to the big houses on the Malone, Shaw's Bridge and Edenderry.

"Tea pot's on, Martin. Help yourself mate."

Tom didn't need to tell him. It had been a daily ritual for the last ten years which Martin and all previous postmen had done since time began.

Martin dismounted the bicycle and propped it against the lock gate. He kept his head down and entered the open door of Tom's cottage to help himself to Tom's almost tar like substance of Thompson's tea. Tom did not like the look of this. Something big was on Martin's mind.

Martin came back out into the light and leaned against the cottage wall beside Tom and spoke to him in almost a whisper.

"The boys on the Belfast deliveries have been getting them thick and fast for a few days now. I've got the first ones in my bag this morning, three of them; know them all," reflected Martin as he shook his head with a sigh, inhaling heavily.

"Would one of them be for here?" asked Tom, as he also inhaled, looking into Martin's face.

"No, thank God, or I wouldn't be standing here. I'd have sneaked in and left it when you were hammering. Couldn't do it mate, what with Davy being all you've got," replied Martin, still looking straight ahead.

A silence descended over both men as Tom gathered his thoughts in temporary relief.

"How many have you got did you say?" asked Tom.

"Three. One for Ballydrain House, two for Lily Bamford in Edenderry," croaked Martin as his emotions got the better of him.

Tom sighed "Not both the twins and Roger," inwardly ashamed of himself for his relief that it was not Davy.

"Poor Lily Bamford, she's already a widow since her old man got caught in one of those machines at Edenderry Mill. Now she has nobody," gasped Martin, as he pulled himself from the wall.

"I'd better get going. Sooner I have this done I can go and get drunk." continued Martin, as he walked over to his cycle and the bag of misery.

"They say a trouble shared is a trouble halved," mused Tom to Martin. "If it helps, you can give me the one for the Big House and I'll get it up there. That just leaves you with Lily Bamford."

Martin leant down to his bag, shuffled through it, retrieving one brown envelope, and walking wearily towards him.

"I would really appreciate it, Tom. I owe you, big time," thanked Martin as he offered the brown envelope addressed to Sir James Arthur, Ballydrain House.

Martin turned, got on his bicycle, and pedalled urgently over the bridge at the lock and up the short cut lane to the Ballylesson Road and Edenderry, hoping Tom would not take cold feet, change his mind, and call him back.

After Martin disappeared beyond the bend in the lane, Tom stared at the envelope before he went into the cottage and set it on the kitchen table. He spent the rest of the morning and early afternoon forging, hammering, dowsing, fitting, and working out how to best deal with Sir James and the terrible news. He knew Sir James would cope, but he feared the effect on Lady May.

By about three in the afternoon, he had made his decision. He dowsed the fire in the forge, got himself washed, put on his clean shirt, lifted a small parcel in his hand and stuck a note on his door.

"Urgent business to attend, back 7.00. Sort the lock yourself."

Tom hitched the horse and trap and headed in the direction of Shaw's Bridge and up to Ballydrain.

He took his time. He knew from a conversation with McCracken earlier that morning, that Sir James was at a meeting in Belfast and would be arriving back home about five in the evening. His Rolls Royce would be easing its way through the main gates of the entrance to the estate.

Tom sat on the trap outside the gates of the estate, leaning back, thinking of the best way to deal with Sir James. By ten to five in the evening, by Tom's pocket watch, he could hear the noise of the Rolls Royce engine before it appeared at the bend opposite Dunmurry lane.

As the chauffeur driven vehicle approached the entrance, Tom dismounted from the trap, walked slowly towards the gate entrance, and waited. McCracken, slowed cautiously, as his duties also included being protector of Sir James from any unsavoury characters that might take exception to Sir James's affluence. When he saw it was Tom, he changed his speed enough to make a leisurely turn in to the estate driveway. As he turned in to the gates Tom was standing alongside.

"Stop here a moment, McCracken. I believe Thomas wishes to speak with me, though why in God's name he hasn't gone up to the house is beyond me," mused Sir James from the back, as he lifted his gaze from the Times.

"Good evening Thomas, and to what do I owe the pleasure?" he uttered from the back of the car.

"Need to speak to you in private, Sir James," asked Tom, in a soft voice, as he glanced in the direction of the chauffeur.

"McCracken, would you mind getting out and checking the wheels like a good man and have a cigarette while you are out there. Open the door for Thomas and let him in please," he instructed.

As McCracken opened the door, he searched into Tom's face to get some sort of message, but Tom just kept his head down.

Tom dropped himself into the leather seat in the back of the car beside Sir James, who folded his newspaper and set it on his knee.

"Martin the post man called this morning," said Tom with a heavy heart.

Sir James leaned back and looked upwards to the upholstered roof of the limo.

"Ah Tom, I am so sorry. David was indeed a good son," replied Sir James, filled with remorse.

"No Sir James, it's not addressed to me," sighed Tom apologetically, as he pulled the brown envelope from his jacket pocket and slid it across to Sir James.

Sir James did not take the envelope, preferring to let it balance on his lap after Tom let go of it.

"The postman didn't have it in him to deliver it. He's two more for the widow Bamford," advised Tom, trying to keep his emotions together.

The two men did not speak for a full minute, which seemed like an hour to Tom.

Sir James finally lifted the envelope, checked the address, leaned forward to a pouch on the side of the car door and pulled out a silver letter knife.

Tom watched the letter knife in Sir James's hand just in case he plunged it in to either of them. Sir James slowly inserted the

239

knife inside the flap, as if it might change or delay the event. With the top of the letter fully opened, Sir James inserted a shaking hand into the envelop and removed its contents. As he read each word, Tom could feel the seat they sat on shake slightly. When Sir James finished reading, he just handed it back in the direction of Tom and let it drop on Tom's lap. Tom picked up the letter and scanned it until he saw the words

"Killed in Action."

"I took it off the postman. Thought it best you got it before Lady May." sighed Tom, still looking straight ahead.

Sir James did not speak, just nodded his head slowly, lost in his thoughts.

"I hope, with all my heart, that you never get one of these letters for young David," replied Sir James, as he tried valiantly to keep his emotions stable.

"Now, I would appreciate it if you would leave me to my thoughts, Thomas. Tell McCracken to make himself useful out there. I need a bit of time to myself, please."

Tom dipped his head and slipped out of the car, patting the door on the outside as he walked away. McCracken looked across from the far side of the Rolls Royce, but Tom did not look at him. He kept walking purposely over to the horse and trap.

He lifted the brown paper parcel and walked back over to the chauffeur and handed it to him and said,

"He wants you to find something to do while he gathers himself."

McCracken looked despondently at Tom. "Roger?"

"Roger," replied Tom as he turned to the haven of the trap.

As he removed the nose bag and checked the reins, he looked over at McCracken.

"Bamford lads didn't make it either. No idea what's the score with Davy. What a fucking senseless mess. God and Ulster!" Tom just shook his head.

"Neither of them has done those lads any favours."

McCracken put his head down, then looked up.

"Let's hope there's no more of those envelopes, Tom.

"No news is good news, eh.

"Amen to that!" replied Tom.

By the middle of August there was still no letter for the cottage at Newforge. One evening, as Tom was shutting down for the night, he could hear the Rolls Royce engine in the distance. It stopped a few hundred yards on the Milltown Road at the top of the lane down on the far side of the canal lock opposite the forge.

Tom anticipated the arrival of the chauffeur in a few minutes, but instead it was Sir James himself. He was carrying an envelope in one hand and a parcel in the other. His walk was steady and purposeful as if he meant business.

Tom's mind ran in different directions as he was getting no message from Sir James's blank expression.

"Good evening Tom," said Sir James calmly. "I am sorry for not speaking with you since that evening at the gate. I have had rather a lot to deal with one way or another."

As he got level with Tom, "I got this telegram from Anna, delivered to me this afternoon. David is alive. He's in a hospital now," explained Sir James, with a sense of relief.

Tom lowered the heavy hammer he was wiping down and let the head drop to the ground.

"How bad is it, Sir James. Will he get home in one piece?" asked Tom, in concern bordering on panic.

"No Tom, he's fine. He is not wounded, other than a few bits of shrapnel to his back and shoulders. He's working in a frontline hospital unit," blurted out Sir James.

"I am sorry I alarmed you. Bad choice of phrase. Sensitivity never one of my strong points."

Tom's legs almost gave way under him, but he covered it by bending his knees and putting his hands on his thighs and looking at the ground for a few seconds. As he gathered his composure, he looked up at Sir James as he straightened himself, and said,

"Thank you, thank you Sir James, I just wish I could have been able to give you the same message."

"Just celebrate the moment, Tom. War is a cruel lot. We must deal with its consequences. Please do not let this moment of good fortune be clouded by my sorrows," assured Sir James as he handed the telegram to Tom.

Tom looked at it but without his reading glasses it was a waste of time.

"Come inside Sir James while I get my glasses; can't see to read without them," said Tom, as he ushered Sir James inside.

Tom rummaged for his spectacles in a cupboard, found them, and gestured to the table in front of them, as they both sat opposite each other. The telegram was sent by Anna and the first few lines were about Roger and reassurance that she was safe and well. Tom's eyes were searching for the bits about Davy.

"David survived the battle and is now assisting in surgical. His skills as a butcher are in high demand. Joseph has been killed. William Johnston has been wounded, injury to his ear. His war is over. Johnston Price has lost a foot. The Bamford twins both missing, killed in action. Please look after Roger's garden for him. I am sorry for being so horrible to you before I left. Your loving daughter, Anna."

After Tom finished reading the telegraph about six times, he looked up at Sir James, who had in the meantime unwrapped the parcel and slid it slowly across the table to Tom.

Tom nodded, retrieved the best two glasses he could find, and set then on the table.

"Your pleasure," he said to Sir James gesturing for him to fill the glasses. Sir James filled them to the brim.

243

"To Anna and David," toasted Sir James as he raised his glass and Tom instinctively did the same. The glasses chinked, and Sir James drank the Bushmills Special Malt in one.

Tom not wanting to be outdone, lifted his glass to do the same.

"Didn't think Jimmy Craig's, Dunville[37] would be appropriate. What do you think Thomas?" asked Sir James.

"He'd be wise to not show his face around here, or I might find something useful to do with some hot metal rods. Fuck you and your Ulster, Craig," rasped Tom with venom.

"Nothing personal Sir James," he apologised as he swallowed the contents in one.

"I have similar feelings Thomas, but it would do me no good to express them," responded Sir James. "I'll leave that pleasure with you!"

As Sir James filled the glasses again, Tom continued.

"Last time we did this it got a bit out of hand," he chuckled.

"It did that Thomas, which is why I gave McCracken specific instructions to get me out of here if I was not back up the lane in an hour. I have meetings in the morning."

"Ah well we should be able to do a bit of damage to this bottle by then. To the pair of them and safe home!" toasted Tom.

"Excellent toast Thomas, excellent!" agreed Sir James, as the second pair of tumblers emptied.

---

[37] Jimmy Craig's Dunville reference to James Craig's Dunville Whisky empire.

By the time the chauffeur arrived at the door to collect Sir James the two fathers had almost drained the bottle of Bushmills. As Sir James began to leave with McCracken, Tom rose stiffly to his feet and followed them to the door.

"Well God, maybe you have just earned yourself a second chance old son," thought Tom to himself as Sir James and McCracken ambled up the lane on the far side of the lock bridge back up to the Rolls.

Chapter Twenty

Aftermath

By the middle of September, the Somme campaign lingered on, neither side wanting nor giving an inch. Rab and Jonty had survived the first day unscathed, Bill was posted to training duties back in England, thanks to being totally deaf in one ear. He also sported a blue scar from the base of his jaw to his ear, containing the remnants of shrapnel that were too difficult to remove and best left.

Roger, Joe, and the twins were all gone, Roger's body was retrieved from no mans' land. Joe and the twins were listed as KIA "Killed in Action." Their remains were never recovered.

Jonty survived the first day, but one week later caught his leg on barbed wire while doing one of his message runs. The leg turned septic, gangrene set in, and it had to be removed just above the ankle. His war was over.

Sergeant Quinn had reported back to his Major, explained the loss of his officers and men, and was returned to his unit to continue the campaign. Quinn would survive the war, only to return to his wife and family to find himself shunned and insulted by the local Nationalist population and let down by Craig sacrificing Donegal, Monaghan, and Cavan Protestants to protect the rest of Ulster from the Nationalist ballot for a hundred years.

Quinn, like many others, had been the sacrificial lamb by both the generals and the Unionist cause. Quinn crossed the Atlantic with his family and joined the Boston police force.

He had also suggested to senior officers after the Somme that Rab would be more use as an assistant to the padre than his limited military abilities. The Major approved, Rab spent the rest of the war assisting the overstretched Anglican padres who came and went on a regular basis. Rab was there throughout the rest of the war and got affectionately known as Tuck for obvious reasons.

By December 1916, Jonty had been discharged from convalescence in England, having been given an artificial stump to replace his left foot. He was given his tickets back to Belfast with his discharge papers, a handful of medals and a brief handshake.

By the time the Heysham boat docked at Donegall Quay two weeks before Christmas, he leant against the side of the metal shed on the quayside. The bitter damp wind that raced from Divis and Blackmountain straight out on to the Lough, froze him to the bone. It was raw, but he was home.

He knew that there would be no job for him at Ballydrain as a stable lad. Too much of that required two quick feet. Those days were over. He knew he would have to go up to the big house to clear out his belongings. He would ask Sir James if he could stay for the night in his stables' quarters and he would be on his way. To where he had no idea.

He hobbled past Tedford's shop near the corner of Anne Street opposite the exit of the quayside. He was surprised to see his old boss the Head Groom, McCracken, leaning against the wall, pipe in hand.

McCracken stepped forward as he knocked his pipe against the brick wall.

"You look like a man that could do with a lift home. It'll take you all day at the rate you are going," said the groom with a rueful smile, trying to disguise the sorrow of seeing young Jonty, who had left full of cheek and youthfulness, return in such a poor condition.

"I could do with a lift to the stables to collect my worldly goods and I'll be away on, if that's ok with you, Mr McCracken," asked Jonty, exhausted already from dragging his left leg and carrying his kit bag.

"That won't be a problem, young Price," replied the groom, as he offered his hand to take Jonty's bag. McCracken placed it on the back of the trap. They both pulled themselves up on to the seats. The groom took the reins and the trap horse trotted slowly through the city and headed up Anne St, Donegal Place, Bedford St, through Shaftesbury Square, past Queens University, Malone and finally up through the gates of Ballydrain House and along the elm lined driveway.

248

They had not talked much on the journey back. Jonty was deep in his own thoughts and when McCracken asked about the war, he got short answers of only a few words. McCracken quickly accepted Jonty did not want to talk about it.

"The Jonty I know is still at the Somme," he thought to himself.,

As they entered the red sandstone gates, Jonty asked.

"How has Sir James taken Roger's death, Mr McCracken?"

'Sir James, sure you never know what he's thinking. He's buried himself in his work to take his mind off it. Lady May, on the other hand, has gone to pieces. You'll see yourself soon enough, son."

By the time they arrived at the stable courtyard, Jonty, intending to retrieve his belongings, noticed they were all stacked at the bottom of the steps to the loft which had been his home.

Jonty sighed, and without turning to face McCracken said,

"Well, that's one idea knocked on the head. I was going to ask if I could stay the night and be on my way, but somebody must want me gone before then."

McCracken grunted a contained laugh.

"Is that right now, young Price. The war has robbed you of your brains as well as your foot then."

Jonty, confused, looked at McCracken.

"Don't give me that look son, your belongings are down here because you aren't going to be sleeping out in the loft from now on. Don't want you breaking your other leg trying to get up and down the loft ladder on one leg."

McCracken grinned again as he pulled his pipe from his pocket but refrained from lighting it as he was beside the stables.

"Come with me and I'll show you a better billet that's on ground level; make it a bit easier for you," sympathised McCracken, as he strolled from the stables into the courtyard, finally striking his match and sucking life into the tobacco embers.

They walked down the side of the rear courtyard towards a door and room that Jonty remembered was used for storing supplies right beside the scullery and kitchens.

McCracken opened the door and gestured Jonty to go inside. Jonty shuffled through the door twisting on his crutch as he did. Inside there was a bed, table, couple of chairs, a bit of bench seating below the window, and a fire already set to be lit.

"That's a bit more Protestant looking for you, Jonty lad, then?" smiled McCracken.

"But I can't do my old job anymore, so I won't be able to work for Sir James. He'll not want me about the place."

At this point, Jonty was a few steps inside the room with his back to the door.

A voice from behind him made him jump.

"Do not think I am providing you with tip top accommodation, to sit and feel sorry for yourself!"

Jonty turned to find Sir James standing in the doorway. Jonty automatically leant himself against his crutch and saluted as if he was being addressed by a Brigadier.

As Sir James strolled into the room he tapped his walking stick against the best chair in the room. "Take yourself a seat young Price, while I explain a few things to you."

Jonty eased himself into the chair, his head spinning in confusion. Sir James, pulled up a spare chair and sat opposite him, placing his walking stick between his legs, both hands clasped on top of the brass nob on the top of the stick.

"Roger, wrote home many times, telling me about all of you young men. How you were his comrades and friends. He asked me, if he did not return, to promise to be as loyal to you all as you," Sir James paused, swallowed hard and briefly looked with glazed eyes at the ceiling, "had been to him. "

Sir James dropped his gaze to the floor, then raised it to look at the embarrassed invalid soldier.

"I do not intend, until my last breath, to let any of you down. I gave that promise to Roger and while, I admit, I am not a man who is lavish with generosity, my word is my bond as the great Bard wrote. So, young Price, these quarters go along with your duties as part time groom and part time apprentice blacksmith to Tom Gibson. He is short of help down there with David gone. Both jobs are yours if you are up for them and do not think you can get away with shirking. I promised Roger I would show loyalty to you all. I did not promise to be a soft touch as they say."

Sir James leant forward and offered his hand to Jonty who extended his own without thinking. "So that is it then, agreed. I am glad you are back. I think some of the staff even more so. Well, I am away to Hilden Mill for a meeting."

Then, as he was leaving, he turned one last time with a straight face asked.

"What exactly did you mean by Sir James is Sir James?"

He laughed quietly, as he saw Jonty's face freeze, as he turned again to disappear out of the door.

Jonty sat on the edge of his bed, trying to take stock of his unexpected good fortune and the even more unexpected benevolence of Sir James. He sat in the sanctuary of the small but comforting space and then his next hurdle came to mind.

He sat with his thoughts, knowing he would soon have to make the journey across the yard and try to get himself down the narrow stone steps that lead to the kitchen where the staff had their meals. He was reluctant to make the journey. He feared the stares of shock that would greet him as he would stumble into the kitchen with his crutch and wooden foot. He really was not looking forward to it.

Just as he was about to drag himself over to the kitchen and face the reception, a strong burst of thumps made the door shudder.

252

"You in there Jonty? I'm fed up waiting on you, coming over for your grub, so I've brought it over. Hope the army hasn't turned you into a lazy wee sod!"

Jonty laughed to himself. He would know that unmistakable voice anywhere, it was Martha.

He lurched towards the door and lifted the latch to find the big girl, with a smile from ear to ear, holding a large tray in both hands.

"Ah Martha, I see you're the same shrinking violet I always remember," laughed Jonty.

"Looks like you've done a bit of shrinking yourself. Jesus, did they feed you at all in that Army? Have you been living off frogs' legs? I'll have to get a pile of grub into you and get you back to the cheeky wee blighter we all know and love!" mocked Martha.

"Well, you haven't shrunk any, big girl," he teased back as he gave her a slap on her hip as she set the tray covered with a clean linen cloth and silver plate on top, down on the table.

Jonty looked up at Martha and smiled a drained smile. Martha looked down at him as she dropped her guard. She looked into Jonty's face and deep into his eyes, leant forward and hugged him. Jonty said nothing for about ten seconds as Martha maintained her bear like grip. Jonty returned the compliment as best he could.

"Martha I never thought I'd be so glad to see you. Sit down there while I eat this before it gets cold. There's a spare spoon, tuck in and we'll share it. Tell me what's been happening while I've been away," he asked.

The pair enjoyed the grub. Jonty sat relaxed by the fireside as Martha updated him on all the goings on at Ballydrain and all the local scandal since he had been away.

By the time they stopped talking it was nearly midday when Martha rose to her feet and looked down at Jonty relaxed in the chair.

"You were missed, Jonty. I've had no one to get a laugh out of in donkeys," she bantered, hands on her substantial hips, as she smiled at Jonty.

Jonty struggled to get his balance as he rose from the chair. Martha leaned forward and held her forearm out for him to grab and pull himself upright.

"Come on over with me and get the hero's return bit over with, smiled Martha." Jonty adjusted his balance on the crutch.

"Next you'll be telling me you fancy me, big girl." laughed Jonty wearily

"Ah I'm working on it," laughed Martha.

As the unlikely pair linked arms across the courtyard at the rear of the mansion house, Jonty pressed her arm with his and laughed.

"Hey Martha, I've got an idea. Next Easter Monday, the Edenderry fete. We could pair up and win the three-legged race, no problem."

Martha gave him a nudge with her hip which nearly caused him to lose his balance, but she strengthened her grip under his arm as they negotiated the steps to face the world of Ballydrain.

For the rest of the war until it ended in November 1918, Davy never saw the battlefield again after he had been transferred to the Medical Unit. Anna and Kitty worked to their physical and mental limits, healing, caring, and acting.

Davy dealt with the constant flow of casualties, which continued to occupy his skills right up until armistice. By the time they were all finally given a release date it was spring of 1919.

The morning they were leaving to return home they were gathering their baggage and saying farewells to colleagues who had become friends, Davy and Anna noticed Kitty was nowhere to be seen.

"Where's Kitty?" asked Davy.

"I'll go and find her. She's been strange this morning, nearly as bad as the Somme," sighed Anna shaking her head.

"Watch our bags please and don't let the transport go without us. I'll go and get her."

Anna retraced her steps back to the nurses' quarters, passing corridors, until she reached the open door of the dormitory she and Kitty had shared with several other nurses. As she entered, she could see Kitty sitting on the side of her bunk, hunched forward, hands clasped downwards staring at the floor, bags packed neatly on the floor beside her feet. Kitty did not lift her head to acknowledge Anna but continued to stare in the direction of the floor.

"Kitty, the transport has arrived to take us home. Shift yourself girl," coaxed Anna, trying to make light of the obvious mood that had enveloped Kitty.

"I'm not going back to Ballydrain, Anna. It's your home, not mine," sighed Kitty in almost a whisper.

"Don't be daft Kitty," replied Anna, standing with her hands on her hips.

"Ballydrain is your home and always will be. I will see to that. You are as near to the sister I never had. Come on, let's get moving," she coaxed as she bent forward to pick up one of Kitty's bags.

Kitty looked up at Anna.

"Leave them there, Anna. You're not listening!" ordered Kitty raising her voice in a tone of frustration.

Anna dropped the bag, shocked by Kitty's disobedience.

As Anna sat down beside Kitty to put an arm around her, she noticed Joe's rosary was clasped between her knuckles, white with the tension in her hands. Anna sat down rubbing Kitty's shoulders in a vain hope to settle her mood.

After a few seconds Kitty, still staring at the floor, said,

"This is my home."

"You can't stay here, Kitty. This place will be knocked down as soon as we leave," pleaded Anna.

"No, I don't mean this room Anna. I mean here; this place," said Kitty assuredly.

'But why, there's nothing here for you?" asked Anna.

Kitty still staring at the floor said.

"My life is here, Anna. Joe is my life. He is still here. He said he would wait for me. He is waiting for me, and I want to be near him."

Anna sat silent for a few seconds.

"But where will you live? How will you fend for yourself with no friends or family?

"Come on Kitty, you are having one of your dark days. Get a move on," stressed Anna, unable to conceal her confusion any further.

"I'm going to St. Claire's, it's not far from here. It looks after wounded soldiers. The ones that will never go home. They need my help and Joe will be at my side. I must stay here.

"Anna, leave me to sit here. Go and find Davy. Get yourselves home and get on with your lives. Make the most of everyday. Never regret being who you are. It is your destiny, this is mine. Davy is the man for you. Love him and care for him as I love Joe. Promise me Anna."

Kitty leant forward to raise Anna up from the bunk in another effort to encourage her to leave.

"But St Claire's is run by the Poor Clare's nuns, Kitty. They'll not let you work with them," replied Anna as she got up from the bunk edge.

Kitty, still sitting, looked up straight into Anna's face but did not speak. Anna stared down to her in silence, as the reality of what she was being told formed in her brain.

"Are you saying you're joining them?

"Don't tell me that, Kitty?" begged Anna in a state of shock and concern.

"You are a beautiful, young woman, with your life ahead of you. Joe would not want you to throw it all away. He would want you to live your life to the full. Do not throw it all away."

"God Anna, you just don't get it. Joe is the only one I will ever love. I don't want a life with anyone else. It would betray him. If I go to the Passion, I can help other Joes and I will be here with him always."

Anna was about to argue further, but Kitty got up, placed her hands onto Anna's shoulders, turned her round to face the door and gave her a gentle push. Anna turned her head to face Kitty, who just put her hand to Anna's lips,

"There's nothing more to be said. Anna, please just go. This is my life, not yours. Just go, please."

Anna turned, leant forward, gave Kitty a long hug, turned again, and walked out of the room, back into the still cold morning air to where Davy was standing impatiently.

"What kept the pair of you? Where is she?" asked Davy, aware that the last tram was drawing up.

Anna tried to look at Davy, but the tears in her eyes made it impossible to focus.

"It's just you and me going home, Davy," sobbed Anna.

"Why, what's.....?" Davy searched for an explanation.

"Not now, Davy. Let's get out of this place. We've all done enough for God and bloody Ulster."

Part Three

Redemption

Chapter Twenty – one

Home coming

Anna and Davy left the Channel port and said goodbye to the British war effort. On the long journey home between the French coast until they disembarked at Donegall Quay, Belfast, they had the chance to unwind and be themselves for the first time in almost three years.

As they stepped off the gang plank from the Heysham boat in the early dawn they mingled with the crowds jostling at the quay side. As they walked towards Customs Square and Anne Street, they both stopped instinctively and looked up at the Cavehill, Blackmountain, Divis, the Castlereagh Hills and down the Lough.

"Well, Anna," laughed Davy,

"If they need anyone to fight anymore battles, they can leave us out of it. We've better things to do, eh girl?" Davy smiled as he set his bags down and put his hands round each side of her beautiful face.

For the first time since the evening at Ballydrain, in the Autumn of 1915, Anna's expression of innocence and love had returned. The strong expression she had to portray throughout the nightmare had disappeared. They were once again just Anna and Davy.

"Forever Anna, forever," whispered Davy.

"Forever Davy," smiled Anna as she leaned forward and rubbed his back with both her hands.

"Just the small matter of Sir James then?" grinned Davy nervously.

"We'll deal with that together, my love," assured Anna. "Let's go home."

The pair lifted their bags and Davy began to walk in the direction of the quayside to Mays Field, intent on getting a lift for them both on a lighter up to his cottage and then leave Anna up to Ballydrain in the horse trap.

"Where do you think you're going, big lad?" teased Anna, in her best broad Belfast accent, mimicking the factory girls chat up line.

"Getting us a lift home, wee girl!" replied Davy mirroring the humour.

"Well, you don't think you are taking me up to Ballydrain covered in coal dust? I have had my fill of roughing it." teased Anna.

"We are taking one of those horse cabs sitting across the street and we are going to ride to the front gates and walk up the driveway together just like we did in the spring of 1915. I have dreamt of it since the day I arrived in France. You and me Davy. You had better get used to going through the front gates with your head held high," assured Anna in a tone that meant there should be no disapproval.

As they reached the first cab with the horse's head still deep in its nose bag, munching contentedly, Davy asked the cabbie, "Ballydrain boss, please."

The cabbie looked at Davy in his tired demob suit and Anna in quality, but well-worn clothes, probably bought second hand, up and down slowly.

"That'll cost a bit, sir," grunted the cabbie, not taking his pipe out of his mouth, as he lifted the nose bag from the horse.

"That will be taken care of at the House," interrupted Anna from behind Davy's shoulder.

"Oh, will it love, and exactly which house in Ballydrain?" asked the cabbie with a smirk.

"Ballydrain House, now kindly just help me on if that's not too much bother," hissed Anna.

The cabbie was considering continuing his line of attack, when he caught Davy's eyes suggesting, he leave it. The cabbie took the hint and offered his hand to Anna without saying anything more.

As they settled into the hard seats of the horse cab, they both sat silently with their thoughts, just taking in the streets and avenues that had been etched in their memories.

As they rode up Bedford Street and towards Shaftesbury Square, the cabbie could not contain his curiosity any further. The two passengers were both only in their early twenties. She

263

was dressed in quality, but well-worn clothes, with an attitude older than her years and she was not short of confidence with the posh accent she was putting on, which did not fool him. The young man seemed to have his wits about him, but he was no toff.

"Going to work for Sir James Arthur then, are you pair?" asked the cabbie without turning around.

"Something like that," replied Davy from the back.

"The best of British with that, folks. From what I hear he's not easy to work for. Bit of a tyrant is the word. Thinks he owns Belfast. Then again, he probably does, come to think of it," informed the cabbie.

Anna looked at Davy and rolled her eyes. Davy gave her a wink.

"Do you know the man well then, mate?" asked Davy from the back.

"No never met him. Just see him passing by in his fancy automobile, head stuck in his paper," replied the cabbie before continuing, after a short silence, broken only by the sound of the horse's hooves.

"Lost his only son at the Somme, I hear. Wouldn't wish that on any man," reflected the cabbie respectfully, dropping his head slightly.

Davy and Anna exchanged glances. Anna was about to educate the cabbie in no uncertain manner but, just as she was about to lean forward and react to the cabbie, Davy leaned across her and pointed as they reached Shaftesbury Square and the butcher's shop where Jack Graham had taught him his trade.

"Look there's the shop. It's had a lick of paint since I was away. There's old Hugh Liggett still chatting up the ladies at the door.

"Hugh, Hughie, leave them ladies alone!" shouted Davy.

The man in the butchers' apron looked in the direction of the insults being launched at him and stepped towards the kerb to confront the abuse.

"Ah Jez it's not you, Davy son, is it? Ah Jez it's great to see you back safe!"

Hugh turned his face back to the shop doorway and shouted into the shop.

"He's back, Davy's home, and he's in one piece, thank God." As he said it the whole shop staff and customers came out, some waved, some nodded, some leaned in and shook his hand.

"Well Hugh, and how are you all?" asked Davy.

"Ah, getting by, son. Too many of the lads in Sandy Row[38] and the Pass around here didn't get back. Others, like yourself, are just glad it's all over."

"Look Hugh I'll have to get on up to see my Da and get Anna home." said Davy, as he nodded in Anna's direction.

Hugh looked across the cab to Anna who had sat smiling, silently as she took in the attention Davy was receiving.

---

[38] Sandy Row and the Pass districts surrounding Shaftesbury Square.

"Ahh, so this is her Ladyship herself. Heard a lot about you girl. All good it was too," greeted Hugh as he lent across to grab her hand.

"What do you see in him? You'd be far better off with a man with a bit of experience that knows how to give a girl a good time," teased Hugh, giving Davy an approving smile.

The cabbie in the front, who had sat holding the reins had listened to every word, closed his eyes, shook his head ruefully wishing the ground would open in front of him.

"Did that old fella say, Anna, and taking her home?" he thought to himself.

As everyone waved the horse cab off, a silence returned which was only broken by the time they reached Queen's University.

"I'm sorry, ma'am. I didn't catch on you were Sir James's daughter. The one that's been at the war. My missus always tells me I've a big mouth. I'm sorry and I'm sorry about your brother, ma'am."

Anna, still simmering at the venom he had launched against her father, raised her eyes to the morning sky, leant forward towards the cabbie and patted the back of his shoulder.

"Never worry, at least you know you'll get your fare paid!" snapped Anna.

"I'll not be taking any money ma'am. It's the least I can do in the circumstances," replied the cabbie, by this stage totally deflated. He never spoke the rest of the way home.

As the horse cab turned into the gatehouse at the entrance of Ballydrain, Anna asked the cabbie to stop.

She gestured to Davy that they should get out. Anna walked round to the cabbie as she fumbled in her purse to find the cabbie's fare.

"No ma'am I will not take your fare. I'm sorry I opened my big mouth," pleaded the cabbie, full of remorse.

"We all make mistakes, sir. God knows I have, and so has my father," reassured Anna, as she pressed the fare into the man's hand.

"Please drive on up to the stables, leave our bags, freshen your horse, and tell the kitchen to get you something to eat. Davy and myself have waited three years to walk up this drive, and I have a few friends to see on the way." Anna smiled at the cabbie and waved him off.

Davy was a bit confused at this but decided that whatever Anna was up to it was best in the circumstances to let her get on with it. This was a watershed day. It was best to go with the flow.

As they walked slowly up the driveway, below the elm trees to the House, Davy could hear the thud of horses' hooves cantering towards them from the field on the right.

They knew it was Anna and they sped up, only slowing as they got to the white railings.

Her favourite pushed its way through and nuzzled against her face. Anna whispered, as it bounced its head up and down.

Davy just stood back and began to imagine what his potential meeting with Sir James might be like. Asking him for Anna's hand in marriage.

After a few minutes Anna turned away from the horses, wiped her eyes with her handkerchief, and linking arms again with Davy walked on up the driveway towards the front of the house.

The noise of the horses and a horse cab with no passengers trotting into the courtyard at the back of the house had attracted the attention of Sir James, who had been reading his paper after breakfast, and Lady May, who had just begun some embroidery. Sir James looked at Lady May, both had the same thought as they rose and looked out of the window to see two figures walking slowly up the path, arm in arm, towards them.

"It's Anna, she's home!" shouted Sir James, loudly enough that half the household could hear it. Gone was the unflappable patriarch. He was consumed by relief and joy that he had not experienced since his youth. Sir James and Lady May embraced each other like a pair of young lovers. The staff present had never seen the pair drop their facade before.

Sir James and Lady May went out to the top step outside the mansion door when Davy and Anna were still about fifteen yards from the bottom step. Anna ran towards her parents while Davy stood back and leaned against a stone plinth at the bottom of the front doorsteps.

He didn't feel that he was part of this Arthur family reunion.

After the three finished their intimate reunion, Sir James looked down the steps at Davy, cap taken respectfully off his head, grinning at the pleasure Anna was enjoying.

"David!" Sir James shouted. "David do not stand there like a wet rag, my boy, come inside please," waving him forward as he spoke.

"Thank you, Sir James, for your kind offer but it might be best if I left you all to it. I'm sure you want a bit of time to yourselves. I'll just head down to the cottage and surprise my father," replied Davy.

"You can surprise Thomas after you have had a good breakfast; the least May and I can do in the circumstances."

Davy smiled slowly and looked towards Sir James who extended a waving arm in the direction of the steps. Davy could not deny a good breakfast was exactly what he wanted and allowed Sir James to guide him in the direction of the mansion door. Sir James walked to the bottom of the steps and beckoned Davy inside with his left arm outstretched.

269

"Thank you, Sir James, your hospitality is appreciated," still remembering his father's advice to keep it short but respectful when dealing with the 'big noises.' Old habits die hard.

Sir James laughed quietly.

"Tom taught you well, young David. Never give those big noises any excuse to get at you. Was not that what he told you?"

Davy looked at Sir James in disbelief. How could this man know what his father had told him? He did own just about everyone and everything in the southern parts of Belfast and the Lagan Valley, but he didn't think Thomas Gibson was part of his inner circle.

"Thomas and I have had several conversations over the last three years. Some of which have helped keep both of our sanity. Fair to say we dug each other out of considerable holes in dark days. That war has changed everything and everyone. You, Thomas, Anna, May, Kitty, myself."

He took in a large breath.

"We survived it. Not like poor Roger and Joe, the Bamford twins. We owe it to them to make amends. Get it right. Make the most of every day. Give misery to no man or woman."

Sir James stared into Davy's face as he spoke, stiff upper lip trying not to tremble, but his throat muscles gave the game away.

Davy, for a few seconds was not looking at the man of power and influence, but a tired, ageing man, who was doing his best to keep himself together. A human being after all.

"Well, Sir James, I know where Anna got her strength from," said Davy.

Sir James, grinned and recovered his facade.

"Ah, Anna, the apple of both our eyes it would seem."

"I cannot deny that Sir James," smiled Davy, as they both started to follow in the direction of the drawing room.

"We are both, hers," added Davy.

"Do you believe so, David?" asked Sir James. "After the way I treated you both before you left."

"Sir James, Anna, if you don't mind me saying, your daughter, is strong willed and can be as stubborn as a mule when she takes a notion. She is her father's daughter. She is also the most caring and beautiful girl I will ever know, and without her I might as well be ....."

Davy cut the sentence short, sensing he had said enough.

As Sir James ushered him into the morning room, Anna, and Lady May, were sitting beside each other smiling and wiping away tears from silk handkerchiefs Lady May had been embroidering.

Anna instinctively got up and walked to Davy's side and linked her arm under his, making it obvious to Sir James that she and David would not be separated again.

When they had finished breakfast, Sir James gestured that they move to the drawing room. Sir James stood looking out of the window, Lady May and Anna sat side by side on a luxurious "chaise longue." Both looked every bit the ladies of the manor.

Davy decided to remain standing, mirroring Sir James's position of authority.

"This is indeed a day to enjoy, after all this misery. We must embrace the present and the future, all of us," mused Sir James. "Now I have a meeting at Edenderry. I am late already, and as the wheels of industry wait for no man, I will have to bid my leave.

""I can give you a lift to Shaw's Bridge, which will get you down to Thomas quicker. He has waited long for this day.

"David, Lady May and I invite you and Thomas to dinner this evening. McCracken will collect you at seven o'clock. We have a lot to discuss. Need to get a few things established. Make up for lost time," said Sir James, showing no hint of emotion in his voice, which bothered Davy.

"Right, things to be done. Let us say our farewells to these ladies of ours and get on."

Davy said his goodbyes to Anna and Lady May, giving a smile to Anna. "See you this evening."

Anna looked puzzled. Davy shrugged his shoulders and looked in Sir James's direction as he followed him out the door.

Davy stepped out of the Roll Royce at Shaws' Bridge and grabbed his kit bag. As he walked on past the bridge to the Milltown Road, he turned left down the lane that would take him the short cut down to the lock quay on the far side opposite his cottage. As he walked the two hundred yards his heart tightened in excitement. As the shallow bend in the lane brought the cottage in sight, he could see the smoke rising from the chimney of the forge and the sound of the hammer hitting metal. As he reached the lock gate, he saw a small figure with a hobbled gait carrying a bucket of metal hinges, steam still rising, freshly forged. Jonty, sensing the presence of someone nearby, looked up and saw Davy standing on the side of the lock as he dropped his bags beside him.

Jonty was about to speak, but before he could open his mouth, Davy signalled to him to remain silent. The two friends walked quietly toward each other, Davy reached into his waist coat pocket and drew out two Woodbines, offering one to Jonty, who proceeded to light a match and offered the flame, sheltered from the breeze, in his hands, to Davy. When they had both ignited and inhaled, Jonty whispered first.

"Take it you are both back. Jesus, it's great you're back mate. How's the lovely Anna, then?"

'She's the same Anna that left, but how, considering what she went through, God only knows," sighed Davy.

"Aye there's a few strong women up at that the House. Lady May, Anna and Martha," grinned Jonty.

Davy smiled and gave Jonty a long questioning look, as he inhaled his Woodbine.

Jonty laughed, "Seems like you are a bit behind on what's been happening around here since you've been gone."

'Aye,, so it would seem," replied Davy, still not wanting to give Jonty the satisfaction of being one step ahead of him.

Jonty was about to expand on the conversation but was cut short by Tom's voice coming from the bowels of the forge.

"Jonty, need that bucket back in here now. Not next Friday kid!"

Davy gestured to Jonty that he would take the bucket inside.

Jonty nodded smiled and whispered,

"I think I'll find something useful to do out here for a bit. Away in and put him in a better mood."

Davy lifted the bucket and quietly walked through the door of the forge. Tom had his back to him. Davy placed the bucket just short of Tom's right and silently stood back near the entrance. Tom, without turning, picked up the bucket and took a pace towards the anvil to lift some horseshoes still cooling to drop into the bucket.

He noticed the shadow on the wall ahead reflected from the open door, which was not the shape of Jonty, much bigger, and the gait, head cocked, shoulder leaning against the door frame. Tom knew instinctively it was Davy. He had such a surge of elation in his body, his legs quivered and started to buckle, but he collected himself and managed to halt his collapse by bending his knees, placing his large stumpy hands against his thighs, just as he had done over two years earlier, when Sir James gave him the news his son had survived the Somme. He stared at the ground, still afraid to look round, afraid it was all a cruel trick of the morning sunshine.

"Please God tell me it's you, Davy!" he exclaimed, dropping his hammer as his strength left him.

"It's me, Da, I'm home. Anna kept her promise," sighed Davy, as he walked towards Tom who could still not dare turn around even if the power in his legs had returned, which it hadn't.

Davy reached Tom's side, leant forward, gripping him under the right armpit and helped him to rise.

Tom turned and placed his hands onto Davy's shoulders.

"Looks like a boy left and a man has returned, son," smiled Tom, his face as white as if he had seen a ghost.

"Maybe just a wiser boy, Da. Wise enough to know what's important to him," mused Davy.

"Anna and you, that's all that matters, Da."

Tom lowered his head, shook it, looked at Davy again.

"Well, there's no more work in me today. Lot to catch up on," as he led Davy out into the sunlight.

"Jonty, there'll be no work done here today, kid. Take yourself off home and give that big woman of yours a hug, a big smacker on the cheek and tell her it was from me," laughed Tom.

"Ah you're full of great ideas, Tom. Maybe Davy should come home every day," bantered Jonty as he grabbed his jacket, mounted his pony and trotted off up to the bridge and back to Ballydrain.

As father and son watched Jonty disappear up the tow path Davy looked at his father and asked, "What's that all about. Fill me in the gaps?"

Oh Jonty, nobody told you? It's Martha Price now; married last Easter. They both live up at the mansion; got their own place in the courtyard."

Davy shook his head, "Big Martha and wee Jonty. Never saw that coming. Ah good luck to him. He seems in good form."

"Aye the Lord makes 'em. The Lord matches 'em. They're as happy as pigs in muck," laughed Tom, "and long may they be so."

"Aye there's a few thought Anna and me sticking it out would never happen, but we did. You should have seen her out there, Da. She was something else. Never cracked under it and stayed the same Anna," reflected Davy admiringly.

"Just the small matter of telling Sir James we'll not be separated."

"The war changed us all, including Sir James," smiled Tom as he looked at him from the corner of his eye.

Davy was about to ask more but Tom raised his hand.

"Leave that to Sir James. Best you speak to him about that. She's his daughter not mine," advised Tom.

"Aye, last thing he said to me when I left the mansion this morning was that he wanted us both up to Ballydrain this evening. It seemed a bit official. He said McCracken would be down at seven o'clock to bring us up," replied Davy.

"Well tonight will come soon enough. Come on into the house and we'll get a cup of tea and break open some of the Armagh brew son."

Tom came out of the cottage a few minutes later to hang a sign across the lock gate.

"Sort the lock yourself. Davy's home."

Inside the cottage the pair, talked, laughed, held back their tears together, sipping the brew as they made up for lost time. Eventually, sleep took them over as they slumped in the two chairs by the fireside.

By three in the afternoon, they were woken by Stan Young, a lighter man from Moira who could not resist a long run of blasts from the hooter on the old barge sharing the celebration of Davy's return.

In the meantime, back up at Ballydrain, Anna was also making her first adjustments to home life. When Davy and Sir James left in the Rolls, Lady May and Anna walked out to the front garden and looked over the lake and the Italian gardens, where Roger had spent so many happy hours.

Anna turned to Lady May and placed her hand against her cheek.

"How are you, Mama? How have you been coping? I had the war to keep me focused, but you had to relive Roger every day. It must have been horrible."

277

"It was horrible, Anna. I had many dark days and nights. Your father and McCracken had to pull me out of the lake on a few occasions. That's how bad it got."

"Oh, my dear Mama." sighed Anna, as she cuddled her mother as if she was her child.

"I live for each day, and now I have you back, little one," replied Lady May, wiping tears from her eyes.

They both continued their walk through the garden and did not speak as they strolled arm in arm.

"Those azaleas need cutting back or they'll be a mess in the summer and the japonicas are not much better. What if we get to work on them? Roger would like that, Mama." said Anna as she stared wistfully down the length of the swathes of clematis, just starting to bud, hanging from the pergola in the spring sunlight.

"That would please him Anna, we will start that tomorrow, my dearest," smiled Lady May.

"What about you? It must have been hard. I do not know how you coped. Your father and I are so proud of you."

Anna paused as she thought to measure her answer.

"It was all those things, Mama, but you get caught up in the here and now and the urgency of it all," she paused, "and I had Davy, my love, my life.

"I am sorry if it disappoints you, but Davy and I will marry, and we will deal with wherever life's destiny takes us. How can I get father to accept David, Mama? What do I have to do?"

Lady May turned full face to Anna and placed her hands on each side of her face, gathering her hair in bunches. She stared into her daughter's face and smiled,

"Anna, destiny will look after itself. Father has told David and Thomas they are to be up here for dinner this evening. McCracken is collecting them. Things will work out for the best. I will say nothing more. Your father will no doubt have his time this evening. He is not the same man he was before the war; we have all been changed by it. None more so than James."

Anna looked at her in silence, screwing up her face in confusion. Lady May gripped Anna's arm tighter, as she turned her towards the path back up to the house.

"Well then, my dear, what do you intend doing for the rest of the day?" asked Lady May.

"I want to do what I have dreamt of doing for almost three years."

"Oh, my dear! and what is that?" asked Lady May as she pulled her face in pretend panic.

"I am going to have a hot bath, soak in the finest soap and drink a significant quantity of the best Chablis we possess. I have smelt and breathed carbolic soap, antiseptics, and other less pleasant smells for so long that the thought has been a dream. I need to lift the smell from my pores, the taste from my lips and breathe in Ballydrain once again; soak in the joy of being home." said Anna.

279

"Shell shock and nightmares haunt many poor survivors of battles. The smell haunts the nurses nearly as much as the cries of pain and the wounds. It will take a long time for it to fade, but that would be a start."

Lady May said nothing at first, just kept walking back to the big house steps, still linking arms with Anna. As they reached the entrance hall Lady May turned and hugged her daughter as they walked on through to the main hallway. Anna turned to face her mother.

"The war did not separate David and I, Mama. It made us even stronger. We will be together for the rest of our lives. If father does not approve, it will not change anything, but I would so love him to share in our happiness."

Lady May placed both her hands in her daughter's hands and said in a way she would have kissed her goodnight as a small child.

"Anna my dear, the war in France is over; so is the war in this house. Your father has a peace treaty drawn up. You know how he must be the man in charge. Just sit back and listen tonight and let him have his moment. This evening with come soon enough."

Chapter Twenty-Two

The Deal

By six thirty on that spring evening, Tom and Davy were both taking in the air as they leaned against the outside wall of the cottage, letting the last of the evening sunshine calm Davy's, if not Tom's, nerves. Both had washed, shaved, polished their shoes, and put on their Sunday best. Tom had gathered daffodils and tulips from the riverbank as token gifts for the ladies and a brown paper covered bottle of Armagh's finest for Sir James.

A few minutes later, McCracken in the Rolls, bumped and bounced, along the gravel lane from Newforge Lane side of the canal to the door of the cottage.

"Good evening gentlemen, especially to you, Davy," as he ambled towards him, trying to avoid the mud in the potholes at the front of the house. McCracken extended his hand to Davy as they shook hands for at least ten seconds, and as he did, looked at Tom and winked. "Well, big night then, Tom."

"Aye, it looks that he has you doing a bit of overtime," laughed Tom to McCracken.

Davy did not join in the fun, as his thoughts were full of the concerns of coping with Sir James.

"Well, best get up there. Over the top one more time. No shots fired this time son, so nothing to worry about," laughed Tom, as he gave Davy a push with his heavy hand.

"Aye, into the Valley of Death rode the six hundred, Davy. Nothing to worry about!" laughed McCracken, as he threw another glance at Tom.

"Your moral support is much appreciated, Mr McCracken!" said Davy dryly.

Between the cottage and the journey up Newforge Lane, up Malone Road, past the Dub and on through the large gates of Ballydrain, McCracken filled in as much detail as he could to Davy about the fates of those at the House, Milltown Road, Edenderry, and Lambeg.

William Johnston had already returned to the Edenderry Mill as a maintenance man. Jonty had married Martha, and she was expecting, which lifted Davy's mood as he considered where Jonty got the step ladders. The news that most surprised him was when McCracken said,

"You know the Bamford twins both copped it at the Somme."

"I was there, McCracken. About twenty yards from them. They were just behind me. Shell exploded, then they were gone. Never saw them again, just like that," sighed Davy softly, as he broke the match he was about to light, between his fingers.

"Ah Davy, I'm sorry. Knew you were in the thick of it, but I didn't know you saw them fall; wasn't thinking when I asked.

Roger getting caught by a sniper nearly killed Sir James and Lady May. Sir James was in a rage for weeks. You couldn't look at him without getting the face bit off, and as far as Lady May, she went to pieces. After her worst episode that Sir James and me, got involved with, it seemed to sort Sir James out. Brought him to his senses. Knew he had to put a brave face on it to bring Lady May round. I'll say no more than that.

Anyhow, Sir James started to change his attitude, changed his way of operating. Still as hard as nails in business matters, but he has time for people now. Very loyal to anyone he decides deserved it.

He went down to the widow Bamford, the twins' mother. I'll never forget it. He asked me to drive him down to her house in Edenderry village. Sir James sat all the way, holding a legal document. I thought it was her eviction notice and he was giving it to her personally. With the twins and her husband dead and her not being a mill worker, she could neither pay rent nor had any ties with the mill tenancies. The lads' wages from the war covered it for a while but that ran out.

So anyhow, I drove into the village right up to Mrs Bamford's door. Jesus, every curtain in the street was moving. Sir James knocked the door, still holding the official looking document, went in by himself. I stayed out at the car. Then things started to get a bit tight. Half the village, me included, thought he was

283

delivering her an eviction notice. The night shift men started to rise from their beds and gathered in the street, not looking too friendly. I felt about as safe and welcome as a fox in a hen run.

Anyhow, after about half an hour, out he came alone, shut the door behind him. Walked towards the Rolls clutching a parcel. He looked at the village men and women straight in their eyes, almost taking time to make eye contact with each one.

"Morning gentlemen, ladies," as he doffed his hat. "Just collecting some of Mrs Bamford's finest soda bread. Did any of you wish to speak to me or are you queuing for some soda as well?"

He stepped into the back of the motor himself, as I was already in the front, engine running, to get away as soon as possible.

"Drive on McCracken, before they gather their thoughts. Drive, please!" was all he said.

It turned out the legal paperwork wasn't an eviction notice, just the title deeds to the terraced house.

Sir James had explained to her that Roger had written to him and told him of his pride of leading the Edenderry Boys and the loyalty they had given him. He told her he could not bring back her sons, but he could return the loyalty they had shown to Roger, handed her the documents, and asked her to tell no one for fear he would be seen as a 'soft touch.'

For twenty minutes of the half hour, he was in the house, he had sat opposite Mrs Bamford, as she shook and sobbed in her chair. Sir James did not do public shows of emotion and could only hastily offer his finest linen kerchief from his suit jacket pocket. He sat and stared at the ceiling for what seems an eternity, waiting for her to settle herself.

"Well, Mrs Bamford, I will bid my leave if that is agreeable to you?" asked Sir James, hoping to remove himself from a meeting he found harder than any industrial dispute.

They both stood up. Mrs Bamford could see the crowd gathering in the street through her small front window.

"Here Sir James, take this soda bread I've just baked on the griddle this morning. That should ease their mood outside. Never thought I'd say it, but you are a good man Sir James, and I'll not have anyone say otherwise."

"I fear I have a few more deeds to carry out before I can wear that compliment with any confidence. I have a lot of catching up to do. Might be best if I see myself out. That and this soda bread will keep your neighbours out there guessing," assured Sir James as he lowered his head on his way out of the front door to the intimidating gathering in the street.

By the time McCracken had completed his tale, the Rolls Royce and its passengers had arrived at the front of the mansion steps. McCracken ushered father and son inside and led them through the outer entrance hall, past the drawing room and straight to the partially closed door of the large lounge, normally used for formal engagements and business meetings. Fitzsimons the butler graciously opened the door and announced,

"The gentlemen Thomas and David Gibson, Sir James," as he ushered them both into the lounge.

As father and son entered the imposing grandeur of the room, intended to both impress and intimidate anyone who entered, they encountered Sir James standing alone, with no sign of Lady May or Anna.

Davy, still wary of Sir James's methods, felt a certain anxiety about the situation.

Sir James was clearly setting out his stall for some ruse up his sleeve. Sir James stepped forward.

"Fitzsimons, drinks for Thomas and David, if you would please," ushered Sir James to his butler.

"Well Tom, this is the day you have waited for far too long, my friend."

Davy flashed a quizzical glance at Tom. "You've got very friendly with Sir James, while I've been away," thought Davy.

"Aye, you are not often wrong, James," laughed Tom, causing another sideways glance from Davy.

"It's James now is it then? Before I left you couldn't say a good word about him," thought Davy to himself.

Sir James did not extend his hand to Davy, but placed it firmly in his trouser pocket, the other still gripping his unlit pipe.

"Ah David, the prodigal son who hath returned. I have heard a lot about your exploits and your hidden talents," said Sir James, with only the slightest sign of a smile.

"Nothing more than I was trained to do. Would have preferred most of it never happened," replied Davy, respectfully.

Sir James stepped forward to the low coffee table and the leather chairs that surrounded it in front of the glowing fire, and ushered father and son to take seats, as Fitzsimons stepped among them with a tray, whiskey decanter, and fine crystal glasses.

"Well Gentlemen, the ladies are still powdering their noses, so it gives us the chance to get a bit of necessary business sorted out now," announced Sir James, as if he were talking to two linen merchants.

Both Davy and Tom looked at Sir James but said nothing.

Davy was filled with dread.

"Correct me if I am wrong, David, but my understanding is that you intend to marry Anna, my Anna," asked Sir James, as he raised his glass to his mouth and tasted his first sip.

Tom and Davy both copied his action. In Davy's case it was intended to fortify himself for a tirade from Sir James. In Tom's case, it was a man enjoying himself watching how his son would deal with Sir James.

"That is correct Sir James. I have saved most of my army pay and I will soon be able to start my own butcher's shop. I will provide for Anna; she will want for nothing. You have my word,

287

Sir James," assured Davy slowly and with a slight touch of defiance.

"I have no doubt you would do your best," replied Sir James, as he sipped his whiskey.

Davy sipped his whiskey in similar fashion, remaining silent. Sir James paused, and looked wistfully at the ornate ceiling, for what seemed an eternity. Davy held his ground and said nothing, waiting for Sir James to display his hand.

"Let me explain something, young man," advised Sir James, pointing the end of his pipe at Davy.

"I cannot allow my daughter to be turned into a skivvy for the love of a member of the artisan class, however well intended. It would not work. She has been brought up with the finest of everything and good standing throughout the length and breadth of this island."

Sir James inhaled deeply.

"I will not have her demean herself in any fashion. I will not allow that to happen in any circumstances," pressed Sir James, with conviction, as he leant back in his chair, waiting for Davy's response.

Davy thought to himself, all the time looking at the pattern on the carpet at his feet.

"Well Sir James, I understood that you had changed since the war, but it would appear I was wrong," sighed Davy, as he set the glass on the coffee table in front of his knees and started to rise.

"I would be obliged, Sir James, that when Anna comes down, you let her know I will be outside, and tell her I am waiting to take her home. Good day to you, Sir."

Davy stood up and was about to step around the coffee table to the doorway of the lounge.

"Sit down David, please. I have not finished," demanded Sir James, still talking in a quiet tone.

"I heard you clearly. You do not think I am good enough for your Anna, but that is for Anna, and no one else, to decide," replied Davy, again copying Sir James's quiet tone, as he continued to stride to the door.

Sir James, still sitting casually in his chair, trying valiantly to keep his face devoid of emotion, looked at Tom.

"Davy, son, sit down!" growled Tom, impatiently looking over at Sir James, not turning his gaze to Davy.

"What's the point Da, he doesn't want to know!" answered Davy, staring at the back of Tom's head, as his father still sat sipping the whiskey, facing Sir James, who was looking across at Tom.

'Davy son, if you don't sit down and listen to Sir James, I swear to God, I will lay you out on that floor. You are a guest in his house. He is entitled to better manners than you are returning.

Sit down son!" ordered Tom, in exasperation.

"And you, Sir James, stop winding him up. You find the humour in this; Davy does not. The pair of them have been through hell and back for each other. He is too wound up to think straight. Just explain to him, please!"

Davy sat back down but did not retrieve his glass.

Sir James still sitting, leant forward over the coffee table towards Davy, as if to emphasis a point.

"Did I say you could not marry Anna Arthur, spinster of this parish?"

Davy looked across at Sir James in defiant mood.

"I have said," continued Sir James, "I could not allow my daughter to marry below her station and live below her standing," continued Sir James.

"But I am what I am, Sir James," replied Davy proudly.

"Yes, you are David, a fine young man, who has proven himself in life and love, and, a man, who can, with a little help, do himself justice."

Sir James paused to take another sip of Bushmills.

"And, at the same time, content his future father-in-law, if you are prepared to partake in a plan I have in mind."

Davy was about to open his mouth to speak again but Tom slammed his large hand on his son's knee.

"Just listen son, shut it!"

Sir James grinned at Tom and continued again.

"David, you have spent over two years working in surgical on the front. I have had incredible reports back from fellow Campbellians, including Brigadier Nugent, of your abilities. I also had a conversation with Professor Dundee, another old school pal at an Old Campbellians' Dinner last Christmas. Turns out he knows you.

Do you remember serving a gentleman who admired your ability at cutting the meat in Graham's? He said you would have made a good surgeon if you had an education."

Davy just nodded slowly. Sir James had now got his full attention.

"Well David, I have spoken to the powers that be at Queen's Medical School and with more than a little help from Professor Dundee there is a place for you in the Medical School this September."

Davy remained silent for a few seconds trying to take this all in.

"But I left school at twelve like the rest of the lads. Granted I was right and good at my spelling and arithmetic but that's another league."

"Precisely David, which is why you should get yourself down to Methodist College and ask for the headmaster, who, courtesy of a small bursary, has agreed to give you intensive tuition; bring you up to speed and narrow the academic gap by September."

Davy sat in silence, the proposition still running through his mind.

"But if I'm working at Graham's, how can I do both?" asked Davy, still seriously confused.

"Professor Dundee has said he would take you on as a part time surgical assistant for the duration of your studentship. I can provide you and Anna with one of the houses I rent in Mount Charles beside the University. Take that as a wedding present. No rent, you should manage," smiled Sir James.

Silence overcame the room, each man with his own thoughts.

"Does Anna know anything about your idea?" asked Davy.

"Not a thing, this is a deal between you and me. I get peace of mind. You get Anna with my complete support. You will have standing in society which you will have earned in your own right. I will have a surgeon for a son-in-law, and Tom will not have to worry about the toffs looking down at you. Good bit of business for us all I would say. Is it agreed then?" asked Sir James as he stretched his hand across the table.

Davy hesitated, turned to Tom.

"You knew all about this, didn't you Da?"

"Not much goes on about Shaws Bridge I don't know about son," replied Tom, as both smiled like mirror images.

Davy retrieved his glass of Bushmills, took a sip, stood up, extended his hand to the already outstretched hand of Sir James.

"I hope I can match your confidence in me Sir James," said Davy.

"Well, that is agreed then. I'll expect you both in church Sunday morning," beamed Sir James.

"I'll arrange for a formal announcement. Would be best if you are there."

"Seem to remember I wasn't so popular last time I was up there," teased Davy to Sir James, as the adrenalin of joy released his thoughts a little too much.

"For which, I can only beg your forgiveness," replied Sir James.

All three stood and drained their glasses in one.

As they finished, the sound of expensive evening gowns brushing against each other could be heard in the open hall outside the lounge. A smell of expensive perfume invaded the room.

The three men turned to see Lady May and Anna at her shoulder, enter the room.

Anna immediately made eye contact with Davy, as she picked up the gleam in the eyes of the three men. She looked at Davy searching for clues.

Sir James stepped towards Lady May, and clasped her hand, raising it. Anna moved slowly towards Davy and relaxed when he threw her a reassuring wink.

"Well then, my dear, it would seem a new hat is required," said Sir James to Lady May.

Anna stood beside Davy, linking his arm with her own.

"What have you been up to, father?" asked Anna coyly.

"Just agreeing a bit of business with David," replied Sir James, straight faced.

Anna looked up at Davy.

"It's sorted Anna, bit different to what I expected, but you will have to get used to Anna Gibson," smiled Davy, more than slightly relieved.

"You have asked father and he said yes?" asked Anna excitedly.

"Well, the way it worked out, I didn't actually have to ask." Davy smiled in relief.

Anna drew back.

"David Gibson, there is more romance in a Belfast Brick. You are not getting away with that. Ask my father properly," scolded Anna, in mock annoyance.

"Dada, David has something to ask you."

"It's fine Anna, I approve. David and I have come to a gentleman's agreement," assured Sir James.

"You may well have come to an 'agreement,' but I have not had the pleasure of hearing you, Davy, asking, and you, father, approving," chided Anna.

David and Sir James looked at each other for mutual support. Anna stared them both in the face, trying to hide a smile. She was setting out her stall; she wanted them to complete her romantic dream. She had also still not forgiven Sir James for the day at the church before the war and wanted to have the last laugh.

Sir James and Davy both knew what she was doing; both were happy to play the game as they would both have died for Anna. A little orchestrated embarrassment was a small price to pay, so they went through the ritual routine. Davy asked for Anna's

294

hand, Sir James approving after a few seconds of over theatrical angst and rubbing the back of his head.

At dinner Sir James explained to Anna the great plan he and Davy had agreed. She teased David with Doctor Gibson the entire evening. After dinner, Anna requested that all the staff join in the celebrations. A long and happy evening was spent at Ballydrain. Martha had to half carry Jonty home across the courtyard!

Far away in France a young novice nun sat in her spartan room, knees on the hard stone floor, rosary in hands, praying for the soul of Joseph Shannon, ending,

"See you on the other side. Wait for me Joe."

Chapter Twenty – Three

Requiem

Anna and David married on the 28th of June 1919, Bill was best man, Jonty, Allen, and Adam Bamford and Rab were all ushers. The twins were not phantoms haunting St Patrick's Church at Drumbeg that day. They were there in body and soul. They had strolled into Edenderry village in April 1919 where they had to grab hold of their poor mother as she fainted in front of them. Davy had assumed they had been blown to kingdom come, but fortune certainly favoured the brave for those lads.

The shell that had landed near them had not killed them. It had blown them off their feet beyond Davy's sight and left them stunned and disorientated, until they were captured by German soldiers in the aftermath, as they wandered shell shocked into the German side beyond the second trench.

They had been sent off, along with a few hundred others, through Belgium on the way to a prison camp near Frankfurt. As they were being marched through the huge expanse of the Ardennes forests, they slipped away like ghosts in the night, confident that they had the skills to disappear and survive.

The Ardennes was one huge Ballydrain Estate, ten thousand times and more over.

From August 1916 until Spring 1919 they had hidden in the Ardennes Forest. Lived off the land using every poacher and scouting skills they possessed, made shelter, foraged, and trapped food.

They were hundreds of miles from their comrades and didn't fancy being caught trying to get home through open ground, or villages, so they settled for what they did best. For two years until the Winter of 1918, they pushed their skills and endurance to the limit.

They knew the war was still going on throughout the two years because on occasional forages near the roads they could see units of German forces heading West.

By December 1918 they noticed most were coming back heading East in the direction of the Fatherland.

They decided to sit out the winter of 1918 keeping warm with the furs they had trapped and a cave they had dug and sealed with thatch. They dared not move too far for fear the snow would reveal their footprints and they could not be sure if the Germans were returning in victory or defeat.

In early spring, when the snow started to melt, they ventured out to the edge of a main road.

They sat and watched, concealed from view. No Germans had passed through. Only locals walking, cycling, talking, occasionally laughing.

In the evening as light began to fade, two young men of about their own age staggered past them on the road below. Far too much Belgian beer had been consumed as they staggered home from the local inn. They were singing a song at the top of their voices. The twins could pick out Boche and Kaiser while the local lads made kicking movements with their feet. "Fuck Le Kaiser." was easily understood in any one's language.

Allen and Adam looked at each other and smiled.

Content that two drunk Belgians might not even remember this evening, they slipped out of the trees and stepped onto the road. Allen in front of the drunken lads, Adam behind.

At the sight of Allen, rifle raised, soldiers' boots and trousers patched with skins, a fur waist coat and army cap, they turned to run. They stopped suddenly when they saw Adam blocking their retreat. How could this man be in front and behind them at the same time?

They turned again to run the other way. Allen again blocked their way.

"Take it easy boys," whispered Allen. "We confuse a lot of people."

"Angleterre?" spluttered the larger Belgian.

"Oh! fuck no!" laughed Adam from the rear. "Irish, sort of."

"Ulstermen!" announced Allen, keeping his face straight.

"Le Guerre est finis. Le Boche." The younger Belgium swung his boot again. "Au revoir!"

"Nous voudrais departer, Irelandais," asked Adam, whose regular chats with local French girls when back from the front line had stood him well in more ways than one.

"Allez, le village. Hotel de Ville. Vous parlez avec le gendarmerie," advised the drunks, pointing back down the road they had come from.

The two Belgians turned to speak to each other and then back to face the twins.

Allen and Adam had disappeared like the ghosts they had become.

After tortuous attempts at explaining themselves, and a night in the unlocked cells of the police station, they were returned to a British Army station near Calais. They were interrogated by an army officer to ensure they were not deserters. The possession of rifles they had "requisitioned" from a German supply truck stopping at the roadside of the forest, and obvious attempts to preserve their uniforms, assisted their claim they were not deserters. British prisoners being taken through the Ardennes was well known.

The difficulty for the Lieutenant in Calais was that, as they had escaped on route to the German Stalag, they had not been recorded as prisoners. Details were only processed and sent on to the Red Cross on arrival at the Prisoner of War camp, long after their escape. As the officer finished his notes and assessment, he raised his head.

"Right chaps, I'll get the paperwork sorted for your return to the Emerald Isle. There is, however, one matter that you pair will have to deal with yourselves."

The twins both looked concerned at the officer.

"You two are both dead. Missing, presumed KIA. Killed in Action; have been since July 16. I suggest you tread carefully with your poor mother."

David entered Queens Medical School in September 1919, and six years later started work as a qualified surgeon. During his time at Queen's, he regularly met Big Rab, who was attending Theological College, also courtesy of Sir James's support. Rab remained in the ministry and eventually became Canon of Belfast, a title that always caused him amusement before his retirement in the late 1960s.

In Easter 1941, Davy had to return to the horrors of explosive trauma again, not on the battlefield, but the streets of Belfast. This time it was repairing broken bodies caused by the Junkers and Dorniers of the Luftwaffe attempting to set Belfast alight with high explosive incendiary bombs.

After the war he received the title of "Sir" for his contribution of leading teams of surgeons retrieving and repairing the shattered bodies of traumatised civilians caused by the five-hundred-pound bombs that fell on a woefully under protected

Belfast. Seven hundred souls could not be saved that night, but many more were more fortunate.

Sir David Gibson and Lady Anna Gibson in their own right; Sir James would have liked that. His business deal had worked out better than he had hoped.

In France, Sister Josephine, as Kitty became, worked with the terminally ill at the hospice throughout her entire life, facing the horrors of war again between 1939 and 1945 in Northern France, treating Allied and German troops alike, as both armies ebbed and flowed through Northern France.

By 1958 she had become Mother Superior of the Hospice. She was known affectionately in the area as Sister Joe, the nun who walked the fields and hedgerows of the farmlands that were once the battlefields; stopping now and again as if she was searching for something or someone, often seeming to talk to herself.

David and Anna had three children. Roger, Joseph, and Kathleen, called Kitty unless she was being told off, which, being her mother's daughter, was quite often.

Tom had died in his sleep in 1936. His liver finally gave in. Davy had warned him for years that Armagh's finest would be the death of him. On the evening of his demise, Anna wrapped him in the same shawl he had given her twenty years earlier. His last act was to pull it up to his face and close his eyes with a smile.

Sir James died in 1942 with lung cancer, caused by his preference for a large consumption of Gallaher's Blues. A much better quality of killer than a working man's Woodbine. Davy had stopped smoking by the time he finished medical college. He had seen the insides of too many decaying chests to consider otherwise. Lady May died later the same year. She simply gave up the will to live.

Up to the mid-1950s Anna took official control of the Arthur business empire, rarely going to the factories, leaving that to Bill Johnston whom she had made her General Manager of the entire business empire after Sir Arthur's demise.

Bill Johnston called to Ballydrain every Friday afternoon to give full reports on every enterprise. Anna made the big decisions. Bill was her eyes and ears. He made sure everything was carried out. Her father would have been proud of her business qualities.

Davy never had any interest or had anything to do with that side of things; Never felt it was his place.

From the mid 1950's Anna took a back seat in the business and allowed her son Roger to take charge of the business empire. Joseph and Kathleen both followed their father into medicine and were quite content to let him get on with it. Sir James's wish had come true. Roger had taken over the business.

In July of 1975, Anna received a letter from France, that Sister Josephine had not long to live. The arteries in her brain were hardening rapidly and she was prone to regular bouts of rambling, seeing visions, and talking to people who were not there, according to the nurses and nuns who cared for her as if she was their own mother.

Anna and Davy travelled to France, earlier than they had intended, to be at her bedside. They knew the route to the Hospice in their sleep. They had travelled it every year without fail since 1919, apart from 1939 to 1945. They loyally visited Kitty each year on their way to the Arthur family villa in Villefranche on the Mediterranean coast; always leaving a sealed, embossed envelope which was handed each year to Anna from Bill Johnston. The content of the envelope was a £100 bankers draft made payable to the St Claire Eglise Hospice from the Edenderry Orange Lodge. Bill had become Lodge Master at Edenderry and a senior member of the Grand Lodge of Ireland and as far as Belfast and District was concerned, he ruled the roost.

Bill, courtesy of his damaged Orange Order medallion which had stopped shrapnel from penetrating his heart, only suffering a heavy thump on the chest on that morning in July 1916, remained staunchly loyal to the Order. The Order had, in his mind, looked after him, the Order deserved his unquestioning loyalty in return.

When Bill had returned from the war and met with his Lodge brethren he did not speak much about the Somme. He talked more about his pals, their loyalty, their bravery, none less than Joe. As he sat sipping a bottle of stout in the Homestead Inn, Drumbo, after a Lodge meeting, he explained to the other members gathered around the scratched and stained table.

"Davy, Jonty, Rab and me would never have returned if it hadn't been for Joe. He was our Dutch Blue Guard."

The others sat round him, looking at Bill with confused expressions; none spoke. There was a common desire not to disrespect Bill as each of them sipped their beer in silence.

"You don't know what I'm on about, none of you, do you?" grinned Bill looking each one in the eye, slowly.

"Can't say we do," replied old Sam McCombe. "Need to educate us on that one, Billy boy."

"Got plenty of time to read on quiet nights in the training camps in England; history most. Turns out King William's best unit at the Boyne was the Dutch Blue Guard.

They led the assault; waded across the Boyne up to their chests, holding their flint locks above their heads. They took the brunt, got an awful hammering, heaviest losses of his army that day in July 1690. They made the breach for the rest to cross. They were Catholic to a man, but they were William's men."

Bill took a long sip on his beer.

The group sat in silence sensing he had not finished.

"Joe, God rest him, was our Dutch Blue Guard out there," whispered Bill, staring at the table, before raising his eyes to stare at the faces around him.

"Returned two grenades back to the Hun bastards; never saw the third." As he hung his head both in shame and sorrow, the group remained silent.

"Need to do something in his memory at the Lodge, lads, we owe him that," Bill continued. Silence engulfed the group, as they thought of Joe's sacrifice and what could be done.

"I know a man lives up at Derriaghy, great old painter who's done some for the Malone Road mob. Only problem is they pay him well and he's got used to it; wouldn't come cheap," suggested Sam Montgomery.

Bill looked across at Sam and although Sam was a good forty years older than him, gave him a look as if he was a child. Bill took in a deep breath to contain his emotions, annoyed that Sam brought the matter of money into the conversation, yet knowing Sam meant no harm. He just did not understand. He had not been there.

"Sam, just contact him. See if he would come and have a talk to us, please," asked Bill, almost demanding.

"Take it as done, young William," replied Sam, regretting he had touched a raw nerve, but letting Bill know that he was the senior member present.

The meeting took place, the artist, to their surprise, refused to accept any payment and completed the painting, which was hung in pride at Edenderry Lodge, for many years until Bill became District Grand Lodge Master.

The first day he walked into his plush office in Dublin Road Belfast, long before it moved to the Cregagh Road, he carried under his arm, the painting. As he entered the impressive entrance hall, he scanned the walls and spotted the very place for the work of art.

Bill hung the painting on the wall, stood back and looked at it for several seconds and said to himself.

"Well Joe, this the best I can do for you, mate."

As he stood lost in his thoughts, the Grand Lodge secretary, a middle aged, quite proper lady, carrying a teacup and saucer walked towards him.

"Good morning Grand Master," said Molly Potter. "Finest Thompson Tea, Mr Johnston. I see you are putting your stamp on things."

"Just bringing a loyal friend with me, Miss Potter," he sighed. 'Left him behind on the Somme, I'll not leave him behind again."

Molly stood and stared at the painting.

"Most of the other paintings have a few words inscribed below them," she mused.

Bill thought for a few seconds, "That's easy," sighed Bill again. 'See you on the other side.'

"I will contact the engravers and get it done Mr Johnston," assured Molly.

"That would be fine, Molly. Get them to send the invoice payable to me please."

As the elderly couple entered the main Hall of St Claire's they were met by Sister Therese who guided them into her office and explained that Kitty, Sister Josephine, was not expected to see the morning and that her physical appearance would shock them. As Davy and Anna entered the small, but comfortable room, they could see a frail figure deep in the quilt and sheets. Kitty tried to raise herself, but the effort was too much. Two young nurses appeared from behind the elderly visitors and gently propped Kitty up as best they could.

Davy and Anna, now both nearly eighty years old, sat each side of the bed. Anna brushed Kitty's forehead gently. Davy sat quietly, sensing that this was, as so many years before, not his place.

Slowly Kitty's eyes opened and tried to smile, and just as slowly, she dragged a few words out of her dry throat.

"You waited for me," she swallowed. "All of you."

"Time the four of us went home." Her voice only a faint whisper.

Anna flashed a glance at Davy.

"I'll be dancing with Joe tonight, won't I Joe?" whispered Kitty as she stared at the end of the bed.

"You will for sure!" Anna replied to the tiny figure she hardly recognised.

Kitty's head sank deep into the pillows and sighed contentedly.

Anna and Davy sat as they listened to Kitty's breathing get slower and fainter until she breathed her last.

They sat silently for a few more minutes before they rose and began to walk out of the room.

"It was as well Sister let us know she was at the delusional stage," whispered Anna.

Davy agreed. "Yes, Anna, let's go home."

As they got to the door, they turned to face Kitty for the last time.

Kitty's hand was outstretched at the side of the bed, blankets ruffled as if someone had taken her by the hand.

Davy and Anna looked at each other. Anna put her hand to her mouth. Davy rubbed the side of his head as they left without a word.

A week later as they sat on the veranda of their villa overlooking the harbour in Villefranche, just below the Villa Rothchilde Gardens, they reminisced of the days before the War. The perfect days which they had been so fortunate to repeat so many times in their lives since. During a pause, Davy, still staring down at the harbour below said,

"Anna, do you remember when we left Kitty that day. Did you notice the smell of Woodbine in Kitty's room as we left?"

"I did, but I didn't want to say anything in case it was just my subconscious remembering Joe. He always smelt of Woodbine," replied Anna wistfully.

They both sat in silence, knowing that someday they would be with Kitty and Joe again, and the days at Shaw's Bridge would never end.

Chapter Twenty – Four

Balancing the books

"Well Danny, now you know the whole way of it," smiled Norman Johnston as he sipped his pint, looking across at the young accountant. It had taken a few lunchtime golfers' fries at Belvoir to relate the tale.

Danny sat silent and after a bit of thought said, with a wry smile.

"Aye, truth can be stranger than fiction and Belfast is a village. Somebody always knows somebody, who knows somebody."

Danny looked Norman straight in the face, letting him know he knew he had left a certain detail out.

Norman stared back, almost defying him.

"William was right, you are a sharp lad, Danny. No flies on you then," smiled Norman.

Danny laughed in both irony and embarrassment.

"So, William Chambers is behind all this, then?"

"Yes, he thought that with me being Bill Johnston's grandson, it was better coming from me," grinned Norman.

"How did he make the connection?" asked Danny.

310

"Your personnel file in Coopers, Danny. Next of kin, mother, Bernadette Marie O'Connor, maiden name, Shannon, address in the Markets, off Cromac Street. Might have been a coincidence but it was worth a shot.

"So that's why William gave me the audit for the Lodges. He knew I would be intrigued by the painting and the payment, and that you would be only too glad to tell the tale."

Norman rocked his head slowly.

Danny leaned down to open his brief case and lifted out a sturdy A4 envelope and handed it to Norman.

"When you mentioned the name Shannon at the very start, you knew it would get my attention. Well, I called down at my grandmother's house, the other day and asked her about her uncle Joe because I had never heard him talked about much in our house. He was apparently a source of embarrassment because he fought with the Ulster Division. Anyhow, I went up into her roof space where an old bag of family photos was left, brought it down, and among the pile, found this."

Norman reverently opened the envelop, and slowly, pulled out the yellow hued cardboard backed photograph of a hundred years earlier.

Norman sat back in his chair in silence, studying the handsome face, with the cheeky grin and the shoulder insignia of the 14th Battalion; put his head back to the ceiling and then looked into the face of Joe Shannon.

"I've told the tale many times, but this is the first time we've met face to face, old son," whispered Norman, as he spoke to the brown weathered photograph, and after a contented sigh, asked, "Any chance you could get me a copy of this, Danny?"

"Already done," chuckled Danny as he pulled out a second A4 envelope and handed it to Norman.

Danny beamed from ear to ear, content that he had been one step ahead of Norman.

"I'll keep the original, I have plans for it, Norman," said Danny.

The next evening Danny sat in the meeting room at Deramore Park, in his role as Treasurer of Bredagh Gaelic Athletic Club. Near the end, when it came to any other business, and the other committee members were already starting to shuffle in their seats, Danny spoke up.

"I have one other matter to be discussed lads. It won't keep you back from the bar too long. It's the matter of one Joseph Shannon and if you don't know who he is, this will get you acquainted."

Danny slid a copy of Joe's picture down the long table which each member glanced at, passing on round. Each member studied the image in silence.

Connor Toner was the first to speak,

"Explain Danny, I'm getting thirsty, and I don't really want to delay it too long for a Brit soldier," he scoffed, with a smile that was a shroud of contempt.

"That Brit soldier was my great uncle and from what I've heard about him he deserves your respect, Connor, not your contempt mate," replied Danny coldly.

Connor looked at the table and did not speak. He had too much friendship for Danny to destroy that, but he was not happy.

After a short silence, Finbar McShane, spoke.

"My great grandfather fought at Messines 1917 with the Dublin Fusiliers."

"I had two great uncles in the Connaught Rangers; never came back," sighed Paul McGlone, face never leaving the table.

The other four at the table sat silently still weighing up the tone of the meeting.

"Ok Danny, give us the craic, please. Time is moving on." Liam O'Malley interrupting the silence.

"I propose that this picture is framed and hung up beside the other Belfast Harlequins/Collegians War Dead photos in the pavilion entrance hall, alongside the Harlequins memorial wall, and his name is added to their memorial list."

Connor stared at the table shaking his head in disbelief, scanning his eyes slowly round the table. All refused to make eye contact with him. The silence was deafening. No one was prepared to put their head above the parapet on this one.

"Joseph Shannon, a great uncle of mine, served in the not so 'Great War.' He died on the first day of the Somme. Saved the lives of several of his friends and comrades before he caught it. The only thing left of him was his rosary beads and they were found by his girlfriend, a frontline nurse. Born in Sligo, worked in Ballydrain House, now better known as Malone Golf Club to you boys. Kathleen Breslin never came home. Joined the nursing convent only miles from the Somme, became a nun and waited to be re-united with Joe. She waited nearly sixty years."

The silence returned to the room.

"I wish to propose the motion. Do I have a seconder to take it to a vote?" continued Danny as his eyes scanned the room.

Connor gave Danny a look that suggested the idea was not going to be supported.

From the far corner of the table a quietly spoken voice muttered.

"I will second the motion."

All heads turned to Eugene D'Arcy, who was also the young assistant priest from St Bridget's Chapel, less than a mile down the Malone Road from where they were sitting. The same Chapel Joe and Kitty first set eyes on each other and that most of the Bredagh club now attended, although a lot less diligently than their ancestors. Father D'Arcy was a keen footballer, who played for Bredagh as much as his parish duties allowed him.

Connor looked daggers at Father D'Arcy.

"Connor, have you ever wondered about the small cross with the name of Sister Josephine, St Claire's Hospice, France that sits in the right transept. It's got a date on it of 1975?"

"Can't say as I have, Eugene," replied Connor, calling the young priest by his first name, not wanting to give him any sense of superiority.

'No neither had I, to my shame. But I would lay odds that Sister Josephine is Kathleen Breslin. Too much coincidence I would say."

Connor was about to reply but he was cut short by Finbar.

"Connor, do you agree the First World War was nearly a hundred years ago?"

Connor nodded and tried to speak again, but Finbar cut him off short.

"And do you agree the War here of the last forty years is over?"

Connor looked ahead. "You know it's over, Finbar. Don't need a history lesson about that!"

"Then what harm does it do if we respect Danny's relative if it means that much to him?"

The rest of the heads in the room either nodded or shrugged their shoulders in a show of indifference.

"Lot's wife, lads, Lot's wife. She looked back and turned to stone," added Eugene.

"Can we have a vote then, lads?" asked Danny.

315

One hand remained down, two abstained, and five approved the motion.

A few weeks later, Danny, by now well settled in his own manager's office, signing off a set of accounts was interrupted by a tap on the door quickly followed by William Chambers himself entering.

"Morning Danny, settled in well I see. Everything under control then?" asked William.

Danny looked at William over the top of his reading glasses as he put his pen down and leant back in his chair.

"Thanks William," replied Danny.

"Nothing to thank me for Danny. You got made Manager on your own account. No reason why you won't be in my chair someday," said William, raising his right hand dismissively.

"No, I don't mean the promotion; I mean him," smiled Danny as he pointed to the wall behind William's large head.

William turned around in the chair. On the far wall were three photographs. One of Bredagh GAC with Danny four from the left on the back row; a second, Siobhan, and the third of Joseph Shannon.

William turned back to Danny,

"My pleasure Danny, my pleasure."

Printed in Great Britain
by Amazon